THE LOST GOSPELS

Stephen Taylor

SAPERE
BOOKS

THE LOST GOSPELS

Published by Sapere Books.

24 Trafalgar Road, Ilkley, LS29 8HH

saperebooks.com

ISBN: 978-0-85495-129-1

ACKNOWLEDGEMENTS

After I started writing this novel there was, by coincidence, a BBC2 TV series on the subject of bible hunting. This added to my research. I would like to acknowledge this. My thanks to the presenter, Dr. Jeff Rose and his team of contributors, Dr. Edward Adams, Prof. Simion Goldhill, Dr. Andrew Bednarski, Dr. David Grange, Dr. Michael Ledger-Lomas, Dr. Scot McKendrick and Dr. Dirk Obbink for telling the stories of the real the men and women who travelled to Egypt to uncover the earliest Christian texts.

My thanks also to the many scholars who have written about the Gospel of Thomas who have provided me with much of the basis of my fictional Gospel of Thaddeus Jude. Thomas gives us an alternative view of Jesus.

PROLOGUE

Carberton Hall, Nottinghamshire 1845

Crisp, streaky bacon greeted me as I lifted the lid of the silver serving tray. Leaning forward, I inhaled the wonderful savoury aroma of it. I took the tongs and lifted two rashers onto my plate. I went along the silver line, raising the lids in turn and adding scrambled eggs, two sausages, and some fried kidneys.

As I sat at the dining table, the morning sun filling the breakfast room with its warm rays, Alexandria came and joined me. She touched her lips tenderly to my forehead before she sat down and picked up her copy of *The Lady's Magazine*, which had just been delivered. A cooked breakfast was not to her taste; she was satisfied with hot chocolate and some buttered toast liberally spread with cherry jam. The footman came and filled my glass with a draught of ale, and I set about eating my breakfast.

The bacon was particularly good, and I asked the footman to send to the kitchen for some more rashers. I sat back in my chair with the ale and contemplated my good fortune. I looked at my wife, smiling inwardly. Her face had an ancient Egyptian look, her large dark eyes drawing the attention of onlookers to her like moths to a flame. I wondered briefly if I had chosen her because of that look; I had travelled extensively in Egypt and even her name brought back memories of that country.

My inward smile must have become visible, because Alexandria seemed to pick up on my contentment.

'What are you so pleased about, Robert?' she asked over the top of a slice of toast.

'I am just happy, my dear,' I said, my tone matter-of-fact, though my grin widened.

'I don't know why it has taken you so long to come back to Carberton. It is years since your father died.'

'I am an academic, my dear. You know my work has kept me away,' I lied. Of course, I kept my reasons even from my wife.

'But the responsibility of running the estate ultimately rests with you, Robert. Our wealth is based here; the rents from the tenant farmers are our primary source of income.'

''Tis true enough, my dear, but I trust my estate manager. He has run things most efficiently in my absence.'

'Well, I am pleased to see you are *now* so contented then, even if it has taken you so many years to realise it.'

We exchanged glances, but I knew she did not suspect my intentions.

'And you, my dear, are you pleased that we have come to live here at the Hall?'

'I am, Robert, indeed I am. Living in London, but not being allowed to be part of the social season, is frustrating.' She gave me a petulant look; it was a long-standing source of conflict between us. 'And it will be good for Edward to grow up here, and soon —' she patted her stomach — 'perhaps a brother for him.'

'Aye, 'tis true, my love,' I agreed.

'You know that your position here will oblige us to entertain; we will not be able to hide here as you have done in London.'

I nodded; I am not a recluse by nature. 'We should invite our neighbours to dinner,' I said enthusiastically. 'We've been here for a month now.'

She looked up from her magazine, surprise evident in her features. 'Yes, my dear,' she said hesitantly. 'Shall I arrange it and send out the invitations?'

'That would be capital, Alexandria,' I said, wiping the fat from my mouth with my napkin. I saw her face light up.

The footman arrived with two more rashers of bacon. The succulent smell tweaked my hunger, but as I spied them it was clear they were not crisp and streaky: it was not side bacon cured of belly pork, but meaty back bacon cut from the pig's loin. I was disappointed, but it was more than that; a potent memory had been awakened.

My mind drifted to past conversations with a long-lost friend. *That is another rasher of bacon altogether*, he would say. My smile broadened.

'That is another rasher of bacon altogether.'

Alexandria looked up at me, her forehead creased. 'What, my dear?'

I coughed, snapping back to the present. 'The bacon, my dear; it's not streaky.' I relaxed when I saw her eyes fall back to her magazine.

My mind wandered back to my long-lost friend and our time in Egypt. We'd been young and adventurous — two of the first few Englishmen to have travelled the country extensively. Camels and turbans, *pashas* and *beys* came vividly into my mind; *chaoushes* and *kawasses* followed. I could still picture the silk dresses in vibrant red and gold with diamond insignia. I sighed heavily as the images kept coming: magnificent Arab stallions, resplendent with gem-studded bridles and covered in red silk trimmings; a boat trip on the lazy Nile; palm trees guarding its bank; thousands of white butterflies taking to the air as we walked among the lush greenery of the flood plains.

I was momentarily nostalgic for my life of adventure. The fact that my life had been in danger so many times was disregarded; so was the insufferably fiery clinging heat, and the endless chattering, biting insects.

I looked out of the large bay windows: fluffy clouds were speeding across a blue midsummer sky; the trees were swaying in the breeze. I snapped back to the present and looked around me.

I *was* contented with my present life, but it had taken a long time to get here. I sucked on some bacon caught between my teeth, playing with the gold ring on my little finger as I considered my life. For much of it, I had felt like a man running from a hue and cry, but now I had found my place. *I am Robert Babcock, eleventh Baron Carberton of Carberton Hall, Nottinghamshire*, I thought, reminding myself again of everything I had. I was also a scholar and adventurer, and much more besides. However, that part of my life had to remain a secret.

PART 1

CHAPTER 1

London, 1st June 1835

I gazed down fearfully at my shadow running before me, then shot an anxious glimpse skyward and cursed the dazzling moon. As I darted through the narrow city alleyways, the sound of my pounding boots echoed back at me from the walls of the overhanging houses.

This is stupid, I thought, *I am just drawing attention to myself.* I stopped and listened intently to see if footsteps were still following me. I could hear nothing but my own heart thumping against my ribcage, the blood pumping in my ears — were these sounds hiding the progress of my pursuers on the cobbled streets? My terror heightened again, and I slipped uneasily under the shadow of an overhanging eave, flattened myself against the wall, swallowed hard and tried to hold my breath while I listened again.

Nothing; I was safe. Well, for the moment — but that damned moon! I looked at my pocket watch: twenty-seven minutes after twelve of the clock. I pulled back my arm quickly, returning the watch to my waistcoat. I had only until dawn to save myself, to at least find a bolt hole until the cover of darkness again tomorrow night. But this was June; dawn would be just after four o'clock.

Oh Christ, I cursed to myself. I had spent money recklessly when I had had it. I looked down at my clothes; even in the shadows, my frock coat declared itself the best that money could buy, and my whole ensemble was the finest of tailoring. I stood out like a tiara on a fisherwoman. At that moment, I knew I had not only to flee my pursuers; I had to flee London. I owed thousands of pounds in gambling debts, and gambling debts were a matter of honour. I could owe money to my grocer or wine merchant, and the worst that could happen was debtors' prison, and even then only after years of skilful evasion. But I had gambled at Molly Jasper's Rooms with dukes and earls, and all debts were recorded in his ledgers — and Molly Jasper made sure they were paid. My name was inscribed there; *John Campbell-John*, it would say, and that meant the debt would be vigorously pursued.

Molly would assume I would, on the threat of agonising violence, get the money from my father, from his estate, or face the dishonour of being a gentleman of society unable to pay his gambling debts as a gentleman should.

In the shadows, a thin, humourless smile slithered across my lips. I had no honour; there was no gentleman father, no estate in the country — it was all a fabrication, an illusion I had created. I was nothing but a silver-tongued, penniless rogue. I knew what my fate would be when my deception was discovered. I would be disposed of — a body fished out of the Thames; a message sent loud and clear to any other scoundrel that might look to deceive the gentlemen of society and then fail to pay his debts.

The sweat on my back cooled as I stood rigid with terror. My life hung by a thread, and so I had to employ all my animal cunning. But then that slithering smile broadened: there was no one more cunning than me. If cunning was a pack of cards, I would be the ace of spades. It was time to do what I did best.

I tiptoed down the alleyway, keeping to the shadows. When the alley opened into a wider thoroughfare, I peeped round the corner, but pulled my head back immediately. My worst fear — it was one of Molly Jasper's men, magnificent in his livery. He wore black satin with gold braid and epaulettes, as well as white stockings, white gloves and a powdered white wig. He was surrounded by street urchins, skin-and-bones boys eager for a farthing or two to feed their shrunken bellies. He was sending them out into the dark streets to find me.

I set off in the opposite direction, a plan forming in my mind; it took me to the nearest drinking establishment. The Bell Inn was an inferior sort of place, the light from the lanterns inside spilling dimly onto the alleyway. I found a dark nook, avoiding the spilling light and the dazzling moon, and listened; there was singing and the clamour of chattering voices as the last of the drinkers kept up their evening's revelry. I could not enter the way I was dressed, so I waited, heart thumping.

The door opened some moments later, and a large man came out and started to relieve himself against the wall. He was humming an out-of-tune song as he went about his business; it made it easy for me to creep up to him and put a knife to his throat. The stream of piss stopped instantly.

'Don't cry out, my friend,' I whispered.

The man grunted a sort of agreement.

'Now, I want you to take off your clothes, slowly, without any sudden movements.' I felt him stiffen at my words, unsure what his attacker had in mind for him. 'Don't worry, I am not a *molly*, we're just going to exchange clothes.'

The man stood motionless for some moments, so I pressed my knife harder against his skin until a trickle of blood started to run down his neck. '*Now!*' I shouted to encourage him, but the word fell away as I realised I might draw the attention of the man's friends inside the inn.

The man started to comply, removing his tarnished jacket. I pointed at his grubby breeches, and he reluctantly removed them as well, standing then in his soiled drawers. I took off my stylish frock coat, managing to pass the knife from one hand to the other, and threw it at him, seeing the man's face light up at the uneven trade. I ran back up the alley, looking over my shoulder at his bewildered face. When it seemed safe, I stopped, put on the worn frock coat, and slid the dirtied breeches over my own. I now smelt foul, but that was good, I thought.

I saw one of the street urchins searching the alleyway, and this time I did not hide from him. 'What you doin' out this time of the night, young 'un?' I asked, working my mouth and spitting out a gob of saliva, my idea of a crude action to match my shabby appearance.

'Got a ha'penny to look for a finely dressed gent, mister.'

'I've just come from the Bell,' I said. 'Your gent is in there, if I am not mistaken.'

'Ta, mister,' the urchin said, running off to find Molly Jasper's liveried brute.

I flattened myself against a shadowed wall and waited. Sure enough, I heard the cry go up as a gang made its way to the Bell Inn. I crept away in the opposite direction, then made my way back to my lodgings.

When I arrived, there was another liveried brute outside. I crept around the back and let myself in through the rear door. I spent the rest of the night filling two chests with my belongings, stumbling, unable to light a lantern, lest I draw the attention of Molly Jasper's man outside. I needed my wardrobe; the clothes were the tools of my trade as a master imposter.

When dawn broke, I lay on the floor as much as I could. My only companions were a bottle of claret, some cheese and a chamber pot. I spent the day drinking, sleeping and pissing, all three achieved with considerable discomfort.

But it did allow me to formulate a plan. At four o'clock, the blackguard could not be seen — he'd probably gone to relieve himself, or to fill his belly. I let myself out of the back door, dressed in the clothes I had stolen, and made my way to the docks to enquire about ships that were ready to sail. I found a captain who was to sail for Venice by the morning tide. At first he looked at me suspiciously, as if I could not afford the cost of the passage, so I told him I was enquiring on behalf of my master.

'Tell your master that we sail on the morning tide. If he is not here by six-thirty, I will not wait for him,' he said. 'And tell him no credit — if he cannot pay, I will not take him,' he added over his shoulder as he walked up his gangplank.

As soon as night fell again, I manhandled the first of my trunks out of the back door and carried it to a corner two streets away. I could not drag it, for I had to be silent. By the time I had reached my destination, sweat was pouring down the side of my face and I had to sit on the chest for some time to recover. I returned for the second chest; my first thought was to leave it, but I found the strength somehow to carry that one too.

I changed in the backstreet, threw away the filthy clothes I had stolen, then gave a street urchin a penny to bring a hackney. When he returned with the carriage, I helped the coachman secure the trunks at the back, looking around me all the time, knowing Molly Jasper's brutes were only a couple of streets away. As the iron-clad wheels rolled over the London cobbles, I sat as far back in the seat as I could, still fearful that I would be recognised. By midnight, I was securely settled in my cabin on the good ship *Trinacria*, thirsty, hungry, but — I hoped — finally safe. The captain did not recognise this finely dressed passenger as the vagabond that had enquired only a few hours earlier; I knew he would not.

The bunk was too small for my long frame, but sleep took me kindly — so much so that half past six came and went, and I slept through the sailing. When I finally woke with a start, the ship was rolling gently. I went on deck, leant on the rail and looked around. We were already out of sight of land; England was gone. There was the taste of salt on my tongue as I ran my hand over my heavily bristled chin.

I paused, gathered my thoughts, and wondered what my father and mother might be doing. I had not seen them in years and had not even sent them a letter, rarely thinking of them. I shivered — a pang of unwelcome conscience, perhaps. It had come to this, running away in fear of my life. I prodded my thumb into my chest. 'This is your fault, John Campbell-John,' I mumbled, 'nobody else but you.' England was gone. I wondered if I would ever return.

CHAPTER 2

My first view of Venice was at dusk, from the deck of the *Trinacria*. There was a menacing sky above the city, the dark, angry clouds picked out by the oblique light of the setting sun. The calm water of the Venetian lagoon was a rose colour, contrasting the silhouetted Gothic buildings. I could see the domes and spires of St Mark's Basilica, with its campanile — the bell tower — standing tallest of all.

So this is the most beautiful city in the world, I thought. I should have been elated, for I had never travelled outside of England, but I was taken with a melancholy that had lasted for the whole fourteen days of the voyage. I leaned over the ship's rail, breathed in the salty air and mused at what my life had sunk to.

My harrowing escape was not the source of my melancholy. At twenty-seven years old, living by my wits had always been part of my life. I had always lied, cheated and impersonated to raise my perceived station in life so that I could con my way through the world. I had frequently outwitted those who had wealth and privilege, and I saw it as their own folly if I relieved them of some of their money. Whenever I saw a condescending face, sneering at those of a lower station in life, I took even more pleasure in outwitting it. My low birth had denied me their privileges but that would not stop me taking theirs.

I stood upright, doing my best to defy my melancholy as I mused on my past. My upbringing was unusual to say the least. I was born to an intelligent, pretty but naïve governess who had been employed to educate a squire's children, a task she was rather good at. So much so that when she became pregnant by him, rather than sending her away he arranged for her to marry his bailiff. For many years afterwards, the squire continued to enjoy the best of all worlds: he had a first-class governess, well-educated children, and a mistress at his beck and call whenever his thoughts grew ardent or to be more precise, whenever his consumption of claret left him feeling lecherous.

Added to this, the lady of the house turned a blind eye to the whole affair. It seemed that everyone was happy — with the possible exception of the bailiff, one Campbell John. But he was only too aware of his place as a servant and knew better than to complain, so he kept his feelings to himself and got on with his job. In return, the governess was a good wife to him. As the years passed and her youth faded so did the squire's interest in her, and eventually Campbell John had my mother to himself.

Into this unorthodox, but by no means unique, world I was born. Campbell John accepted me as his own, and I always thought of him as my father, but somewhat perversely my mother christened me 'Edward John'. Perversely, because the master of the house had already fathered two legitimate sons, the first of whom was also called Edward, and was five years old when I entered this world. The second son, George, preceded me by just four months.

As we boys grew up, we were allowed to play together, and it was acknowledged that I was an acceptable playmate for my half-brothers, especially George, so long as the boundaries and conventions were not infringed. The problem was that I was unaware of these limits, and as I grew up I showed no inclination to learn them. There was also the problem of my name; as the mistress of the house was often heard to remark, 'You cannot have three boys playing together with two of them answering to the name of Edward; it is all too confusing.' So whenever I was at the big house, I was called 'John', and only on Sundays was I known by my given name — and even then, only by my mother.

As I grew older, I was accepted into the big house despite my blatant disregard for conventions. This was because the squire took a shine to me and indulged me, much to the annoyance of his wife. I was everything George was not. I was outgoing where George was timid. I was entertaining where George was a bit dour. I was rugged where George was scrawny — it was not that George was frail, he was just undersized. We both did well at our studies, but I was quick-witted where George was more of a quiet academic. The problem for the squire was that I was everything he wanted in a son, whereas poor George was a bit of a disappointment. Every day, as he watched us boys play, I must have reminded him of this fact; I even looked like him, whereas George did not — nor did he resemble his mother.

I supposed I did not, as a young boy, rationalise this, but I certainly took advantage of the squire's liking of me. We boys got into more and more mischief, but it was me who was the main perpetrator, though I always had enough nous to taint George with my roguery. And like many children of that ilk, I had a natural ability to get away with it. I would look at my natural father with a twinkle in my eye, and the squire's stern face would twitch uncontrollably into a smile and, after dismissing us, I would hear him roaring with laughter; I could play him like a fiddle. I could do no wrong in the squire's eyes, but his wife grew to hate me, as did the elder Edward, who became jealous of his father's affection for me. George, on the other hand, loved me.

When I was nineteen, the squire died. He had promised to look after me in his will, but it was claimed that no will existed. The estate was entailed, the first son Edward inherited, and my continued residence was at the mercy of the new young master of the house, who soon had the excuse he needed to rid himself of his young half-brother. I had been bedding the daughter of the local coal merchant and when her father came round to the big house, enraged and armed with a pistol with the purpose of emasculating the man who had defiled his daughter, I was banished. I went on my way with five guineas, a horse and a change of clothes, and was expected to be thankful for that. I had no trade and only my wits to sustain me, but I had been sheltered from any sense of responsibility in my youth. Within days, I was penniless and forced to sell my horse. Within days of that, I was again penniless. And so I turned to soldiery — I took the king's shilling and joined an infantry regiment. If the squire had lived, perhaps he could have purchased me a commission, but my lot was now as a common foot soldier.

To my amazement, I loved it. There were many hours of boredom in a soldier's life that needed to be filled. There was endless scope for mischief — for gambling, for wenching, for pranks. I was just the man to fill this space. My time in the army, however, added guile and worldliness to my array of talents.

And then, on one drunken evening, a plot was hatched and a bet was proposed. The officers of my company had been invited to a country ball, along with officers from the rest of the regiment, and the bet was that I should go and pass himself off as an officer. Impersonating an officer was a very serious offence, but even after sobering up, the notion took hold of me. I had the education, some Greek and Latin, the accent, the knowledge of the big house — I would do it. I bribed a laundry girl and an officer's uniform was purloined. The success of the venture astounded even me. I was accepted entirely — even officers from my own company failed to recognise me. I knew that officers never really looked enlisted men in the eye — but it was much more than that. I learned that evening that some people only saw what was in front of them. If I looked and sounded like an officer, then to all intents and purposes I was an officer. A life lesson had been learned.

And so I deserted. I invented the persona of 'Captain John Campbell-John'. I went to London with the uniform of an infantry captain, which complemented my fine physique and good looks. I strode about with my shoulders squared, accentuating all five foot eleven inches of my frame, and my blond hair escaped and flowed from the back of my shako. My intention was to use this invention to con my way through the city — to make my fortune. I had thought little further than that. And make my fortune I did; in the last four years, I had become Captain John Campbell-John, to the point that the fiction now almost felt real.

As I looked down at the lagoon, I again tried to shake my melancholy. This was Venice. There would be endless scope for excitement, endless scope for roguery, and I was just the man take advantage of it. I had read of the legendary Carnival of Venice; there would be dancing and carnival masks. I had been to masked balls in England and I knew they were an excuse for debauchery. Masks gave anonymity and with that the rules of society were blurred, and so sexual favours were bestowed that would normally be withheld. At a masquerade, I would be desirable, I mused. My blond hair and athletic build would trump the wealth and position of the noblest gentleman if he were bloated by the indulgences of good living.

I returned to my cramped cabin; this was a trading vessel, not a passage ship. There was room for little more than the bunk, which was nailed to the floor and was the length of the cabin, somewhat less than my own height. Other than that there was just a railed stand, holding in place a tin pitcher and a bowl for washing. The rest of the space was filled by my two trunks full of fine clothes, one piled on top of the other. The clothes were the best that money could buy, but I had left without paying my tailor's bill, of course.

I stumbled to the bunk and lay on my back, looking at the wooden deck above me and trying to think of what knavery I would pursue first. I could hear the sailors scurrying about above me as the ship made ready to dock. I had run away with just ten guineas; I knew that would not last me long, but they were in gold coin and, as such, the money exchangers could easily check the weight of the gold and swap it for the local currency. I would then register at the best hotel in the city and, I thought, play the man of means.

Yet my thoughts still drifted; my glumness would not leave me. It was new to me and I did not know how to handle it — though I did know the cause of it. I had grievously wronged the only true friend I had ever had, a man named Samuel who had shown nothing but friendship and generosity. Try as I might, I could not forget that.

CHAPTER 3

The following morning I took a finely tailored knee-length frock coat from one of my trunks and put it on. It was blue-grey and had a high stand-fall collar. The skirts of the coat were cut away at the front, and the sleeves revealed the frill of my shirt cuffs. I also wore black breeches with white stockings and shiny black, buckled shoes. The fineness of the outfit made me want to strut about the cabin, but it was too cramped, and I could only manage two or three steps.

Mid-morning, I strode purposefully into the foyer of the Hotel Danieli. The ship's captain, himself a resident of Venice, had recommended it after he had spied my fine clothes. The hotel's main building was on the Palazzo Dandolo, close to St Mark's Square with a rear façade on the Riva degli Schiavoni's quayside promenade overlooking St Mark's Basin. It was palatial, exactly what I was looking for, and — as the captain had advised — also offered guests the services of interpreters. I gave instructions for them to pick up my trunks from the ship and then enquired where I might take lunch.

First, though, I wanted to see something of the city. I was offered a guide who advised me that there were only two ways to get about: on foot or by water. Venezia was, he said exuberantly, the City of Water, the City of Masks, the City of Bridges, the City of Canals. For an hour or so we walked the Piazza San Marco and he proudly showed me its treasures. I was particularly taken with the Horses of St Mark, a replica of the *Triumphal Quadriga* apparently captured in Constantinople in 1204 and carried to Venice as a trophy.

However, Venice in June was hot, and I realised that, excellent as my clothes were, they were made for cooler climes than an Adriatic summer. At my request, my guide hailed a sandolo, a traditional flat-bottomed rowing boat designed for the shallow waters of the Venetian lagoon. It was smaller than a gondola, but was also rowed whilst standing up.

By one of the clock I was ravenously hungry. Spurred by the fact that I had dined meagrely on board the *Trinacria* for the last fortnight, I asked to be delivered to the Caffè Florian, a coffee house situated in the Procuratie Nuove back at the Piazza San Marco. It had been recommended by the hotel because it attracted the notables of the city and beyond, including artists and women; I liked that idea.

I stood outside the front façade and could see what an elegant establishment it was, but then I realised I had not visited the money exchangers, and had only golden guineas as a means of payment. I contemplated turning and calling back the interpreter and the sandolo boatman, but I was then taken by an idea. I would use this to my advantage; perhaps I could procure a free meal — sharpen my skills, so to speak.

The interior was just as elegant: a long narrow room, the walls of which were decorated with panels illustrating classical scenes. I was led to a table on my own, but I looked about, hoping to spy another Englishman. About three tables down on the opposite side sat a young man, reading absorbedly, and I knew instinctively that he was English from the style of his dress. I strode purposefully to his table and stood tall before him.

'Captain John Campbell-John, at your service, sir,' I said in a fierce military whisper. He slowly looked up from his book, his eyes taking me in as they ascended. I could see the puzzlement on his face at this imposing figure standing above him.

I gave the smallest of nods and continued, 'I wonder, sir, if I might request your assistance? I find myself on the horns of a dilemma. I docked only this morning and in my haste for luncheon, I am afraid I have forgotten to go to the money exchangers. I have only guineas on me.' I plucked a golden guinea from my waistcoat by way of illustration.

The man did not reply immediately; he just raised an inquisitive eyebrow. I would have to work my silver tongue a little harder, I thought. 'Do you think, sir, that this establishment will accept my sterling?'

'Why don't you ask them?' he asked, sucking his teeth.

I bit my lower lip; he was not responding as I had expected him too. 'Yes, yes, you are right sir; I shall enquire of the management.' I turned slightly to return to my table, but then I saw him twitch the merest smile.

He sat upright in his chair and his expression softened. He pointed to the chair opposite him. 'Please, sir, take a seat with me,' he said. 'I must apologise, but I have travelled extensively, and I have become wary of strangers and their intentions. I can see that you are a gentleman who wishes to avoid embarrassment. Please, you must be my guest for lunch.' He thrust out his hand, and I shook it; both our grips were forceful, which I found reassuring. 'Robert Babcock Esquire, sir,' he introduced himself.

'Oh, I couldn't possibly intrude,' I said, still maintaining my deception.

He stood and pointed to the chair again. 'No, please, sir. Sit, I insist.'

'Your servant, sir,' I nodded, using my finest manners.

Before I sat, I took in this man. He was lean and tall, perhaps an inch taller than me. His hair was dark brown and luxurious, with long sideburns, a small, manicured moustache and the dark shadow of a beard on his face. He was ruggedly handsome, as masculine a man as you could meet.

He raised his hand to call the waiter, then looked at me inquisitively. I noticed a golden ring on the little finger of his left hand, with a green agate mounted in the centre that was engraved with the image of an eagle, its wings spread in the style of a Roman Legion standard. 'What shall I order for you?'

I had not thought. 'What would you recommend?'

'The Venetians like their seafood.'

'Well, I'm game,' I said.

He turned to the waiter, said, '*Bisàto, per favore*,' and looked back at me, his face creasing into a smile. 'Marinated eel,' he said. He must have seen my face turn sour at the thought, for he laughed. 'It's better than it sounds, I promise you. Coffee or wine?'

'Wine, please.'

'And a bottle of Pucinum, *per favore*,' he added.

He was right: the eel was splendid and so was the wine — a light, sparkling white.

'What brings you to Venice, sir?' I enquired.

'After I came down from Cambridge, I was keen to undertake the Grand Tour. So that is what I have been doing for the last four years.'

'Is that not a long time for the tour?'

'Aye, 'tis true enough. I have been more rigorous than most. But then I studied classics at Cambridge, ancient Greece and Rome and the like, so I came at it from an educated angle. Many of the young men on the tour are more interested in drinking and wenching their way around Europe than education. That was not for me.'

But that sounds good to me, I thought. I looked at him pensively; he seemed a strange cove. His appearance put him down as one of those Englishmen who would indeed drink and wench his way through life. He had all the physical attributes that I saw in myself and which I used to my advantage, and yet he said he was more interested in academia. 'So where have you been?' I asked.

'Calais to Paris, then Ostend, the Spanish Netherlands, Flanders, Geneva and Lausanne. Then I traversed the Alps to the German-speaking parts of Europe: Innsbruck, Vienna, Dresden, Heidelberg, Berlin and Potsdam. I then went south to the Italian cities of Milan, Turin, Pisa, Florence, Venice, Padua and Rome. Finally, I took a boat to Spain to visit Barcelona, Madrid and Seville, and then I should have gone home.'

I blew out my cheeks and gave a long whistle at the extensive list. 'But you came back to Venice — why?'

'Because I have not finished travelling!' he said. 'I want to go to Egypt.'

'That will mean crossing swords with Johnny Turk, will it not?'

'It will indeed, sir; it will indeed. Egypt has been an Ottoman province for hundreds of years.'

'You are not afraid, sir?'

'Granted, Egypt is another rasher of bacon entirely — it is a journey into the unknown, but I wouldn't be the first European to visit Egypt. Did not Napoleon take an army there in 1798? I am preparing myself.' He pointed down at the book he had been reading. 'I am learning Turkish in preparation.'

'So you will travel to Egypt from Venice?'

'Yes, it's the obvious choice; for hundreds of years the city has been the centre of trade between Western Europe and the rest of the world, and that includes the *Mahomedan* world.' He took the bottle, looked at what was left in it and then shared the wine out between us. 'And you, sir, what brings you to Venice?' he asked as he brought the glass to his lips.

'Adventure, sir,' I answered haughtily. 'I was growing bored with the London scene. I thought Venice would be a fine escapade.'

We talked together easily for an hour or so as we consumed another bottle of the Pucinum. When we stood to take our leave of each other, I offered to stand him dinner. I could not explain even to myself why I did so. He was supposed to be just another person of privilege to be duped by my silver tongue, but I found the man fascinating.

'Your offer is generous and I am happy to accept, sir,' he said, thrusting out his hand as if to complete a commercial transaction.

As I shook his hand, I noticed his large hazel eyes. They were expressive, but it was more than that — they suggested genuineness, as though this man was truthful, trustworthy. It was a look that I had practised many times as part of my own deceptions. I wondered if, in his case, this was also a falsehood.

CHAPTER 4

I met with Robert Babcock again that evening, and then dined with him every night for the next week. He was not the sort of man I would have normally chosen to be my companion in the beautiful city of Venice, but I could not have found a more informed one. I had never found the privileged in England to be the sharpest swords in the armoury. In fact, I thought the English were a narrow-minded breed of men, an arrogant and intolerant race who believed that the sun rose and fell in London. The only time they thought deeply was when they lay in bed at night, fearing that the revolution in France would cross the Channel.

But Robert Babcock was not of that breed; he knew everything about everything, but he wore his intellect lightly, as well as being manly of countenance and athletic of build. He was the ideal of the dashing young guardsman, but with the conversation and intellect of a Cambridge don. I was taken with the idea of making him understand that he ought to put to good use what God had granted him, but, I have to admit, my terms of reference were inclined towards the pleasures of the flesh, not the mind. I enquired of him when the famous carnival was to take place. I had a picture in my mind of us dressed in black capes with elaborate masks, complete with lace and feathers, taking our pick of the beautiful ladies of the city.

He just laughed robustly at me. 'But you are thirty years too late, sir! The Emperor of Austria outlawed it in 1797, along with the use of masks. They are now strictly forbidden.'

I was rather crestfallen. His amusement at my naivety stung me, and he must have seen that in my countenance. I looked at him, holding his gaze firmly. 'How do you know *everything*?' I asked sarcastically. 'Did you never play out in the sun when you were a child? Did you always have your head in a book?'

'Forgive me, my friend,' he said as his face softened. 'Yes, 'tis true, I've always had a thirst for knowledge, and books have always been my companions, but there is more to me than book learning, I assure you. I was blessed with athletic ability too; it seems to come naturally to me. I fenced at university. I shot there too, *and* I am a fine opening batsman. So yes, I *have* played out in the sun many times.'

I relaxed at his friendliness and smiled back at him. 'Would you also regard yourself as a man about town, then?' I had a night's wenching on my mind.

We exchanged glances and I could see that he understood the nuance in my question. He cocked his eyebrow. 'Well, I don't waste my life supping and wenching all night and then spending the next day hungover and sleeping it off, if that's what you mean.'

I ground my teeth, disappointed at this response — then I saw his eyes flash.

'But I have learned that we have to take our pleasures where we can,' he went on.

'And do those pleasures include the ladies?' I sat forward in my seat.

'I would say it explicitly refers to the fairer sex,' he said, giving me a knowing sideways glance.

We laughed, raised our wine glasses and clinked them together. 'And where do we find these fair ladies?' I enquired playfully.

'If we are talking about fine ladies of breeding, the opera is a good place to meet them, but it will need guile and delicacy to arrange a tryst. Or there is another festival, the Festa del Redentore, that takes place next month, when everyone turns out to see the fireworks. That may be easier, but I'll have left for Egypt by then.'

'But what about *tonight*?' I persisted.

'I suppose there will be women about offering their services, but I have no knowledge of how to go about meeting them,' he said, shaking his head.

'Then you must let me be *your* guide tonight,' I said. 'Venice is a port, after all, and all ports have delights to offer after dark. Are you game, sir?'

I scanned his face expectantly, then saw a roguish smile spark behind his eyes. 'Aye, sir. You lead on; let us see where the night takes us.'

I hailed a gondola and tried to tell the boatman that we were looking for entertainment, looking for women, but my few words of Italian were not up to the task, and Robert took over the consultation. The boatman took us to a *taverna* near the Santa Margherita Bridge, a middling sort of place. It was certainly not a place frequented by the common sailor, nor was it a place where the members of the noble families of this beautiful city would venture. Nevertheless, it was relatively clean and inviting.

From the walkway, we entered through a large Gothic doorway of an old but impressive stone building. We then climbed some stairs, as the *taverna* was on the first floor. The room was dimly lit with lanterns, but it was warm and enticing. In the corner, a guitarist was playing and singing a folk song and the customers were quiet, listening intently. We took a table and ordered wine from the *proprietario*. When it came, it was non-vintage, coarse on the palate, but we just shrugged as if to say it was to be expected. I looked around; the clientele was placid and respectful to the entertainer, and my first thought was that the gondolier had not brought us to the type of low establishment that we were intent on sampling. There were women present; however, they were with their partners. Then I spied the *proprietario* talking eagerly to a woman who I assumed to be his wife. She then left the *taverna*.

I thought little more of it, but a few minutes later she returned with four young women who were dressed decoratively, their dresses cut audaciously low to reveal acres of bosom. Their faces were heavily powdered and rouged, their eyebrows plucked and their lips painted a vivid red. I smiled knowingly — perhaps the gondolier knew what he was doing, after all. We did not need to go looking for wenches, they would come to us.

I caught Robert's eye and nodded in the direction of the young women. They came over to us, closely followed by the *proprietario*, who knew his business well. This may have been a foreign country to me, but I knew that we were expected to buy them wine and the women knew that they must encourage us to keep drinking. The only person at the table who did not seem to know the rules of the game was Robert, but I quickly educated him whilst he acted as interpreter.

The table began to groan under the weight of empty wine bottles and half-drunk goblets. As the evening wore on, I became anxious that inebriation might lead to unconsciousness rather than tupping. A young woman came and sat on my lap, trailing a finger down my face. She then placed her warm wine-laced red lips sensuously against mine, her constricted bosom rising and falling as if fighting to escape her stays. I knew that she had the same thoughts as I, if from a different motivation: if I passed out, she would not get paid. I tried to ask where we should go to complete the transaction, but I failed dismally; she had incomprehension writ across her face.

I looked at Robert, but his face was hidden by the wench who had commandeered him as my wench had commandeered me. I didn't need to worry — all this had been spied by the *proprietario*; this was everyday business to him. He came and rapidly spat Italian words at me, and I called for Robert to interpret. We were being offered rooms upstairs for our use, and Robert negotiated on our behalf.

I spent the night in the arms of Gabriella, a young dark-haired beauty with flashing green eyes and the body of a Roman goddess. It had been over a month since I had lain with a woman, and this *giovane donna* was as perfect a creature as I could have found.

I lunched with Robert the next day at the Caffè Florian. He had already gone when I finally stirred and left the *taverna* in the morning. His constitution, it seemed, was stronger than mine. With the coarse wine from the previous evening lying heavy in my stomach, I took only coffee and a little bread.

'You, sir, look as if you have got the stench of the lagoon in your nostrils,' he teased.

'And I feel as if I've got the dregs of the lagoon in my belly as well,' I replied, trying to raise some wit.

He laughed robustly as he tucked into his lunch of risotto, blackened with the ink from a cuttlefish. Each mouthful I saw him shovel into his mouth made my guts churn. He saw my discomfort, but it only made him relish his meal the more. When he finished, he sat back in his chair and looked at me intently, as if he were contemplating something. Then his eyebrow arched.

'What — what is it, sir?' I asked.

'Whilst you were sleeping off the night's excesses, I went to see a shipping agent this morning. I have secured a passage to Alexandria; I leave in six days' time.'

I was a little disappointed; I had grown to enjoy his company. 'I shall be sorry to see you go,' I said, surprisingly honestly for me, 'but why the rush?'

'My time is limited.' I was not sure what he meant, and he must have seen he needed to explain further. 'Last night was agreeable, most pleasant; it was good to behave as though I have no responsibilities, but this morning ... well, this morning has made me realise that I do.'

I was still not sure that I understood him; after all, I had always pursued a lifestyle devoid of any responsibility. It must have been plain from the confusion on my face.

'My father will be sixty next year,' Robert continued. 'He is getting old, and I won't be able to continue travelling should he die.'

I gave a hollow laugh. 'But you would never be able to get back for the funeral,' I said. 'It would take weeks even before a letter reached you! You can't let guilt consume you.'

'No, you don't understand, my friend. It will be my responsibilities that draw me back. My elder brother was killed in the 1812 war against the Americans. When my father dies, I will inherit the barony. *I* will become the eleventh Baron Carberton. I will have to go back and run the estate in Nottinghamshire, and find a wife so that I can produce an heir.'

'So you're a *lord*?'

'Well, not yet, but I will be one day.'

35

'I didn't take you for a lord; you are far too bright for that.'

'I'm not sure I understand you,' he said, 'but I thank you anyway, sir, if a compliment *was* intended.'

'So you have to do all your adventuring before you become part of the landed gentry?'

'That's about the size of it.' Then he paused, looked down contemplatively at the condiments on the table before us. 'I have a proposition for you. I'd like you to come with me.'

I liked the sound of that, two young men with mischief on their minds in a far-off country. 'That sounds capital, sir!' I enthused.

He gave me a disturbed glance. 'No, you misunderstand, sir; what I am proposing is a different rasher of bacon altogether. I am not suggesting a young man's escapade; it will not be a follow-on from last night. I am first and foremost an academic, and the purpose of the trip will be a quest: I am going in search of antiquities. And anyway, Egypt is a Mahomedan country, so there will be little opportunity for alcohol and, I would think, little scope for wenching.'

I sat back, somewhat crestfallen, but then I paused and gathered my thoughts. Suddenly, my betrayal of Samuel, my old friend in England, came rushing back to me. 'So what will my job be on this *quest*?'

'I noticed you last night. You had no knowledge of Venice, yet you instinctively seemed to know how to find what you wanted, and then you had the negotiation skills to obtain it. I think you have a natural cunning, sir, which would be invaluable to me.'

I knew that assessment of me was correct. 'And what sort of antiquities are we looking for? Mummies?'

'No, no,' he said, 'religious texts.'

'What do you want with Islamic texts?' I was confused.

'Nothing — I'm talking about Christian religious texts.'

'But Egypt is a Mahomedan country.'

'It is now, but it wasn't before the Arab conquest in the seventh century. Before that, Egypt was inhabited principally by Coptic Christians. The European Monastic Movement began in Egypt.'

I shuffled forward in my chair, leaning my elbows on the table. 'So where do we find these texts?'

'In the monasteries, or what is left of them. Some go back fifteen hundred years to the fourth century, and so do their libraries.'

'And will we be able to understand these texts?'

'Good question, John,' he said, arching his eyebrow again. 'I have studied Coptic Egyptian.'

'You would have!' I said mockingly.

'In its written form, it is an adaptation of the Greek script with some additional letters added to represent Egyptian sounds not found in the Greek language.'

'I studied some Greek as a boy,' I said enthusiastically. 'Would I be able to understand it?'

'Maybe —' I could see he was being coy — 'with some study.' He stared at me, but his face remained unchanged. Then he exhaled, as though he had been holding his breath in anticipation. 'It's a big decision, I know. You think on it, sir, and let me know — shall we say tomorrow evening?'

CHAPTER 5

I spent the next morning in my hotel room at the Hotel Danieli; my melancholy had returned. I took luncheon in the hotel, for I was not yet ready to see Robert. After lunch I walked for miles beside the canals, but thoughts of my previous betrayal stabbed at me. I had grievously wronged Samuel, the noblest of men.

I knew what my nature was, a scheming rapscallion without empathy for my victims. I looked down, felt the inquisitive nose of a snuffling dog around my groin. It was hot in the midday sun and wanted attention, or, I thought, had this mangy animal sniffed the scent of my lost honour struggling to reassert itself. I realised I saw in Robert Babcock the honourable character of Samuel — the man I had cheated and betrayed. That evening I dined with Robert, as promised, at the Caffè Florian. He poured me a glass of wine and I fingered the stem rather than drinking it. Then I played with a loose thread on my sleeve. Robert must have seen my unease.

'You do not have to be so coy, sir. If you have decided against my offer, then out with it and say so. I will not think less of you; I know I ask a lot of a man I have known only a week.'

I looked at him, but then dropped my eyes submissively. I had decided that afternoon that I would unburden myself to Robert. If I were to become his companion, then at least he should know the type of man that his life may depend upon. But I could not look him in the eye as I spoke.

'Sir,' I started, but then I paused — the words were not to come easily — 'you are clearly a principled man...'

'I hope so. I am an Englishman, after all.'

'I too am an Englishman, Robert,' I stumbled, 'but I am *not* a principled man; I am not the man that I purport to be.' I glanced up and saw him looking directly at me. I had to drop my eyes again. 'I need to tell you exactly the type of man I am. When I have done so, you must think again about your offer. If you do not want this man to be your companion, then the matter will never be spoken of again.'

He opened his mouth to speak, but then closed it, and gestured for me to continue. Fear gripped me, but then I started to unburden myself and the words flowed until they became a torrent. I told him about my upbringing, that my real name was Edward John, that Captain John Campbell-John was an invention; I had only been a common soldier. I said that I did not even have enough money to pay my hotel bill or my account at the Caffè Florian, and I intended to run out on both. And then I told him of the real reason I had come to Venice.

'Sir,' I said, 'on my first day in London as the invented infantry captain, John Campbell-John, I met a young Jewish pugilist, the now famous Samuel Medina. I have always been a lucky man; this was no more than a chance meeting. I encountered a youth involved in a street fight and I stood second for him; the lad turned out to be exceptional, and I offered to be his manager. He stood a mere five feet eight, but he beat everyone they put in front of him, besting men who were so much bigger. He eventually became the Champion of All England, and he earned huge purses from his victories. However, they were paltry compared with the gambling winnings we made. He looked much too small, so the book always ran against him. In those early fights, I regularly got five to one against him, or even more. We made prodigious amounts of money and lived like kings. But more than that, Samuel, the most honourable man I have ever met, became my friend; the only true friend I have ever had.

'But I became addicted to the gaming tables and I was an excellent card player. Well, I was when I was sober, but my love of cards was matched by my love of claret. I started to lose heavily, so I needed those fights, to keep replenishing my funds. But then I lost a fortune on the turn of one hand — I was sure that I could not be beaten, but I was. Worse than that, I was at Molly Jasper's Rooms, and Molly Jasper guaranteed any gaming losses that arose on his premises. If your name was in his ledgers, you had to pay, whether you be a lord or a commoner. If you failed, his men sought you out with the intention of inflicting pain until you paid. Additionally, your reputation would be brought to nought; gambling losses were a matter of honour and must be paid in preference to your tailor, your gunsmith or even your grocer. And so I stole the advance takings from the famous fight between Samuel Medina and Big Charles Sweep for the Championship of All England — and bet it on Sweep. Sweep was unbeatable; everyone knew that. But Samuel won again. I was still unable to pay *my* debts, but I had now also plunged Samuel into massive debts; he had to pay all his suppliers for the control of the fight at Newmarket Racecourse.' I paused temporarily and sought out Robert's eyes.

'How much did you steal from your friend?' he asked.

I knew the amount to the penny — it was burned into my mind like a branding iron. 'Two thousand, one hundred and seventy-eight pounds, seven shillings and eight pence.'

He sat upright, his eyebrow arched so high that I thought it would escape into his hairline. 'My God, sir,' he said, 'even dukes would baulk at such a figure!'

I nodded contritely, but I was still intent on telling him the whole truth. 'And so I had only one option, and that was to flee. I took passage on the first ship that I could — and that is how I find myself here in Venice. In England, people are looking for me, not just Samuel. I owe them all vast sums of money. In short, sir, I am a fraud, a swindler, a common criminal. That is the sort of man that I am, and the kind of man you ask to be your companion.'

Robert leant back in his chair and studied me. We entered a long period of silence as he reflected on what I had said. I looked down, embarrassed. He took long drinks of his wine at intervals, swilling the ruby liquid as he reflected. His face revealed irritation, and then his expression darkened and a shiver ran down my spine.

The silence seemed to be interminable; I could see that I was now diminished in his eyes. I stood involuntarily and put down my napkin on the table. 'I'll bid you goodnight then, sir,' I said meekly. I nodded civilly and turned to go.

He gestured for me to stop. 'No, John Campbell-John. Sit, we still have things to discuss.' I sat again as ordered, as if I was a schoolboy being admonished by the headmaster.

He took up his glass again, then put it down and fiddled with the cutlery instead. He exhaled deeply to signal that he was ready to give his verdict. 'We are likely to face dangers in Egypt, sir.' These opening words gave me hope, but then they were dashed as he continued, 'My life may be in your hands. I need to know that I can trust you, but by your own admission you are untrustworthy.'

This honesty I had displayed was new territory for me; it left my silver tongue redundant.

'On the other hand,' he added, inclining his head, 'you have other attributes. The dark arts apparently come easily to you —

perhaps your cunning will be an asset on my quest. You are also educated and have some Latin and Greek — that too will be helpful.'

I sat upright in my chair. 'Does that mean your offer stands?' I asked.

'I didn't say that, sir.'

His words were devastating. For some reason, I wanted this man's approval. The silence returned and he looked me up and down.

'I will ask a lot of you over the coming months, John Campbell-John, but I will ask one thing above all others: whatever lies that devious tongue of yours tells to others, it tells the truth to me. Is that condition acceptable to you?'

'Aye, sir,' I said without hesitation.

'No, sir, think well upon it. Our lives may depend on each other.'

I turned towards him. 'Aye, sir, your condition is acceptable. You can count on me.'

He met my gaze. 'I hope so, John Campbell-John. I sincerely hope so.'

CHAPTER 6

It was on the tenth day of July 1835 that I got my first sight of Alexandria. I was called on deck by Robert to look at the castle and, at first, I came reluctantly because of the searing heat. As an Englishman, I thought Venice in June was hot, but I had never experienced anything like this. As I came up from below, the fiery sun was even melting the tar in the seams of the deck. The passage from Venice had not been by way of a gentleman's cruise; there were no passage steamers to this destination. We were aboard a merchantman called the *Adelina* and, just like my journey from London to Venice, my cabin was small and cramped — but even that was preferable to being on the blazing deck, despite the occasional refreshing breeze. Our passage had been slow, the sea calm for much of the time in the absence of any noticeable wind.

Robert had insisted that I leave most of my clothes in storage, as they would be unsuitable for the heat of the Levant, but I also realised then that my reduced wardrobe, one frock coat and my military uniform, was still decidedly inappropriate. I was stripped down to my breeches and a linen shirt, open at the neck without my stock. Even so, I sweltered.

I strode across the deck to Robert, still holding the book on Arabic that he had given me. He was learning Turkish, the language of the Ottoman masters in Egypt, so I had volunteered to try and learn some Arabic.

'How is it going?' Robert said, nodding at the book.

'Slowly,' I answered. 'I think I am learning more from the Arab cook than from this tome. I am not the scholar you are.'

He laughed at me, then pointed at the castle on the shore for me to take in my first view of Africa, another continent entirely and a new world to me. He seemed so excited by the whole affair. I heard the sea anchor descend and looked around me, puzzled.

'We have to wait for the pilot to take us into the harbour,' he said by way of explanation.

I gestured that I would go below again, but then a rogue wind blew from somewhere to punctuate the oven in which we were imprisoned, my sleeves billowing. The temporary relief was enough to make me stay, and I was glad that I did. We went under the awning to get some relief from the scorching sun and Robert pointed again, this time at a curious-looking boat with a lateen sail. In the stern of the boat sat an old man with a turban and a long grey beard.

'That must be the pilot,' said Robert. He proved to be correct. The pilot saw us safely into the harbour, and we anchored not far from the shore.

The captain of our ship laughed uproariously when I asked him if he could recommend a hotel. 'Go to the Tre Anchore,' he chuckled. 'It's probably the *only* inn in *all* of Africa.'

And so we trundled wearily through the sizzling streets with our belongings strapped to the backs of the mules we had hired. As we walked, we were accosted by half-naked men, each with what looked like a dead pig under his arm. They turned out to be water carriers, and they knew their business as, before we reached the inn, we had given them a small coin, a para — which is the fortieth part of a piastre, which itself is worth about twopence-halfpenny — and they filled a sparkling brass cup with water from their goatskins. I was glad that Robert had remembered to visit the money exchangers of Venice for some local coins before we left.

Our rooms were on the first floor of the inn. The main one was long and narrow with a window at the end, opening onto a balcony that overlooked the main street and the bazaar. It was devoid of chairs. It was dark and dingy, little light entering through the one window, but then that was probably the intention: to keep out the sun's heat.

The balcony was a good vantage point, though, and I spent several hours just watching the scene below us, though I had little comprehension of what I was actually seeing. I didn't know the significance of the picturesque dress, the turbans, the people of various nations and their weapons, but it was all so thrilling to me. Then something wonderful happened: it seemed that the whole of Alexandria came out to parade before us.

'Lord Robert!' I exclaimed. I had taken to calling him that, knowing that it irritated him. 'Come look, it's a parade of some sort.' He was sitting on a cushion in the far corner, fanning himself and waiting for the sun to go down, but he ambled to his feet to come and see. He put his hand on my shoulder and crouched down beside me, and we looked on together in wonderment.

It started with a long procession of men on horseback with golden bridles and velvet trimmings. Then came donkeys, cushions piled high on their backs so that women dressed in what looked like black silk could ride in comfort, their feet resting on the animals' shoulders. Each donkey was led by a man whilst another walked by the side, holding the saddle. Then came two young boys covered in diamonds, mounted on huge heavy horses, the saddles high-backed and seemingly made of gold. I guessed that they must have actually been silver gilt, as they would have cost a king's ransom otherwise.

'We must be witnessing some form of ceremony,' said Robert, 'some sort of rite of passage for the young boys.'

We later found out that he was right; the boys were being transported to their rite of circumcision, which was obviously a significant event in their lives.

A little while later, another procession came before us, but this time the mood seemed less solemn than that of the circumcision ritual. A band of musicians ambled into view, and I watched as they put their various wind instruments to their mouths and started to blow. I did not know what I expected, but certainly not the cacophony that assailed our ears. Robert and I looked at each other in disbelief, then we laughed at this blast of noise.

There followed, with dignified slowness, what looked like a four-poster bed with pink gauze curtains, supported by numerous ample men, their bronzed muscles gleaming in the evening sunshine. A canopy covered the bed, supported at each corner by poles carried by four other muscled men. A young woman reclined on the bed, not veiled, but covered with cashmere shawls from head to foot.

'Do you think she is a bride?' I asked, turning to Robert.

'That would be my guess, John,' he answered, his eyes still fixed on the colourful procession. Pointing, he added, 'The veiled girls walking by her side are probably her bridesmaids, or whatever the Mahomedan version of that is.'

'But we can't see what the bride looks like,' I said naïvely. 'She's too well wrapped up.'

'I think that is the whole point, John. She is for her new husband's eyes only.'

We watched the comings and goings until darkness fell. It came unexpectedly quickly and without warning, and the streets emptied just as suddenly.

Our entertainment, it seemed, was over for the night. Although we were both tired, sleep did not come easily, as the clinging heat took time to dissipate. We spoke in the shadowy room for some hours, and I quizzed Robert as to our immediate plans.

'We need to hire equipment and camels to transport it,' he said matter-of-factly, 'and then we will want a guide to take us across country.'

'Where?' I asked.

'I thought we'd head for Cairo.'

'And where do we find the camels and equipment? The souk, the bazaar?'

'I thought so,' he grunted, 'and that's where your skills will be required. The merchants will probably see us as innocents to be fleeced.'

I lay for several hours, my eyes wide open in the darkness as I conjured a plan. If Robert wanted me for my cunning, then I would not disappoint him.

At first light I roused Robert from his slumber, my mind full of ideas. He was none too pleased, as he'd only managed to get to sleep in the early hours.

'Who's the ruler of Egypt?' I asked. The lines on his face deepened, his forehead creased as he tried to make sense of what I was saying. 'Who's in charge here?' I repeated.

'Muhammad Ali Pasha, I suppose. Why?'

'And who is he?'

'He is the Khedive of Egypt and the Sudan,' he said, turning away from me and closing his eyes in an effort to return to sleep.

'What's a *pasha*, then?' I asked, shaking him as I spoke.

He looked back over his shoulder at me, bleary-eyed. '*Pasha?* It is a title, a sort of … well, a kind of high lord, I suppose.' He turned back on his cushions and I left him alone.

I woke him again a couple of hours later, and this time he sat up, although he looked at me wearily. I thought he could see from my expression that I had something to tell him. He did no more than raise his eyebrow, but I knew I had to explain. 'I've been speaking to one of the other guests of the inn, a ship's captain who has some English.'

'And?' Robert asked, yawning.

'Well, it seems that the *local* man in charge is someone called Boghos Bey Yusufian, and he is like the prime minister of Muhammed Ali.'

'That makes sense — a *bey* is a high-ranking official,' he said.

I continued, still enthused. 'Look, put on your finest clothes. We are going to see this Boghos Bey chap. I have brought my army uniform and I will wear that.'

'What on earth for?' He looked at me with a puzzled expression.

'Well, if a *pasha* is a sort of a high lord, then you are going to be Lord Robert Babcock, an English lord, and I will be your aide, Captain John Campbell-John. By my reckoning, an English lord will trump an Ottoman *bey*.'

'I fear your reasoning may be false, John, but even if it is true, what will that get us?'

'Safe passage through Egypt, Robert. That's what it will get us.'

Later that morning, we presented ourselves across the city at the residence of Boghos Bey Yusufian. We were sweltering in our inappropriate dress, but I was enthusiastic; this was to be my finest deception. We were received with great kindness and civility by the *bey*'s advisers, and it was clear to us both that they had not encountered many European travellers in Egypt and they did not know how to treat us. 'The *bey* is expected soon,' we were told, and we were asked to wait in an anteroom where we were presented with pipes and coffee to drink. The room was quiet except for the ticking of a number of clocks that stood about the room; clocks must have been a favourite of the *bey*. It was a strange collection to find in Egypt — they were of mostly European manufacture, not Ottoman. The constant tickings overlapped so that they sounded like the insects calling and answering each other that I had heard throughout the previous night.

The coffee was strong but sweet. It matched the sweet sherbet and both were most enjoyable to our foreign palate. Then we became aware of a noise outside, and we went to the window and looked out at the courtyard for the cause of it. The gates of the residence had been flung open, so that what seemed a great person could enter. This was the *bey*, I concluded, as he approached on a magnificent horse with a gem-studded bridle and covered in red silk trimmings. He had a number of mounted attendants and some men on foot who cleared the way for him and struck on the head with their sticks those who did not get out of the way quickly enough. They entered the courtyard and a portable platform was brought to the *bey* so that he could dismount.

Sometime later we were presented to him, in an upper room that was a sort of court. He was seated regally at one end on a velvet divan, whilst the lower end of the room was occupied by his *chaoushes* — court officials — and other servants. He was dressed in red and gold with a diamond insignia of his rank displayed on his chest. Our finest European garments suddenly seemed trivial in the presence of his regal attire. I bowed in my full European military fashion before him, introduced Robert as Lord Robert Babcock of Piccadilly and said that I was his military attaché, Captain John Campbell-John of the Seventh Queen's Own Regiment of Light Dragoons.

The *bey* at first just puffed on his pipe, a magnificent instrument about seven feet long. He then leant sideways and an aide interpreted my words by whispering into his ear. I saw a smile flit across his face. He spoke to the interpreter, who then turned back to me.

'Light Cavalry Captain Campbell-John, you are a man after the *bey*'s heart.'

I nodded respectfully to the *bey*, but inside I registered caution, realising that this man was no fool; he evidently knew of European military matters. I would have to be careful with my falsehoods. 'My Lord Robert,' I said and held out my hand in his direction, 'has travelled to Egypt to study the antiquities of your great country.' Robert played his part instinctively and nodded respectfully at the *bey*. I thought it best not to mention that we were looking for Christian antiquities.

The *bey*'s face remained an implacable mask. I quickly realised that flattery and sycophancy were everyday matters in his life, and I could not overdo the obsequiousness. I therefore obliged with my full devious repertoire.

'Our intention is to travel first to the magnificent city of Cairo,' I said, 'but we could not leave without paying our respects to the noble *bey*.' I flourished an arm and then lowered myself over my knee in an exaggerated fashion.

I thought he liked that, although his face still remained implacable. He gestured imperially with a waved hand as he sucked on his diamond-encrusted pipe. The conversation continued in that manner, and I saw Robert several times trying to suppress smiles at my silver tongue and outrageous gestures.

But it worked; the *bey* said that although the *pasha* was in Upper Egypt, he would tell him of our arrival and, on his behalf, arrange for every facility to be put at our disposal in seeing all the objects of interest. He said that he would also write to Habeeb Effendi, the Governor of Cairo, to direct him to let us have the use of the *pasha*'s horses. I saw a look of amazement cross Robert's face, and hoped that he would not undo my good work.

It got better: the *bey*, from his cross-legged position, directed that a *kawass* should attend us. The interpreter explained afterwards that a *kawass* was a sort of armed servant or bodyguard belonging to the government. Each *kawass* bore as his badge of office a thick cane about four feet long, with a large silver head, with which instrument he occasionally enforced his commands and supported his authority as well as the person he was protecting. Apparently, they normally attended ambassadors or consuls; their presence showed that the State protected the person they accompanied.

A man was summoned from the far end of the room and, coming forward, he waved deferentially in our direction and bowed his head to emphasise his subservience; yet that did not diminish his commanding presence. He was a powerful-looking man with a magnificent jet-black moustache extending at least an inch either side of his expressionless face. His seeming self-assurance was emphasised by his broad shoulders, which were thrust back so that his muscular chest was made even more prominent. He wore an elaborately embroidered rust-coloured jacket that was cut off at the waist, and worn over a rich, deep-jade shirt. Material of the same colour was used for his billowing trousers, separated from his shirt by an ornate belt. On his head he wore a turban of the sort that looked like a draped headscarf, again in the same deep-jade colour. At his waist he wore a sword, a *kilij*, which was long and thin and curved backwards, while on his right hip he carried a *kurbash*, a curled whip made from hippopotamus hide, about a yard long.

Back at the hotel, with our *kawass* in tow, we broke into laughter at the implausible success of my ruse, much to his incredulity; he, of course, failed to understand our delight. Robert, with his limited Turkish, elicited his name. He was called Fatma, but we were to address him merely as '*kawass*'.

My ruse had been successful: we had gained a passport to roam Egypt under the *pasha*'s patronage. Robert wondered at the proficiency of my silver tongue, and rejoiced that our adventure in Egypt was starting so well.

CHAPTER 7

We awoke the next morning in the highest of spirits, keen to start, in earnest, our quest. Robert told the *kawass*, in his limited Turkish, that we were to go to the souk to purchase our provisions, but he advised that we should first employ a person called a dragoman to avoid being fleeced. A dragoman, it seemed, was an interpreter, but would also manage all our commercial affairs.

We dispatched the *kawass*, who quickly returned with a man who said his name was Hakeem, which, he was at pains to tell us in his broken English, meant 'wise' in Arabic. '*Salaam Sidi,*' he said, flourishing his hand deferentially, and indicating he would employ all his wisdom to get us the very best deals available. The problem was that he did not, at first glance, look like a man of such acumen; he was grim-faced and hunched, with a jutting black-bearded jaw. He was also shabby, his body wrapped in what seemed like one garment that covered his head and swept around his neck and across one shoulder and then around his lower body, and was finally held in place over the crook of the opposite arm. It was not dissimilar to a toga in ancient Rome, if on a much smaller scale.

In his case, though, appearances were deceptive. It quickly became apparent that this was a man of extreme cunning. No one was going to cheat us whilst he was our dragoman — that was his job. Now, I was also a man that had the shrewd serpent within me — I knew all about the world of the trickster and I quickly deduced the nature of him — but there was little I could do about it. We were to find out later that we would eat and drink what he chose to give us; we would see through his eyes; we would hear through his ears. He would negotiate our commercial deals, and it was *his* palm that was greased by the vendor. He was, on the surface, our servant, but in reality we were his vassals to be used at his will. I naïvely advised him that I was trying to learn Arabic and that his assistance would be most appreciated.

'*Sidi*,' he nodded, addressing me as 'my master' in Egyptian Arabic, 'I will give you every assistance.' But of course he had no intention of negating his own advantage over me.

He started well, however. His advice was not to hire a train of donkeys to carry our extensive belongings on an overland trip to Cairo — that would take too long — so the best plan was to travel southwards by boat. With this in mind, he accompanied us to the souk to purchase provisions and hire Mahomedan servants who would act as our bearers and bodyguards. Then he went off on his own to secure our passage.

Whilst at the souk, I had another purchase in mind. I had come to the conclusion that English breeches and linen shirts were unsuitable for our journey. I had a hankering to dress like a local and I persuaded Robert to do the same. The problem was that there were so many nuances of dress to represent the complex strata of Ottoman and Arab societies.

However, we boarded our dhow in the Ottoman dress of blue cloth, a billowing pair of trousers down to the knee, then tight to the ankle. We wore our own white stockings and European shoes, though, together with our own linen shirts. To my eyes we looked like sons of the Prophet. The boat was small, but it only took us down to Atfeh via the Mahmoudieh Canal, the purpose of which was to link the port of Alexandria with the river. At Atfeh we hired a larger dhow to take us on the legendary Nile itself south to Cairo. The Nile, known as the father of rivers and as Al-Bahr to the locals, was a slothful swirling creature, its fertile muddy waters rolling languidly northwards like a wise old man coming to feed his grateful grandchildren.

I enjoyed our journey immensely, though. I adapted to the languid nature of the river and I was, for some days, at peace with myself, for my melancholy was banished. One morning I watched the cook fill numerous earthenware jars of river water, the insides of which he had rubbed with a paste of bitter almonds. I discovered that the purpose of this was so that, after a couple of days, all the impurities of the murky river would be filtered out, leaving clean drinking water.

I loved standing on the deck, listening to the gentle lapping against the sides of our boat, and to the cries of birds as they swooped over the surface of the river. There were pigeons, white spoonbills and other strange birds stalking amongst the herbage and flying around us in every direction. The captain, or *reis*, put out into the middle of the stream, set two huge lateen sails on low masts and, with the help of the wind, we made our way slowly towards the south. I marvelled at the fertility of the land that swept idly by us: watermelons, corn, figs, dates, limes and all manner of green herbs flourished luxuriantly. The river itself was filled with crisscrossing boats of every description, and reminded me of the most congested thoroughfare in the heart of London.

I was leaning over the rail, feeling the delicious wind on my face, when one of the hired Arab servants spoke. 'Excuse me, sir,' he said as he passed me by.

I looked around, startled at his unexpected use of English. Although dressed like the other Arab men in the *galabeya* — a long white shirt — worn over a pair of loose trousers called a *seroual*, it transpired that he was in fact Maltese, and a Christian to boot. He was a squat, powerful man, with a skullcap over his shaven head and a tattoo of a cross on his neck. He seemed to have an honest face, and he did not drop his eyes the way I observed some of the lower classes did when confronted with someone of a higher status. I immediately commandeered him in my quest to learn Arabic; he was to be my teacher. He answered to the name Rokku and we struck up an unlikely friendship, which, unfortunately for him, made him an enemy of Hakeem the dragoman, who glared at him every time he saw us talking together. I was sure that on one occasion I even saw him make a cutting gesture across his throat, but Rokku did not seem to be distressed by the apparent threat.

On a beautiful morning, with the rising sun giving a pink tint to the muddy waters of the Nile, Rokku waved me over from the open cabin at the back of the dhow and pointed out the tops of some pyramids. I called Robert over and he said they were undoubtedly the great Pyramids of Giza.

I took the opportunity to look at his features. Although I had been unshaven for many days, my dark blond hair and blue eyes still proclaimed me as European. Robert, however, was dark with large hazel eyes, his dark stubble now having reached several days' growth. I suddenly realised that with his semi-Ottoman dress, he could have passed for an Ottoman Turk. I made a mental note; perhaps I could use this in the future.

Later that day we landed at Bulaq, a small port town on the Nile. The place was shambolic, perhaps a relic of more prosperous times, and the population looked shabby and underfed. It was only a short donkey ride from there to Cairo, our first destination. As Robert had advised me, Cairo was close to the ancient cities of Memphis, Fustat and Giza, the great Sphinx, and the pyramids.

CHAPTER 8

'I did play in the sunshine sometimes, you know,' said Robert, playfully thrusting a book into my hands. I looked down at the title; it was called *Modern Egypt* and was by a Mr Edward Lane. 'I have marked a passage for you to read,' he added, 'an account of the population of Cairo.'

I retired to the open cabin at the back of the boat and sat on the carpets that had been spread out. I opened the book and began to read. I learned that in Cairo, the ruling class were Turks who spoke Turkish. Then came the Arabs, the former conquerors of the land who formed the bulk of the population, and were the merchants and farmers of the country. Besides these were the Copts, who were descended from the ancient Egyptians. These main groups, along with the Jews, were subjects of the Ottoman Empire and Muhammad Ali Pasha. In addition there were small communities of Franks, Armenians, Arabs of Barbary and the Hejaz, Syrians, and the Nubian people of Southern Egypt and the Sudan; these were migrants in the land. I was surprised to read that there were also Levantine Christians, who were under the protection of one or other of the European powers. Many of them were merchants and had grown rich in this country.

We spent our first morning in Old Cairo, looking about the city as if we were just tourists. We took the *kawass*, who ensured, with his thick silver-topped cane, that we had uninterrupted access. Hakeem also came along, wanting to know everything we did. I insisted that Rokku came as well, and the two lurked about, casting sideways glances at each other when they thought we were not looking.

The different groups resided in various quarters, separated by high gates at the end of the streets, which were closed at night. This was enforced by the Ottomans to keep the peace amongst the Turks, Arabs, Christians, Jews, Copts and other religious sects. We were to find out that it also kept the drunken Europeans from intruding on their communities.

It was a city of many domes and minarets, towers, narrow streets and flat-roofed houses, and I could hear the *adhān*, the periodic call to prayer. The Nile was never far away, and we saw the gardens of the *pasha* on the island of Rhoda to the left and the avenue of Egyptian sycamores to the right, leading to the *pasha*'s country palace of Shoubra.

I suggested to Robert that if our goal was to visit Coptic monasteries, then we should visit the Coptic quarter. Hakeem took his cue and led us to that part of the city, where he disappeared after telling us that he had many acquaintances amongst the Copts. He returned with a wealthy-looking Copt whose business was that of a *kateb*, a sort of scribe and accountant, and who it seemed was well-educated and knew about the monasteries.

I distrusted Hakeem intensely, but I had to admit that he did have knowledge of all things Egyptian. He interpreted for us in Arabic as the general language of business. Robert had knowledge of Coptic, but he concealed that information from the dragoman. We were invited to the man's house to take a meal with him and his family, and I was pleased with the progress we were making.

We were afforded every courtesy and were treated to an elegant meal of rice-stuffed vegetables and grape leaves, followed by baklava, a rich, sweet pastry with nuts and honey. The food was served with wine, they not being Mahomedan. We engaged in stimulating Arabic: our host told us that the

Coptic language was now understood by few. Although his family understood Coptic, his business was generally conducted in Arabic, and I was able to follow much of the conversation. Robert in particular was keen to take advice on the Coptic monasteries we should visit.

My concentration was interrupted by the distant sound of a woman singing somewhere in the house. I could not understand her words, of course, but there was something ethereal about her voice. My thoughts kept drifting away and the lady of the house must have seen my reaction. She rose from her divan, pulled back a curtain to a door and called out to the singer. A young woman then entered the room — a woman of such beauty that she took my breath away. I assumed she must be the daughter of the *kateb* and his wife.

I had to admit my emotions could be base, yet I did not initially look at this young woman with the lust of a rutting stag, as I would have done back in England. She was a vision of purity, shown in the way she carried herself, with her large dark eyes and long black hair hanging down her back. She was, I thought, about seventeen. Her dress was made of rose-coloured silk that was edged with gold, and it seemed to complement her youth and charm. I caught myself staring, captivated by her loveliness.

Her mother uttered a few words, at which she came and attended me on my divan. I could not speak Coptic, of course, so I attempted to talk to her in Egyptian Arabic. She laughed intermittently at my stumbling words, and I even found *that* engaging. She then brought us pipes, coffee and sherbet and re-joined me on my divan and, to my surprise, she took a pipe herself.

I realised later that she was only extending the hospitality of the house, as she had been taught to do by her parents. But at the time I misread what was being offered. It was as if a capricious artist had painted me on the wrong canvas: I wanted to be in the unrestrained atmosphere of a London gentleman's club, where beauties were procured for the wealthy gent. The rutting stag in me surfaced, fuelled by the wine I had drunk. I reached out and took her hand, stroking her tender forearm. I did not think about it beforehand; it was merely instinctive. She looked down at her hand in mine and that sparkle in her eye turned to distress. It was as though an icy chill had swept into the room through an open window. All eyes shot in my direction, displaying various degrees of disapproval or apprehension.

I saw Robert's eyebrow arch in that way of his, but this time it was not expressing irony or sarcasm. He made a contemptuous tsking sound, accompanied by a sharp intake of breath. I did not know if this had the same meaning in the Coptic culture, but it bit deep into *my* consciousness; I knew I had let him down. At the least I had been ungentlemanly; at the worst I was putting us in danger.

I stiffened immediately and gave a slight nod to the young woman and then to her father. I was contrite, acknowledging my *faux pas*, but I was unsure if they understood me. The atmosphere remained frosty.

Robert turned to our *kateb* host and spluttered some Coptic words, his head held on one side as if in subservience. He told me later that he had used all the sycophantic Coptic phrases he knew to thank him for his hospitality, of which we were not worthy. He made the farewells on our behalf and we took our leave, back to the European quarter where the dragoman had arranged lodgings for us.

Robert went to bed in disgust, unable to speak to me. Hakeem said that if I needed a woman, I should come to him and he would procure one for me. Rokku heard him say that and came and offered the same service. I said that I needed a drink, and he disappeared for a few minutes and then came back and took me to a low sort of place, and we descended into an oven-like room below stairs. Here I drank brandy and water, then arak and, finally, other crude spirits I had never heard of. My melancholy was back with a vengeance — I had let Robert down, despite my promises to him. This was not like me at all; I had always been a self-centred man, with little regard for others' feelings, but just then, I was consumed with remorse.

CHAPTER 9

When I finally stirred my hungover body the next morning, Robert had already gone about his business, taking the *kawass* with him to ensure safe passage. I read the note he had left for me, my head pounding as I tried to focus my heavy eyes. It was curt and although there was no reprimand in his words, it was clear he was disappointed in me. I wondered if he regretted bringing me along as his travelling companion.

The note said that he had gone to visit the Patriarch of Alexandria who, despite his title, had his palace in Cairo. He explained that the Patriarch was the spiritual leader of the Copts and claimed descent, in uninterrupted succession, from St Mark. His purpose was to gain a letter of introduction to the few remaining Coptic monasteries, so that we would be given access when we arrived. I was tasked with going to the souk to acquire everything we needed for the journey, and he suggested that Hakeem should go with me to do the negotiations. It seemed that he did not even trust me to undertake that task on my own.

In Egypt, all business was taken care of in the morning. Most Egyptians disappeared in the heat of the afternoon, and only reappeared again in the evenings, when the heat began to dissipate. Despite my indisposition, I had to make my way to the souk. The bazaar at first made my head throb again, so vibrant was the activity there, but then the magic of it began to take me. There was the piquant smell of herbs and spices, the wonderful aroma of bread baking and the sweet smell of elaborate confectionaries. Metalworkers' hammers tapped their intricate designs into highly polished copper and silver, and the steam from the laundries added to the humidity of the climate. I listened to the merry chatter of the veiled women, their identities hidden from even their husbands when in public. There were many echelons and nuances of Egyptian and Ottoman society, I had noticed, but here in the souk was where they all combined. High status Ottoman women bedecked in gold jewellery, accompanied by their servants and slaves, were avoiding the beggars holding out cups for alms. Elaborately dressed military men strolled with their hands on the hilts of their swords, whilst young boys skipped between the legs of the throng of people.

The negotiations of these people seemed to be fired with extreme emotions. Hands were raised and flourished in what, to me, sounded like insults and counter-insults at the thieving dogs who would demand such high prices, or who would offer so little coin to purchase. However, when the deal was done, they seemed to descend effortlessly into courtesy, so they were the best of friends again. My spirits began to rise, and I charged Hakeem with the negotiations, realising that Robert was indeed right to have suggested him.

I kept Rokku close by me, as I was learning Arabic from him at a pace now, and he filled in the gaps translating the words I was not accustomed to. I told Hakeem that he was to acquire camels, but he advised that we should, instead, procure donkeys. I looked at Rokku, who nodded in agreement; he said that donkeys were the carts of Egypt. We secured tents and kettles, hens and cook pots and other stores, including hams and tea, and all the other provisions we would need for a trek across Egypt.

Yet I was looking for more, a currency to take with us, something that the monks would like, but Hakeem, despite having poked his nose into all things Egyptian, had little knowledge of the Coptic monks.

Rokku pinched my elbow and I turned to him. He was eager that the dragoman should not be in on his secret, so we moved away a few paces, Hakeem's suspicious eyes following us as we did so.

'The monks are Christian, sir,' he whispered to me, making a point of turning his back on Hakeem. It was an obvious statement, and I was not sure what point he was making. He must have seen that he had to explain further. 'They are not prohibited from drinking alcohol as the Mahomedans are.'

A sly smile turned up the corner of my lips; I now knew exactly what he was getting at. He took my arm and we went off together. The dragoman attempted to follow us, but I turned and waved him back to his task. The souk, it seemed, catered for all men, not just the Mahomedans. After touring the narrow labyrinthine streets, we found an establishment trading in alcoholic beverages. In my broken Arabic and with Rokku's help, I asked the proprietor if he ever did business with the Coptic monasteries, but he said he did very little because they were so poor. I had not realised that — my view of monasteries was based on a European observation of large, wealthy establishments and rotund monks growing fat on their own food and brewing their own beer, with the abbot's powerful men taking rents from the tenant farmers on their lands.

The man knew his trade, however, and said he knew what their drinks of choice were. He recommended arak, and my stomach turned, as it was one of the raw spirits that I had been drinking the night before. He also suggested something called *rosoglio* and we were invited to try it. It was a sweet pink liqueur, quite gentle on the palate, unlike the raw arak, and we purchased a number of bottles of each. I swore Rokku to secrecy, as I wanted something to produce in the future that would re-establish my worth in Robert's eyes.

On our way back we passed a strange sort of establishment; it was not immediately clear to me what it traded in, but I was almost accosted by the proprietor, a learned man dressed in European dress, a style that was obviously becoming fashionable amongst some wealthier Egyptians. He apparently recognised me as a European and spoke to me in French. He then took me into his establishment, where he showed me a number of antiquities from ancient Egypt, including what he claimed was a genuine mummy. My own French was very rusty and I struggled to remember the lessons I'd had with my mother, but we managed to make sense of each other. What he did not know was that I did not have the funds to purchase any of them. I had only two golden sovereigns left of the money I'd come with, even after Robert had settled my hotel and restaurant accounts. A notion had taken me, however — whilst Robert was in search of ancient Christian manuscripts, I could undertake a quest of my own. I was sure there existed a lucrative market for such antiquities back in London, should I ever be in a position to return.

CHAPTER 10

Three days later we set out at dawn, travelling north-west from Cairo. The sound of the call to prayer of the faithful was ringing around the city, diminishing as we left it behind. Our journey would mean that we would leave the lush and fertile lands of the delta and enter the desert and the Wadi El Natrun (the Natron Valley in English), west of the Nile. We made a strange bunch, some twenty of us. The *kawass* had reminded us of the promise made to us by Boghos Bey to write to the Habeeb Effendi, the Governor of Cairo, to tell him of our arrival, and direct him to let us have the use of the *pasha*'s horses. He disappeared for a short time to the governor's palace and returned with three splendid Arabian stallions, one each for Robert and me, the third for himself.

We led the little procession, followed by Hakeem, who insisted on riding on a donkey, his stick-thin legs almost dragging along the ground. The others walked beside the remaining donkeys, being either bearers or well-armed men hired for our protection. We also carried guns to shoot fowl to supplement our provisions.

Our destination was the Desert of Nitria, and in particular we were headed for the Monastery of El-Sourian; Robert had been advised by the Patriarch of Alexandria, when he had visited him, that there was known to be a library there. Robert, know-all that he was, told me that it was in this region of Egypt where monasticism, as we knew it in Europe, was first founded and it went back as far as the middle of the second century. He was now talking to me again after my appalling behaviour at the house of the Coptic *kateb*, but his words were businesslike, and I sensed a mocking tone; it was as if I was not worthy to be his companion.

When we camped that first evening, Robert kept himself to himself, writing and sketching in his notebooks like the academic that he was, straining in the little light given off by the campfire and his lantern. The cook prepared our first authentic Egyptian meal, a dish he called *ful*, which was spicy soaked fava beans and onions, served with a flatbread called *eesh baladi* that was sprinkled with bran. The loaves were about eight inches round and half an inch thick. They were also quite dry but were used to scoop up the beans in lieu of cutlery. I quite enjoyed it until we had it again for breakfast, and then again for dinner and breakfast on each subsequent day.

The people of Egypt, I observed, went to bed when the sun went down. I joined them, going to my tent and curling up on my blanket, leaving Robert alone with his scribbling and our Mahomedan servants prostrating themselves towards Mecca on their prayer mats.

For several days we headed northwards, following the west bank of the Nile. Palm trees guarded the majestic river, and it was clear to me that the Egyptians were masters of irrigation, for there was a profusion of lemons, olives, pineapples and dates. When we reached the village of Terrané, we acquired Arab guides complete with their camels to take us across the desert tracts of the plain. The guides answered to the names Awad and Ahmed, and their love of their camels made me smile; they treated them just like their children. They said that camels should have good teeth, a firm hump and big feet, and insisted on us looking into the mouths of the animals and examining them to confirm their quality.

Although they were locals, they were strangely anxious, their eyes always darting at even the slightest sound, and they told Hakeem that these tracks were inhabited by devils and evil spirits. Bobby Babcock Know-all — as I had taken to sometimes calling Robert — had told me about *djinns*, which were supernatural creatures in Islamic cultures.

It was to be a five-day trek and we followed the measured lolloping gait of the foul-smelling camels and took our pace from them, watching as the landscape changed from luxuriant emerald to stone buff until we were encased in a barren, rocky, dusty landscape as far as the eye could see. Trudging from waterhole to waterhole, frying in a murderously fiery sun — the temperature reaching a hundred and twelve degrees Fahrenheit — I wondered why on earth the early Christians would choose such a desolate place to build their monasteries. Robert told me later that the early Christians had seen the deprivations as a sort of test of their religious devotions. I supposed it was not that different from us fasting and giving things up for Lent as part of *our* devotions. They were also out of the way so that in troubled times it brought them security, and they were built behind high walls that made them defendable.

Awad and Ahmed knew where the wells were to be found, so we could refill the waterskins that our donkeys carried. As the arduous burning days passed with what seemed like nothing but gravel and dust to divert us, we came upon a number of stone heaps, and Robert said they were the remains of the many monasteries in this area.

In the evenings when we made camp, the temperature dropped, and at first I thought our Arab guides were particularly susceptible to the cold, as they seemed to shiver so easily — until Rokku told me that they were actually shivering because they were afraid that the demonic djinns would get them whilst they slept.

The next day, as we rode across the tedious landscape, we approached a small isolated hill. A trail rose up it, which we and our guides followed. The trail was not more than a few feet wide, obliging us to go in single file. But then, abruptly, the lead camel was brought to a stop. Robert called ahead to the Arab guide, but when there was no response, he dismounted and made his way up carefully, leading his horse past the camels to the front. I followed him. Awad merely pointed a bony finger ahead of us.

There was a small band of half a dozen Arab men with long-barrelled guns who had been hiding in a crevice and must have been watching our progress. Their weapons were cocked and aimed at us, pointing at Robert and me as we came forward. I turned instinctively and looked behind us, seeking an escape route, but our rear was also cut off as a larger band had appeared from another crevice behind us. From nowhere a gust of wind blew against me, and the sand it carried stung my face, as if it was an omen. A knot tightened in my stomach.

I had been a soldier, if not a very dedicated one, and I had learned how to appraise a dangerous situation. I looked around anxiously in an effort to reconnoitre the position. Looking up at the top of the hill, I saw several more faces looking down on us from behind the barrels of their guns. I heard our own armed Ottoman guards cock their weapons and my head swung round in alarm; they were taking aim at the men above us.

'Hold!' I shouted, then searched my memory desperately for an equivalent Arabic word. I raised my hand in the air to emphasise my command, and thankfully they responded.

I looked down at the only apparent escape route. The sand and rock appeared loose but the hillside, though steep, was not a precipice, and our horses could possibly *just* navigate it — with luck they would not stumble and break a leg. However, that would have meant deserting our own hired men and leaving them to their fate.

My mind was unexpectedly clear; I knew what I must do. I gritted my teeth. They had not opened fire, I thought — why was that? Perhaps they were not just a band of robbers, content to ambush us, murder us and steal our belongings. It was as though there was an invisible hand guiding me. I would negotiate with their leader. My eyes homed in on the obvious man, whose imposing stance made him stand out from the others.

I mounted my Arabian stallion and, squeezing with my knees, manoeuvred him forward. I fingered my expensive Joseph Egg percussion pistol, sliding it forward on my hip; it was not loaded, but I wanted him to see it, nonetheless. As I approached, the guns of his men followed me and he gave me an amused look, his thin lips parting to reveal a gap-toothed grin. His dark beard was starting to grey and was also coloured by the dust of the desert. His bare legs protruded from the bottom of his *seroual* trousers as he sat atop his mount. He looked me up and down, apparently unsure of what to make of me.

'*As-salamu alaykum.*' I used the Arabic *salaam*, a greeting which meant 'peace be upon you'. I was trying to show that we were not his enemies.

'*Alaykum,*' he replied, meaning 'and upon you', but his face was grinning, his words low and guttural. I was unsure of what to make of that. Rokku had told me that Mahomedans should respond with a longer *salaam*. The fact that he did not might have meant that he did not regard us as men of the Quran. We looked eyeball to eyeball for some moments and I tried not to show fear. He then spat out more Arabic words and surprisingly, my sharpened mind translated the gist of them. He was saying that this country belonged to him. I nodded, but I took care not to lower my eyes submissively.

I shouted over my shoulder for Hakeem, and I heard him scrambling forward along the ledge. When he reached us, I saw from the corner of my eye that he had fallen to his knees, his forehead touching the dirty ground in submission. 'Get up, Hakeem!' I shouted to him, my eyes still fixed on the grinning face before me.

At first he refused. '*Sidi*,' he said, his voice muted in the dirt, 'we must not provoke him.'

'Get up, Hakeem!' I shouted again. 'Interpret for me, and for goodness' sake, man, show that you are not afraid.'

He stood, but his eyes remained lowered, as though he was not worthy of looking directly at this tribesman. 'He says this is *his* land,' I advised. 'I want you to acknowledge that we accept that and ask for his permission to cross it.'

I listened as Hakeem spoke. My Arabic was good enough to hear that he was just asking for them to spare our lives. 'Hakeem,' I rebuked him, 'tell him what I said, man.' He looked up at me pleadingly, as though this was the worst thing he could do. 'Tell him!' I barked.

He spoke again, but that sycophantic language was still there.

The leader of the men spoke again and I called on Hakeem to interpret.

'*Sidi*, he says that we are Muhammad Ali Pasha's men, but this land belongs to the sons of Arabs.'

My clarity of thought was still with me. This man and his followers, I reasoned, must have been rebels; they had never submitted to the Ottoman rulers. There must have been safety for them in this remote desert. He must have thought we were the *pasha*'s men because we had the Ottoman garments and the *kawass* was dressed in Turkish clothes too, of course. Fear now came flooding back to me, as I realised the depth of the peril facing us. If I could not convince this man we were not the *pasha*'s men, then death would come our way swiftly.

I continued to hold his gaze to show that I was not afraid of him, despite the bile rising from the pit of my stomach. I swallowed hard, trying to hide it. 'Tell him we are Englishmen,' I instructed Hakeem.

'He says he does not know what an Englishman is, *sidi*,' interpreted Hakeem.

I then remembered that the people in this land described all Europeans as Franks. 'Tell him that an Englishman is a type of Frank — very good people who are friends of the Egyptians and not friends of the Ottomans.'

'They say that Franks do not wear the Ottoman dress, *sidi*.'

Damnation! I had resolved to introduce Robert as our leader. I would call him Emir Robert, a very mighty Frank who'd come to wonder at the greatness of their vast land. However, that ruse was quickly dismissed from my mind as I saw Robert out of the corner of my eye. He was dark-haired and had not shaved for several weeks. Clothed in the Ottoman dress, he looked every inch an Ottoman. I had to be the leader, and a powerful one at that.

'Ask him whom I am addressing.'

Hakeem recoiled visibly, then fell to his knees again in fear. He was useless to me, so I yelled over my shoulder for Rokku, although I resolved to speak for myself with him to correct me. I asked the man that question and watched the grin on his face widen at my faltering Arabic, but I could see that he understood. He introduced himself as Sheik Abd Al-Rashid.

I nodded my head in salutation, still being careful not to drop my eyes submissively, but I waved my hand in the sort of salute that I had observed others perform, hand to heart, to mouth and then to forehead. I was relieved when he reciprocated. Then, suddenly, that grin disappeared as a belligerence took his features and he barked directly at me.

'We are the sons of Egypt, sons of Arabs. We are not fools to be trifled with. I ask again why you come to my lands.' Rokku made it very clear that I had understood correctly. 'You are Muhammad Ali Pasha's men,' he rumbled again.

I felt my heart beat in a rhythm of terror, but my mind remained clear. 'Rokku,' I yelled, 'go to my donkeys and find my English army sword! It is stowed away on one of them.' He gave me a disturbed look, as though I had lost my mind. 'Go!' I barked again.

I held my breath as he scrambled away, trying all the while to maintain an unyielding, implacable expression. He came back holding the sword sideways, avoiding the handle; that was good, there was no challenge handling it that way. 'Take it to the sheik,' I commanded.

Rokku shuffled forward and then held it up to him. The sheik's face registered surprise; this was clearly not the sort of sword that he had ever seen before, and it was a beautiful weapon. I had bought it from Mr Jeffries — sword cutter to His Majesty — at his shop on the Strand for seven guineas, after a large win on the turn of a card. The sheik took it up and drew it from its scabbard, the rasping noise it made punctuating the air like the caw of a swooping bird. He made cutting movements to the left and right, feeling the balance, and then showed it to his henchmen. A heated discussion took place. I wondered if I would get it back; it was to be my bargaining tool, to exchange for antiquities to take back with me.

'Sheik,' I called out to him, 'you can see that this is not the sword of a follower of the *pasha*. This is the sword of an English soldier.'

He looked back at me. 'So you claim to be an unbeliever,' he said.

I did not know how to respond to that: was that an insult? Or was he beginning to believe me? I decided that it was progress anyway. I called for Rokku again. 'Fetch what is left of the ham,' I told him, and he scampered off again. 'And bring some tea,' I called over my shoulder. He returned quickly, carrying what I had requested. I held up the half-eaten ham for the sheik to see. He curled his lip at the sight of the unclean meat. I then showed him the tea. 'Franks drink coffee,' I said eagerly, 'but Englishmen drink tea.'

The distinction, I could see, between an Englishman and a Frank meant nothing to him, but the ham seemed to have been convincing.

'So why do you pig-eaters come to my land?' he said again; however, his eyes were now less threatening.

'Tell him we are his servants,' whispered Rokku.

I was unsure that this was the right tactic, as I had tried so hard to seem unafraid of him, to show that I was at least his equal. Nevertheless, I took the advice. 'Your servants are men of peace,' I said, again with the traditional salute, 'come on a pilgrimage to see the Monastery of El Sourian.'

The sheik turned to discuss our claim with his menacing henchmen and various turbans nodded, with mumbled words that, to me, seemed to accept what I had said. The sheik waved his arm in the air, the long barrel of his gun glinting in the sun, to signal to his men to lower their weapons. The immediate danger was averted; I wondered then how I could get my sword back.

CHAPTER 11

It was in the early evening of that same day when we entered the walls of the Monastery of El-Sourian. It had not dawned on me that we were so close. Sheik Abd Al-Rashid and his men had escorted us across and down the hill and set us on the right path to travel. It was not until then that I realised just how many men the sheik had; in addition to those that we could see, there were probably a hundred more. I realised then just how much danger we had been in; there was no way we could have fought our way out, even if we had not been ambushed and surrounded.

The sheik had been quite friendly when he'd bidden us goodbye, once he had accepted that we were not the *pasha*'s men. I did not feel safe, however, until we had lost sight of his band as they disappeared over the horizon. It was clear that I was a hero in the eyes of the others, but I was mainly glad to have restored my bond with Robert. Unfortunately, I had lost my magnificent sword in the process, which, apart from my gold fob watch, was about the only thing of value that I'd had left in my possession. In the end, I'd had to gift it to the sheik.

At first sight, the monastery appeared like a mirage in an unforgiving landscape. It shimmered as if it was floating on a lake on the horizon. This strange effect, according to Robert, was caused by the layers of hot and cold air. It was surrounded, I saw, by a high imposing stone wall, with a large square tower guarding the narrow iron door. It looked more like a fort than a monastery, but then I remembered what Robert had told me — these monasteries were built here so that they could be defended. Inside we found a substantial square enclosure, which must have been at least an acre or even more. At the centre was the large, well-maintained church, but most of the other buildings were neglected, some almost derelict. In the corner was a garden where the monks grew the meagre food they needed to sustain them.

We were met by the old abbot and about a dozen monks. Robert presented the letter of introduction from the Patriarch of Alexandria, at which point we realised that the old abbot was blind, the milky opacity of his sightless eyes giving him a serene look of contentment, though he needed an attendant monk at all times. They all looked malnourished, and at first I wondered if it was self-denial as part of their devotions; but I soon realised that it was just their poverty — they simply had so little to eat. This was not the oasis I had initially thought. Robert said that since the Arab invasion of the seventh century, these monasteries had not prospered as their counterparts in England had.

The convent garden looked fresh and luxuriant. A mule was constantly employed at the monastery well, going round in endless circles, drawing water to the soil. Waving palms and banana plants grew tall amidst pomegranate trees, which had bright green leaves and vivid red blossoms. The deep green of the carob tree vied with the clusters of limes with their sweet white flowers. Irrigation channels were filled with precious water so that the monks could grow vegetables, and at first I thought that there must be plenty here, but it was clear that there were more mouths than food.

They had hardly anything to offer us, which I could see troubled the old blind abbot, so we shared some of our rice and other provisions with them. The cells they offered us were surprisingly comfortable, though — mine overlooked the garden — with the absence of fleas being particularly welcome.

The next morning, Robert could not contain himself and apart from some tea, he skipped breakfast, eager to get to the library. I rushed after him, gulping down a piece of honeyed flatbread that the monastery kitchen had supplied. The old abbot instructed a monk to accompany us, and we were led to a long, narrow upper room in the high square tower that was the library. I saw all of Robert's enthusiasm evaporate at the first sight of it; it clearly had not had the services of a librarian for decades, or even centuries. There were some manuscripts in niches on the stone wall, but the bulk were just strewn across the floor, like religious flotsam and jetsam. Some were even stuck to the stone.

'This will take months to catalogue,' Robert mumbled, and then he stared into the distance, as though a grand prize had been stolen from him.

I attempted to be enthusiastic. 'You cannot have expected the abbot to direct you to an index, and then produce an exquisitely bound manuscript, surely.'

'Well, no.' He turned and looked at me, shrugging his shoulders. 'But look at this! It's chaos!'

'So you will have to be clever, won't you?'

'But where do I start, John?'

'You begin in the niches; they are obviously the most important, as they have been looked after. Then you start at that end of the floor,' I pointed to the top left-hand corner, 'and work your way down the room.'

'But it will still take months, if not years.'

'It will if you try to catalogue it. But sometimes broad brushstrokes are what are required.'

He gave a hollow laugh, but then he saw what I was getting at. 'You mean I should just start by sifting quickly through it all, eliminating anything that is not an original text?'

'Exactly,' I nodded. 'Look, I can read some Greek. I'll help you.'

He gave a smile of amusement and his eyebrow rose. 'I am glad you came along as my companion, John — but no, even if you are able to follow the Greek script, the Coptic words will mean nothing to you. This is another rasher of bacon altogether — it is a task for me, and the sooner I start, the better.'

CHAPTER 12

I spent the rest of the morning exploring the monastery, but in the afternoon I stayed out of the sun's blistering heat and rested after our long journey. The next day, I went back to the library with Robert and offered my services as a sort of personal assistant. My task, we decided, was to go through all those loose-leafed dismantled folios that were strewn across the floor and try to see what belonged together. Most of those lying on the floor, I determined after consulting Robert, were Coptic manuscripts on cotton paper, many of which had stuck together over the years and, as such, were unreadable.

As I worked, Robert studied the documents in the niches, but he kept tsking as he read; it seemed these were important to the monks because they were the liturgies, records of the various services for their holy days. Many were quite beautiful — illuminated and smelling of incense — but we were only looking for original historical documents.

The following day, he diligently sifted the strewn papers that I had attempted to put together. Again, it seemed a forlorn venture: what bits at first seemed promising turned out to be incomplete, or so badly damaged as to be indecipherable. As the sun began to fall low in the sky, we decided to give up and catch a couple of hours' sleep before the evening meal. Robert opened the door, disillusion consuming his face, and we both took a long disenchanted look back at the neat piles of manuscripts we had left on the library floor — then something caught my eye. I pointed to some large open pots we had been avoiding for the last two days that cluttered the room.

'Robert, what's that — there?'

He followed my finger. 'What, near those pots?'

'No,' I said, becoming more animated, 'the pots themselves — look, what is that wrapped around them?' It was the material that had caught my attention; I saw a much finer quality parchment than the cotton paper. 'Isn't that vellum, you know, made from animal skin?'

He did not answer, but he saw immediately that I was right and rushed over to the pots that we had been overlooking. He took his knife from its sheath at his waist, and calmed himself before carefully cutting the twine holding them in place. Cautiously, he unwrapped these vellum manuscript leaves and then held them lovingly in his arms. He saw at once that they formed part of the same document.

'John,' he said, looking intently at me. 'John, you wonderful man, look what you've found for me!'

I smiled, tilting my head. 'What do you think it is, Robert?' I was infected by his enthusiasm.

'I'll need to translate it to be sure —' I could see he was willing himself to be cautious — 'but it *is* Coptic Egyptian writing true enough. Look...' He pointed at the cover and I looked at the dirt-engrained page, almost illegible. 'This heading says *The Gospel of Matthew*.' He ran his finger down another page. 'Look there — see.' He pointed to some faint notes in the margin. 'These are commentaries made by the early fathers of the Church.'

'So you think it's important, then?'

'John, you cannot comprehend how important this could be. It could be the oldest version of the Gospels ever found. The religious scholars will need to study it to see how old it is, but it could be original, going back to the second century. Or it could be a copy by an ancient scribe in, say, the eighth century of the original. Either way, it is a *very* early translation of the original Gospels.'

'It's still a translation, though?'

'Yes, but that doesn't diminish it. Jesus spoke Aramaic, but the original Gospels were thought to be written in Greek.'

'Well, if it's that important, why have they used it to protect pots of spices and preserves?'

'Because they don't know what it is, John. To them, it must have been seen as something past its day, past its usefulness. There has been no librarian here to stop them. John —' his voice was little more than a murmur, but he turned and looked at me, his expression entreating — 'we have to save this manuscript.'

The next day, Robert spent his time studying the manuscript, jotting endless notes in his journal and making sketches of the monastery. We invited the abbot and his monks to dine with us that evening, even though it depleted our provisions, for we were intent on negotiating a purchase of the manuscript. I produced a couple of bottles of *rosoglio* and Robert gave me a sideways look, trying to suppress his smirk; he knew what I had in mind. The dark-robed monks drank it with relish, and we could see that it had been a long time since they had tasted such a luxury.

Robert tentatively brought up the question of the manuscript and, at the same time, I leaned across and filled the goblet of the grey-bearded blind abbot with more *rosoglio*. He licked his lips and took a long drink, savouring its sweet taste. I saw his sightless features start to display that mellowness that inebriation brings, and it made our task much easier than we had expected. At the mention of a purchase, the deprived abbot's ears pricked up; coin to fund his dilapidated monastery was most welcome, and when we explained that the manuscript had been found wrapped around a jar of long gone preserves, neither he nor his monks saw any value in it.

Afterwards, when the monks had departed to their cells, I produced a bottle of arak. We toasted our success as the insufferable heat dropped to a bearable temperature and I invited Rokku to join us, he being Christian. As we three drained the bottle, I could see that Robert was anxious to talk, and I allowed him to do so into the night.

Robert worked frantically over the next few days, studying his newly acquired manuscript. He wanted to stay longer, but our provisions were running out. We could not continue to accept the hospitality of the impoverished monks; they had barely enough to feed themselves. I took the last few days to explore the monastery further, for I was taken with the idea that we had not been shown everything that was to be found.

With Rokku's help, I questioned the monks, but we were both hampered by our lack of understanding of Coptic and had to speak to them in Arabic. On the day of our leaving, we had mounted our Arabian stallions when Rokku came to me. The sight of us leaving had emboldened one of the monks, who had whispered something to him.

I leant down to listen to him. 'Sir, there are other documents hidden in vaults — I have it from one of the monks.' He looked around to point to the brother, but he had disappeared, hiding himself from view.

It was too late now — but I resolved to come back.

CHAPTER 13

Over a month later, we set out on our next expedition, south on the Nile in a boat hardly large enough to accommodate our party. We hired a larger dhow at Cairo, our destination being the monastery at Deir el-Adra, the Convent of the Virgin, but more commonly known as the Convent of the Pulley, another one hundred and twenty-five miles south on the river. This river journey allowed us to be better provisioned than we had been during our trek across the desert.

Most ancient monasteries were built in inaccessible places as a means of protection, but this one took that principle to the extreme. It was situated on the top of the rocks of Gebel el-Teir, where a precipice of over two hundred feet rose from the waters of the Nile.

To gain access, with the help of the monks, we had to wade perilously ashore, there being no place for the boat to dock, then climb the treacherous rocks even before we could get to the monastery walls themselves. It was more by luck than anything else that we all survived the climb.

The monastery, we were told, was built by St Helena — the mother of the Roman emperor Constantine — in the fourth century AD, as the Copts believed it to be one of the sites visited by the holy family on their flight to Egypt to escape Herod's wrath. Robert's spirits rose, I saw, at the sheer unapproachability and antiquity of the place, making it a prime candidate in his quest.

A Coptic community had built up around the monastery, and they all came out to see us. Although we were greeted enthusiastically, it quickly became apparent that both the Copts and the monks were abjectly poor, and the prospect of alms was their prime motivation in helping us. I enjoyed my time there but, unfortunately, it yielded little for Robert in the way of original ancient documents. He did find twenty-three manuscripts, highly cherished by the monks, but they were all liturgies, books of service.

Robert was downhearted, but I was not going to let it rest there. Whilst he was sketching and making notes, I set about talking to some of the emaciated monks and, with the help of some of our ample provisions, I attempted to bribe them. I asked Rokku to do the same. After a few days, one particular monk seemed to be receptive and we began to feed him from our own provisions to supplement his meagre diet. Bit by bit, a story unfolded of a secret vault where a great iron-bound chest was hidden. When we pressed him about its contents, he again became reticent and I realised that his strategy was to get as many meals out of us as possible. After another couple of days, he claimed the chest was full of ancient books on vellum, which was not to be opened without the consent of the Patriarch.

I got Robert to invite the abbot to a sumptuous meal, and I used the same technique of plying him and his senior monks with *rosoglio*. Despite their inebriation and our promises that we would arrange for a supply ship, their desperate need for alms did not result in any admission of the existence of this chest. They went off happily, though, to complete their devotions for the day.

'Do you think it exists, Lord Robert?' I enquired of him afterwards. We were both as intoxicated as the monks.

'Not sure, John,' he replied. 'You are my captain of the dark arts. What do *you* think?'

I scanned his face. The man looking back at me in his Ottoman clothes, his headdress, dark beard; this was no longer an English lord, this was a Turkish lord. There had been a hint of it before — when we had been confronted by the rebel sheik in the desert of Nitria on our journey to the Monastery of El-Sourian. But now it was more pronounced.

'You know what you look like?' I said, my tone still playful.

'What do I look like?'

'A Turk! I think I shall call you Pasha Robert from now on.'

He laughed robustly. 'So, my captain of the dark arts, your *pasha* commands you to give your opinion: does this elusive chest exist?'

I took a sharp breath. 'Your unworthy servant has two theories. These monasteries are built in such isolated places for reasons of safety. On the same principle, they would not want it known that they have anything of value that might cause a raider to come looking for loot.'

'That makes sense. So there may indeed be a treasure hidden here, but secret for reasons of security. What is your other theory?'

'That our informant monk is just very, very hungry.'

He chuckled. 'Aye, I see that too — another rasher of bacon entirely, if I am not mistaken. I think we'll move on to the White Monastery.'

The next morning, Rokku came to me. My head was still throbbing from our excesses the night before, but I could see anxiety writ large on his face. He gestured me to one side so we could speak privately, and I obliged. He looked about him anxiously, and then put his hand inside his meagre tunic and produced a small silver enamelled box. I recognised it immediately. There was a miniature of Robert's father painted on the lid; it was his snuffbox.

'Where did you get this, Rokku?' My words were clipped as I realised the significance of what he was showing me.

'Sir,' he answered fearfully, 'I have few belongings — extra clothing, a keepsake to remind me of my family, a purse with a few piastres and paras. I keep the money on me at all times, as there are always thieves about, but the others are in a pouch that I keep with my sleeping roll. I went to wash some clothes this morning before we set off again and I found this box in my pouch; it has been planted on me.'

I took a moment to work out what he was saying. 'But who would do that?' I said eventually.

'Isn't it obvious, sir? Hakeem, the dragoman, planted this, I am sure of it, the son of a thief that he is.'

'But why not just steal it for himself?'

'Because he will make more money cheating you if I am not with you.' I could see the sense in his words. 'You have to believe me, sir. Please tell Sir Robert that I did not steal from him.'

'Yes, leave it to me, Rokku,' I mumbled, thoughts whirling in my head.

I went to Robert immediately, but on the way I stopped and looked about me — I did not know why, but I thought I was being watched. I was right: I saw Hakeem's eyes following me, but he scurried away guiltily when he saw that I had noticed him. I found Robert in the cell given over to him by the abbot, packing away his notebooks and sketches.

'Here,' I said, tossing the snuffbox at him. He turned and caught it one-handed, the fine cricketer that he was. 'Lost something?' I added flippantly, trying to make light of it.

He looked down, his forehead furrowing. 'Where did you find this? I did not know I had lost it.'

'I don't think that you did lose it. Rokku found it in his belongings this morning.'

'He stole it?' Robert's eyes narrowed.

'He says it was planted on him, by the dragoman, and I believe him. Rokku was with us last night, dining with the abbot, remember?'

Robert sighed as he considered what I was saying. 'So he thinks Hakeem planted it.'

'That's about the size of it. Hakeem is resentful of my friendship with Rokku — no, more than that — he wants him out of the way so that he has an open door to us. He makes more money that way.'

'So it looks as if one of them will have to go, John; but which one?'

'Well, if it were left to me, it would be the dragoman — it is clear that he is working for himself and not us.'

Robert nodded. 'But he is still useful — he understands the ways of Egypt. Let us wait until we get back to Cairo, and we will decide then. In the meantime, keep an eye on the dragoman — let's see if we can catch him red-handed.'

We took to our boat again, heading south on the Nile to Sohag and the White Monastery, about three hundred and twenty miles from Cairo. The trip was lazy; we shared the river not only with other boats but also with wildlife, in particular the white spoonbills, which I had come to admire. I watched them for hours, but I also kept my eyes on Hakeem and he knew it. I suspected that he also knew that his little scheme had not succeeded.

At the village of Sohag we hired donkeys, and it took only an hour or so to get to the blanched limestone walls of the White Monastery, but the monks were reluctant to let us in. Robert eventually passed the letter of introduction from the Patriarch of Alexandria through the narrow viewing hole in the middle of the door, after which the abbot was sent for and he eventually gave us a warm welcome.

Inside, it was little more than a ruin. There were piles of wrecked buildings, and the ancient church was now roofless, the place a home to chickens and goats. The abbot seemed embarrassed at its state and informed us that it had once been a great monastery founded as far back as 442 AD and at its peak housing a community of over two thousand monks. But it had gone into decline after the Arab invasion of the seventh century, and had also been sacked many times, the last time being just thirty-odd years ago in 1798, when it was raided and burned down by the Mamluks. Some monks had returned tentatively since then and when they were not assaulted, others had arrived; but it was a small community now.

The abbot also said that it had once contained the greatest library in all of Christian Egypt. I saw Robert's eyebrow cock at that information, and he took to scribbling in his journal.

I left him on the next morning to his exploration of the library, but by lunchtime he was back, his spirits drained. The only things he had been able to find were half a dozen liturgies. Rokku and I again set out to bribe some of the monks with food as we had done previously, and we established that there had indeed been hundreds of volumes written on gazelle skins — that probably meant vellum — but they had been destroyed by the Mamluks during their last pillage.

Robert took this very badly. He was keen not to waste any more time, and so we left the next day, returning to our boat at Sohag. Dejected, we sailed north up the Nile, our destination once again Cairo.

CHAPTER 14

Our *reis* took to the lethargic middle of the river, the sail lowered, allowing the natural flow to the sea to aid our progress. The languid journey was in tune with Robert's spirits; he scribbled and sketched for days under the open cabin at the rear. I, on the other hand, enjoyed the untroubled trip and returned to my study of Arabic with the help of Rokku. It seemed that this unlikely friendship was burgeoning. He had had little education, though he had done and seen so much in his life, but it was, I think, a kindred spirit that I saw in him; he had always lived by his wits, the same as me.

I spent many hours leaning over the rail, looking at the verdant Nile valley as it floated past, and at the farmers busy with their honest toil. High in a tree, I saw a huge bird; it looked like an eagle to me, its body black, its head, shoulders and chest brilliant white.

One evening, the boat's cook gave us a traditional Egyptian meal of *molokhia*, which was a plant as well as a dish. I was told that the *molokhia* leaves were stripped from their stems, then minced using a mezzaluna. They were then cooked with ground coriander, garlic and stock and served with rabbit. We enjoyed the food immensely, although the deep green colour was initially off-putting. Afterwards, we lay on our carpets under the canopy formed by the open cabin, Robert, Rokku and I, talking lazily before we turned in for the night. I sat up as I saw a lantern at the bow of the boat held by the cook, and noted that our servants and bodyguards had congregated there. Our cook, it seemed, was going to tell them a story.

I rolled on my carpet and stood, keen to test my understanding of Arabic against this storyteller, and Rokku joined me without any command. To my surprise, Robert followed us and we took our seats at the back of the semi-circle of listeners, almost in darkness, the small pool of light from the lantern held by the cook not reaching as far as us. Even the *reis* came to hear the story, and the only person missing was the steersman.

As the storyteller began, all the men leant forward in anticipation, some puffing on their pipes. In the circle of light, the cook's grey beard twitched with each word, sometimes slowly and at other times more animatedly as he allowed his story to unfold.

He introduced us to the beautiful Ouardi, who was shut up in an enchanted palace to keep her from her lover, Prince Anas el Ajoud, the son of the Sultan Esshamieh. Rokku interpreted for Robert, and I was pleased to hear that my understanding of the storyteller's words matched his own. As I looked up, I saw Hakeem towards the front, visible in that small circle of light, looking around at us and at Rokku in particular, animosity on his skinny features. I thought little more about it at the time.

The story began with the Sultan, who had married seven wives before he had a son, the Prince Anas el Ajoud. The first six wives, on his son's birth, stole the baby away and left him in the desert to die, but he was nursed by a gazelle and later, he returned to punish the six cruel stepmothers. His father rejoiced, because he had been told by these wives that his Sultana, by magic art, had presented him with a log instead of a son, who was to be the heir of his dominions.

The storyteller then moved on to the Prince Anas himself, who was in despair at being separated from his lady love, who would sing laments as he sailed past the walls of the island

91

palace where she was imprisoned. But our prince prevailed and carried off the fair Ouardi. The story was spun out with no little skill and took over an hour to tell; when the cook told us of the laments that were sung, he sung them himself. He finally shut his eyes and threw back his head to signify that his story had ended, to be met by applause.

We went back to our beds as satisfied with the entertainment as our servants, and I slept soundly under the open cabin that I shared with Robert, the *kawass* and the *reis*.

I woke with a start at first light to a cacophony of shouts and wails coming from the deck where the Arab men slept in the open. Robert went first, bleary-eyed, but then he called for me, his words strangled. I rolled over on my carpet and looked down the boat. Robert was standing with the *reis* and I saw him waving at me.

When I got there, I looked down, and what I saw made me go rigid. A body lay face down in a pool of dark, sticky blood. The *kawass* came and took charge on behalf of the government, brandishing his thick silver-topped cane as his badge of office. We demurred and stepped back, allowing him to do his duty. He turned the body over, but I shuddered as he did so, because I knew from the shaven head who it was. Rokku's dead face stared back up at me, his throat expertly cut from ear to ear.

'Jesus Christ,' murmured Robert. Then he put his hand on my shoulder, as he knew I'd been fond of him.

But my mind was racing — that envious, loathing look the previous evening sprang vengefully into my mind, followed by the memory of that throat-cutting gesture I had seen on the boat trip to Cairo. 'Hakeem!' I bellowed. 'Where are you?'

He slinked obsequiously towards us and inclined his head, twitching as he spoke. 'Yes, *sidi*, I am at your service.' He flourished his arm and dropped his eyes sycophantically.

'What do you know about *this*?' I demanded.

But my words were lost in the clamour of the men who all seemed to be chattering at once, pushing to get a look at poor Rokku. There was the cry of a bird as it swooped across the deck, and I looked up at it momentarily, but out of the corner of my eye I was sure I saw an expression of contempt on Hakeem's face.

'*Well*?' I asked, my hands curling into fists.

'I know nothing, *sidi*,' he said. 'I was awoken by all the noise, just as you were, *sidi*.'

'So this is not your doing?' I spat.

He flourished his arm again. '*Sidi*, I am a man of peace, a man of commerce. This is the work of some dog of the street.' He looked round disdainfully at the Arab crew, inferring it was one of them.

I felt that it was my responsibility to get justice for Rokku, but Robert put his hand on my arm and I looked round at him. 'You must let the *kawass* interrogate him,' he said, pulling me away to the open cabin. I sat for some time in a state of distress as I watched the men truss up the body in a sail canvas.

The *kawass* decided we were too many days from Cairo, and in this hot climate the body would not last, so we put into the first substantial village we passed. He left the boat and returned with the local sheik. A kind of tribunal was then set up, and the *kawass*, the sheik and the *reis*, now wearing a long, wide-sleeved striped kaftan over his *galabeya* to emphasise his importance, sat on the roof of the open cabin at the back of the boat, surveying all around them. Robert and I watched the proceedings intently, and they called many of the Arab bearers and bodyguards to say what they knew. The dragoman was also called, where he calmly claimed that he knew nothing of the murder, and repeated that he was a man of peace and a man of commerce.

When I gave my evidence I told them of the snuffbox incident, that it had been planted by someone who obviously had a grudge against Rokku, and that I thought that man was Hakeem.

The three then got into a prolonged discussion. Finally, the sheik then rose to address the assembly and announced they were all agreed: God was great and Mahomed was the Prophet of God. He said he would take the body of poor Rokku away with him. I shuddered; I knew he would not get a Christian burial and I tried to protest, but Robert again took me by the arm and pulled me away.

'John,' he said, 'Rokku is far away from home. He must have known himself that he was unlikely to get a Christian burial. If we could get him to Cairo, we could take his body to the Christian quarter, but we just cannot.'

I knew he was right, but I went down the boat and briefly stopped the bearers taking his body, commanding them to put it in the middle of the deck. All I wanted was to say some Christian words over Rokku before they took his body away, but the sheik would have none of it, cajoling the sailors to carry him away.

I stood in front of the gangplank, again commanding them, in my newly acquired Arabic, to put the canvas-covered body down. We all tried to understand one another, but it seemed none of us succeeded.

The *kawass* came and took charge of the situation; he raised his long silver-headed cane and silence fell immediately — it was clear that his authority was absolute here. But then he gestured for the sailors to take the body ashore, his cane first pointing at the canvas and then to the gangplank behind me. The body was lifted and came in my direction, but I stood firm; I had no intention of letting them pass.

The *kawass* came over to me, our faces no more than a few inches apart. His magnificent jet-black moustache twitched.

'We need just a few minutes to say some Christian words,' I said in Arabic, which I knew he understood.

He scowled — it seemed he had interpreted my action as a challenge to his authority. I shot an uneasy glance at Robert and saw the concern on his face, but my blood was up. I shook my head slowly. 'A few minutes only,' I repeated.

The *kawass* was about the same height as me, but much more heavily built, and I suspected he was immensely strong. He raised his silver-headed cane high above me, and my eyes followed it into the air.

There was no need for this, I thought, but I refused to cower before him. He feigned to strike me, the thick cane coming down just a few inches. Everyone expected me to recoil, but I had sparred many rounds with my wronged friend, the champion pugilist Samuel Medina. I knew how to defend myself with my fists as well as my sword. He had also taught me how to fight with a cudgel, the weapon I was now, in effect, faced with.

At close quarters, the cudgel was a more efficient weapon than even a sword, which needed distance to be effective. The cudgel could strike with the forehand and the backhand, making two blows with the same movement. To be effective, though, the cudgel needed to be swung in small arcs close to the body, but the *kawass* had raised his weapon high into the air — and that had left his face open to attack. I was unarmed, but I had surprise on my side.

I made a forward strike with my left fist. It landed forcefully on his nose, which immediately began to run with blood. He staggered back, more stunned than hurt, I thought. This just did not happen to him.

I heard gasps from the sailors and bearers. A *kawass* was a person of high authority in the Ottoman Empire and was not to be trifled with in this way. I took the opportunity to move to my left, so that I did not have the boat's rail at my back and I could retreat if I needed to.

The *kawass* ran the back of his free hand across his face, looked down and saw the blood dripping from his fingers. His anger rose and he walked towards me, smashing the head of his cane into the palm of his free hand as he did so, his intent obvious. I backed away, circling him, keeping as much distance between us as I could.

He lunged forward, raising his stick. It was four feet long, which would give him leverage, but the arc formed was huge, again opening him up to a counter. I planted my feet and again sent a straight left fist into his face, followed by a right hook that hit him on the side of the head and probably made his ears ring. But the cane was coming down and I now had to evade it. That second punch had been a luxury too far; I had stayed in range for too long. I scrambled backwards to avoid the cane, but I quickly realised that I could not; the best I could do was raise my arm to protect my head.

A severe pain in my left arm made me wince. The realisation of my folly now struck me; I could not best the *kawass* unarmed. I was in for a thrashing.

We circled again and I feigned to the left; the *kawass* lunged at me again, but I stepped to the right. Before I could strike, though, Robert thrust himself between us, shouting at the *kawass* in Turkish that he would report his behaviour to Boghos Bey Yusufian. The *kawass* stood upright at the name of his master and looked anxiously from Robert to me and back again; he was looking for a way out of his dilemma — his pride and his authority versus his duty to his master.

Robert put up his hands, lowering and raising them slowly to indicate that we should both calm down. I took a step backwards and dropped my fists, but the tension remained and silence prevailed — the *kawass* stood statuesque before us, drawn tight as the string of a longbow. Robert flourished his arm in that polite way of the Ottomans, touching his hand from his heart to his mouth and then to his forehead. He then looked at me, and I knew he wanted me to do the same. I followed suit in the direction of the *kawass*, but he hesitated. Robert arched his eyebrow at him, and slowly the *kawass* lowered his silver-headed cane. He had been holding his breath, but now he exhaled heavily and offered the salute to both of us; hand to heart, to mouth, to forehead.

Robert raised his Bible, which he had quickly retrieved from the open cabin at the back of the boat, and then pointed it at the canvas-covered body of Rokku. The *kawass* gestured that he understood and nodded to show his agreement.

Robert and I shuffled cautiously to the centre of the deck and stood over poor Rokku. Robert opened his Bible and flicked through the pages. At first he was uncertain, but then he turned to Psalm 23, which began: *The Lord is my shepherd; I shall not want.* We recited the words together on Rokku's behalf, standing over his body with our heads bowed. I then added some of my own words, telling God that Rokku had been a good friend to me.

CHAPTER 15

Back in Cairo, as the boat was being unloaded, I looked intently at the *kawass*; his manner was regal as usual, but he was passive. I realised he would take no action against Hakeem. The tribunal had taken the view that Rokku had been killed in some squabble with one of our servants, but it was not possible to identify the culprit. There was no point searching anyone for the weapon, as they all carried curved daggers at their waists. It was clear to me that Rokku's throat had been expertly cut as he slept so that he would not cry out; I had no doubt that it was Hakeem.

Yet Hakeem carried on as normal, as if nothing had happened, and even seemed happy now that he had unrestricted access to Robert and me. I watched him directing the bearers as they unloaded, and I decided I was having none of that; my blood was up again. I strode across the deck to challenge him.

'You stole the snuffbox and planted it on Rokku, did you not?' I said in Arabic. I stood over him, emphasising my stature, hoping it would cow him into admitting his crime. I also wanted the other men to know of my wrath.

But his face remained a mask; if he felt intimidated, he did not show it. '*Sidi*, I am your servant. Thieving is for the dogs of the streets. I am your dragoman.'

I realised then that there was little I could do to get justice for Rokku, but I would be damned if I would let Hakeem profit from his crime. 'I do not believe you, Hakeem!' I barked, so that everyone would hear. 'You are dismissed — be gone with you!'

For the first time that mask slipped, and I saw surprise in his eyes. He did not understand why I should be so bothered about Rokku — a man he thought of as far below me. Such dismissal of the lower classes was not unique to the Levant; I had seen it many times in London as well. Hakeem stood motionless, unable at first to find any words.

'But *sidi*,' he said eventually, 'you need me to steer a course through Egypt.'

'I can get somebody else to do that,' I snapped and waved him away, throwing some piastres after him.

Hakeem scrambled to pick them up, then turned slowly and walked to the gangplank. He stopped and looked back over his shoulder, bewilderment in his eyes, but then his face transformed into something darker. A thin, humourless smile took his features and, unbelievably, he repeated that throat-cutting gesture with his forefinger — this time at me. Then he went ashore.

This was not a threat aimed at me, I decided. It was *his* arrogant admission of what he had done. I was glad to see the scoundrel go.

We dismissed the Arab bearers and the bodyguards and found new rooms for ourselves in the small Christian quarter. It was November and the searing heat of the Egyptian summer was abating slightly, although it was still hot, with Robert's thermometer showing the high seventies. Robert began a detailed study of the manuscript of the Gospel of Matthew he had brought back from the El-Sourian monastery; I did not envy him his dour chore, but to my surprise he was clearly excited by his research. I realised that although he was a multi-faceted man, it was his scholarship that was the most important thing in his life. This left me a lot of time to myself;

I would like to say that I filled it equally honourably, but that would be a lie. The fact that I felt guilty was, in some way, evidence that I was changing; but still, I had nothing to be proud of.

I sought out that bar Rokku had found for me — it was not easy, it was an inferior sort of place, hidden away below stairs in an oven-like room — yet find it I did, and I took to going each evening to drink brandy and water, avoiding the arak (I had learned my lesson there). There were card games going on and I had a craving to join in, but I had no stake.

French was the language of the bar, though there were Europeans of many nations, notably Dutch and Portuguese. The first drink each evening I dedicated to Rokku — to me, this was Rokku's place. There were never women there, but on the third evening the proprietor casually asked if I wanted a woman; I did not need asking twice. He sent out a runner.

I had expected the runner to return with the woman but to my surprise he did not. The proprietor came to me and said the runner would take me to her and, reluctantly, I agreed to follow him. I was led down a labyrinth of small streets that seemed to get narrower and narrower, and a fear took me; was I suddenly going to meet a band of brigands who would rob me and leave me for dead? I cursed myself for not bringing my pistol. But I was wrong; the proprietor was not going to lose the good customer I had become. I was led to a modest house in a warren of streets, whereupon the runner bowed and took his leave.

I knocked and entered, standing in the doorway tentatively. The place was unexpected, modest — just two rooms separated by a curtain, although I never got to see that mysterious second room. Yet it was tasteful in a very feminine way, the aroma of spices heavy on the air. On a divan at the far end of the first room lay the prostitute, who was quite lovely, combing her long black hair with extensive gliding strokes. She beckoned me to enter. The proprietor of the cheap inn had apparently chosen a harlot of a higher status for me.

She was wearing over-loose trousers and a sort of extended silk shirt with long sleeves, embroidered with gold and pearls. Adorning her head was a charming ornament called, she later told me, a *koors*. It was a remarkably pretty headdress in the shape of a shallow basin, covered with semi-precious stones. She said her name was Ebonee, which matched her ebony eyes.

I visited her regularly and found her conversation as stimulating as her beauty. She seemed genuinely interested in where I came from and what I was doing in Egypt, although it may just have been part of her trade to act so. She struggled with the concept that I was a Frank, but not a Frank, and had never heard of England or Englishmen.

While talking to her of our expeditions, I began to realise that I should be doing more than just drinking and wenching. Robert's studies had given me some time to myself, and I should not waste it. That notion came back to me: to find some ancient artefacts of my own to take back to England to sell — although I had still not worked out how to finance any purchases, my beautiful army sword having gone with the sheik who had accosted us in the desert on our way to El-Sourian. I had only two golden sovereigns and my half hunter watch left to my name.

The next morning, I took from my trunk my bright red uniform of an English infantry captain; I was not totally sure why, other than, for that particular day, I did not want to look anything like an Arab or an Ottoman. I shaved for the first time in days and set off for the souk. I searched its alleyways in vain for almost an hour, my stiff collar rubbing my newly shaved neck, trying to find that trader in antiquities. I was stifling in my inappropriate dress, so I called across to a *sakis* and flipped him a small coin, a para, and he filled for me a sparkling cupful of water from the goatskin under his arm. He looked on me as some strange breed of foreign man, I noted, something he had never seen before. I flipped him another para for another cupful and saw the amazement in his face that I could speak Arabic.

'Ah, *monsieur*, did your expedition go well?' said a French voice from behind me.

I turned and saw that it was the proprietor of the antiquities emporium; I had forgotten we had conversed previously in French. He bowed before me and I acknowledged him with a small nod. I then realised why my cunning had made me wear my uniform; if I could not find him, then perhaps I had enabled him to find me.

'Some success, sir,' I answered blandly, trying not to show too much interest. This was difficult, as I had little left of the French my governess mother had taught me.

'Will you take tea with me at my establishment?' He held out his hand. 'Perhaps you can tell me about it; we are in the same business, are we not?'

I held myself stiff and nodded again; he bowed before me and I caught his musty scent, evident above all the herbs and spices for sale in the souk. I re-evaluated the sort of man I was dealing with, realising this was not some ordinary trader, sharp but uneducated — there was some refinement in this man. As we walked the short distance to his establishment, I examined him. He was tall, nearly as tall as myself, and there was something European about his dress; the thing that was most striking about him was the scent of pomade, which was heavy on his well-groomed hair. When we entered his establishment, he took me through the small shop front being attended by his man — which had virtually nothing on display — to the larger back quarters, secured with heavy locks. He took a substantial key from within his tunic, opened the door and led me into a well-appointed apartment. He called back to his man to bring us tea and sherbet.

'You live here?' I asked, looking about the shaded apartment room at the dark wooden furniture, unusually consisting also of European chairs.

'I do at the moment; I have new valuable antiquities here. I will not let thieves take them, but usually I live with my family in the Jewish quarter.'

We took the sweet tea together and he introduced himself as Amram Haroun, scholar and trader, and we chatted awkwardly in French, but this was stilted and I suddenly switched to Arabic, to his surprise, as he had correctly remembered that my Arabic had been so poor just a few months before. He was interested in the Coptic manuscripts that we were in search of; I thought he was judging whether it could be a new branch of his business, and was trying to establish if they were of value to collectors. He cooled when he realised that he would need an agent who could not only read Coptic, but who could also interpret the writing and identify the writers. There were so few of these people in the world, never mind in Egypt.

Haroun talked to me extensively about his agents; he said he had them all over Egypt, but especially in the ancient cities of Fustat, Giza and Memphis, and they were constantly looking for ancient Egyptian artefacts new to the market.

'But I am not a collector,' I said, sucking in my cheeks. I was being devious; I did not want to seem too eager, yet still wanted to leave the impression that I was interested.

He offered me a pipe in response, and I knew immediately the game was still being played. I accepted and we were quiet for some time, puffing away.

'My agent at Deir El Medina has recently found a tomb that was previously undisturbed,' he said eventually, between puffs of scented smoke. 'They are very rare; it is an exceptional find.'

I raised an inquisitive eye in the way of Robert. 'So the tomb robbers have not already stripped it clean, you mean?'

'Exactly, *sidi*.' Haroun leant forward conspiratorially. 'Would you like to see something of what was found?' I blew out the smoke from my mouth, nodding.

He stood and went to a large chest standing on a table in the corner. He took another large key from his tunic, unlocked it and then raised the heavy lid. A fusty odour immediately filled the room, a smell of the ancient past. It was not a sweet smell, neither was it acrid. I had never encountered such an odour before. And then I realised why; he reached in and took out a papyrus scroll, handling it as if it were the most precious thing in the world.

'What is it?' I said, abandoning any attempt to be diffident.

'It is the deceased's *Book of the Dead*. Unrolled, it is twelve metres long.'

'But what is it for?' I whispered insistently, my interest having been tweaked. I saw that he had noticed this.

'The ancient Egyptians believed that when they died, they went on a journey to the afterlife. This was their map, telling them how to get there. There is everything they needed: funerary incantations, texts and spells to help them fend off any evil spirits they encounter. It was to enable the deceased to navigate that journey.'

Haroun brought it to me. It was beautifully written and illuminated with pictures, the original colours still vibrant — ochres, blues and greens. I delicately unrolled several feet of it.

'From this, we even know his name,' the trader said, pointing a finger at some hieroglyphics. 'He was called Nykara.'

'A pharaoh?' I asked enthusiastically.

'No, but an important chief and vastly wealthy. He must have been to have such a tomb — they were enormously expensive.' He ran his thumb and forefinger along his manicured moustache. He then went to the chest again and took out a small statue. It was made of wood, beautifully carved, and decorated in vibrant colours like the scroll. He brought it over to me, and I took it as delicately as he had been handling it.

'What is it?' I asked. My guile had drifted away from me, and my pretence of disinterest had gone, I was sure.

'It is a tomb statuette; this is Nykara himself, a likeness of him. This was his insurance if something happened to his body; this would hold his spirit and he could continue his journey.'

'So he was a young man, then?' I was absorbed in its beauty, so much so that I was not even translating in my mind — Arabic was just coming from my lips.

'No, probably not, but he decided *himself* the image he wanted to take into the afterlife. I think he chose the image of himself as a young man.'

'Is there any more?' I asked, as if I were a hungry child.

Haroun hesitated, but then went again to the chest. He reached down into its opulent depths, his body at first hiding what he removed. When he turned, I saw it — and it took my breath away. I sat up in my chair. My eyes widened at the sight of it. *Gold* — rows of gold. Ancient Egyptian jewellery, made of gold interspersed with dozens of richly coloured and moulded amulets.

Words stuck in my mouth. 'What *is* it?' was all I could force myself to say.

'A broad collar necklace. It sits on the shoulders going around the front and back to make a complete circle, row upon row, so that it is almost a foot wide at every point.'

I beckoned him to bring it over, and at first he seemed reluctant to do so, but then he came and draped it over my outstretched arms. I felt the weight immediately, as if I was holding a fortune. I looked up at him again, my eyes questioning — could there possibly be more?

Haroun turned one last time to that Aladdin's cave of a chest, bending deep over it, but what he removed I did not recognise.

'This,' he said, his tone suggesting that this was the prize of the collection, 'is Nykara's death mask.' He pointed to the eyes, the brows and the collar. 'They are made of decorative glass, and the face is covered in gold leaf; they are typically just covered in ochre to imitate gold. But not this — this, my friend, is the best one you will ever see. It is the best antiquity I have ever acquired.'

I could see a fortune for myself, but it seemed out of reach: how could I possibly grasp it? 'How much would these cost me?' I asked tentatively, belatedly adopting my disinterested tone.

Haroun clapped his hands and his man came through from the front. He ordered more pipes and we settled to puff them as we negotiated. 'For the *Book of the Dead* and the tomb statuette —' he hesitated, stroking his moustache with his thumb and forefinger again — 'eight thousand piastres, *each*.'

I tried to remember what Robert had said to me — a para was the fortieth part of a piastre, itself worth about two pence-halfpenny. There were two hundred and forty pence to the pound; therefore, there were about a hundred piastres to the pound. So eight thousand was about eighty pounds. A very substantial sum indeed.

'And the others?'

'For the broad collar necklace, twenty thousand piastres, the death mask, twenty-five thousand piastres.' He took a puff at his pipe.

I leant back and puffed as well; that was two hundred pounds and two hundred and fifty pounds respectively. The whole lot would cost me six hundred and ten pounds — but this was Egypt, and everything was negotiable here. Even so, these were such immense sums, and much more than I had expected. Perhaps I could get the *Book of the Dead* for fifty pounds, but even that would take some raising. That golden broad-neck collar, though, I reasoned, would have added value back in England, not just to the scholars and collectors but to the rich and powerful. However, I knew I was in no position to make any sort of offer. I needed to withdraw with my credibility intact.

'My access to funds in Egypt is restricted, *monsieur*,' I said matter-of-factly. 'I am not in England, where I can consult my bankers with ease. But I register my interest with you; these are indeed magnificent artefacts.'

Haroun nodded politely in response. As I stood to take my leave, he shook me by the hand in the European way but was keen to impart one last thing. 'Nathan Rothschild has an agent in Cairo,' he said, leaning in conspiratorially, his scent once again powerful in my nostrils. 'If you want to purchase, you can perhaps obtain a letter of credit through him in a matter of a few weeks; Rothschild's bank has a branch in London. Such a letter of credit would be acceptable to me.'

'Yes, perhaps,' I lied as I took my leave.

That evening I enthused to Robert about the antiquities Haroun had shown me.

'You didn't tell him of the manuscripts I've found, did you?' There was alarm in his voice, and he seemed more interested in that than in my story.

'Of course not,' I said, without thinking it through — but with hindsight that was probably a lie.

'You know, when I get back to England with my manuscripts, it will provoke an avalanche of people coming to find more. I will have to protect the location of my finds, otherwise every Tom, Dick and Harry will ransack the monasteries.'

I nodded. My conscience was pricked, although I quickly put that to one side — I was so excited. Robert then began to share my enthusiasm, but when I tried to ask him to fund the purchase for me, to be repaid to him out of the proceeds, he just laughed at me.

'That's six hundred and ten pounds!' he screeched. 'That far exceeds my funds for the whole of this expedition to Egypt, and that includes the funds for my own purchases. The allowance I get from my father is generous, but it will not finance such extravagance.'

'I can negotiate a deal, I am sure of it, Robert,' I pleaded, but he just brushed me aside, as if I had lost my senses. I had, of course, and deep down I knew it; but this prize had completely possessed me.

CHAPTER 16

I retrieved my eighteen-carat gold half hunter watch from my room and looked at it wistfully; the case was solid gold, the movement English. I held it in my hand, feeling its weight, its excellent quality. I flipped open the spring-hinged circular metal cover that closed over the watch dial, protecting it from damage, a glass panel in the centre giving a view of the hands; I looked at the handsome and delicate enamel face. I remembered buying it, the best that money could buy. Samuel had fought the Bristol Bonecrusher and the book had run against him. I'd bet everything I had on him, but I knew he would win. I had never seen such money and I had spent it as if I were a prince or a duke. It was as fine a watch as you could get in London.

I closed it again, enjoying its feel, the good memories that it brought. Then those memories darkened; Samuel Medina, the man who had been the source of all that wealth, had been badly deceived — and I was the instrument of that deceit. Guilt consumed me caustically.

I tried to shake myself out of the melancholy, looking down at the watch with more commercial eyes. I took off the heavy chain. This too was eighteen-carat gold, but with gadgets attached: the winding key, a Vesta case, a cigar cutter — all solid gold. The watch was my only source of capital, and I thought I might be able to sell them off separately to maximise my funds, though the prospect of parting with them made me curse.

I grabbed both of them up and went down to the souk to seek out the money exchangers. They weighed the chain and the watch, then took a minute scraping to assay the quality of the gold and seemed most impressed. They offered me six hundred piastres for the gold chain and after negotiation, I accepted six hundred and seventy-five — about six pounds, fifteen shillings.

For the watch, they offered me a thousand piastres and I initially rejected this. I had paid twelve guineas back in London, so an offer of about ten pounds was not too bad, but I was so attached to it; it was a link with Samuel. I also remembered the clock room back at Boghos Bey's palace — he was obviously a collector, so perhaps he would offer me much more. But he was back in Alexandria, and I needed the money right then. Reluctantly, I negotiated a price of a thousand and forty-five piastres, about ten pounds and nine shillings. I left with a heavy heart and one thousand, seven hundred and twenty piastres to add to my last two sterling coins.

That evening I went back to the bar, dressed as a fine English gentleman, and stood over a group of Dutch sea captains who were at an impromptu card table. I was a skilled card player, although it had finally been my downfall, as my skills left me when the effects of John Barleycorn addled my brain. I knew all the games of society in London — ombre, quadrille, quintile, piquet, basset, faro, whist, cribbage, put, loo — but I was not, at first, familiar with the game the sea captains were playing, so I watched intently.

I decided it was a variant of loo, a trick-taking game of trumps, whereby each player replenished his hand after every round by drawing a fresh card from the pack. I tried to see the variants and the four players noticed my interest, eventually asking me to join them. I agreed reluctantly — but this reserve was a ruse. My cunning was still intact.

As I sat down, a pang of conscience took me, however; I had been forced to flee England because of my drinking, wenching and gambling — and I was now doing just the same. I determined to fix a strategy in my mind; I had to stay sober if I was going to win a stake to purchase the antiquities.

Like loo, I saw, the game used a fifty-two card pack. The players were dealt three cards each and the next was turned up for trumps. The players betted and played for tricks, and in each round they could pass, play or miss. The basic idea was that a pool was formed by each player's contributions made before each deal. Each player's aim was to win at least one trick, under penalty of increasing the pool. The winning of a trick entitled him to take one-fifth of the pool.

I enjoyed the game and played conservatively as a learner, but I was disappointed that the stakes were so small; they were betting in paras, not piastres. I had chosen, it seemed, a game where the players were honest, playing merely for enjoyment. They did not see me as a naïve mark to be exploited. I decided to play the long game; I relaxed and enjoyed it in the same way as my fellow players, but all the time I was learning the nuances of the play.

I went back to the grimy bar for the next four nights and played again. The customers changed every few days as the sea captains sailed away on their trade routes, and I noticed that not all the games were so well-mannered. On the fifth night, there was a game in which I noticed that the stakes were much higher. I stood and waited, and eventually I was asked to take a hand, but they were not playing the variant of loo that I had been cultivating.

'Unfortunately, gentleman,' I said in my faltering French, 'I am not familiar with the game you are playing. I do not want to spoil your game.' I knew what I was doing and I watched for their reaction. Two of the players shot discreet glances at each other, but I caught the nuance. I had sown the seed that I was not a skilled player.

'What games do you play, sir?' asked one of the Dutch captains.

'In England I play mostly whist, sir, but some fellow sea captains of yours have been teaching me a new game, a trick-taking game of trumps, where each player adds to his hand after each round by drawing a new card from the pack.'

They nodded, indicating that they knew the game, and the first sea captain extended his arm, inviting me to take a seat at the table. He turned and called for the landlord to bring a bottle of brandy, and I recognised the crude ploy. I was a master of such deceptions — here, though, I was playing the dupe. I took a cup of the brandy, but I took a large measure of water with it.

At first I played like a novice, though losing only modestly, waiting for a round of the game where the pool of money was larger. After a couple of hours, that point came and the pot was more substantial than it had been all night. I sat back in my chair, took out my snuffbox from my waistcoat, put a pinch on the back of my hand and put it to my nose, inhaling it deeply. I flourished my handkerchief as a fine English gentleman would, to wipe the excess from my face, all the time taking in their faces. As the next hand was being dealt, the other two captains both lit a bowl of tobacco in their pipes, blowing out the smoke to mingle with the smoke that already hung in the room.

The slimy heat wound around me, my fine clothes clearly unsuitable, yet I was comfortable; I was treading ground that I had trod so many times before. I had only to await my opportunity to foil my fellow players. The pool continued to accumulate and by the time they had finished their bowls of tobacco, my chance came. I drew a hand of all trumps, including the ace, the highest card. I then took the necessary tricks to loo, feigning surprise at my good luck.

I left with winnings of over seven hundred piastres, about seven pounds sterling, increasing my capital to about two thousand four hundred piastres, or about twenty-four pounds. I did not go back for some days, but then returned and repeated my strategy, when the clientele was unknown to me, and I to them. After three weeks, I had my war chest: four and a half thousand piastres — about forty-five pounds. I could start to acquire some antiquities, if not the very best that Amram Haroun had for sale.

CHAPTER 17

Lord Robert busied himself endlessly, arranging our next expedition. His plan was to go to St Catherine's monastery at Sinai, which would be a long and arduous journey overland of some two hundred and eighty miles from Cairo to the Sinai Peninsula. He wanted to make the trip before the blazing heights of the Egyptian summer.

I had been speaking to Haroun, who had told me that there were ruined Coptic monasteries in the Necropolis of Thebes. That was itself a three hundred-mile or so journey, but it was south, on the west bank of the Nile. It was, for this reason, reachable by river boat.

I was of course being disingenuous; this was the place, Haroun had told me, that had been used for ritual burials in the times of the pharaohs, especially in the New Kingdom, when ancient Egypt had been at the height of its powers. I had my own agenda; I wanted to find ancient Egyptian artefacts, not the Coptic ones that Robert was in search of.

I could be persuasive, though, and eventually I convinced Robert that we could journey to Thebes and be back in time to start the expedition to Sinai by mid-March. We put together the mission quickly after I went to the souk and asked about the services of a new dragoman. I was tempted to try and take on the task myself with my new expertise in Arabic, but without Rokku to help me, I decided against it.

The new dragoman went by the name of Kamil, a younger and handsomer man than Hakeem. He wore the same sort of single garment that covered his head and swept around his neck and across one shoulder, then around his lower body, and was finally held in place over the crook of the opposite arm; but his garment was not as shabby as Hakeem's had been. He stood erect, giving him a more noble stature than our previous dragoman, although I quickly came to realise that he was just as cunning and calculating; I could always spot a fellow conman. But he was efficient, and everything was in order in less than two weeks.

We set sail on the twentieth of January 1836, for Luxor, the site of the ancient city of Thebes — the great capital of Egypt during the New Kingdom, as Lord Robert told me at regular intervals. We took fewer bearers, but the same number of bodyguards, and we retained the services of the *kawass*, a man of few words, to give us access to the places we wanted to visit.

I had come to like this form of boat travel, the tranquillity aiding my intermittent bouts of melancholy. The Nile was at the heart of Egypt; the people talked about it on a daily basis, the way Englishmen talked about the weather. Travelling south and just watching the palm-treed banks was like a window into this country and its people: the sight of turbaned farmers at their honest toil or leaning on their staffs in the high noonday heat; the lush green of their lands; the way thousands of tiny white butterflies would take to the air at the slightest disturbance; the sideways movement of the heads of the spoonbills sifting the water for nourishment; the malevolence of the crocodiles that shared the Nile with us, languidly swivelling their bodies as they glided through the water. In the evenings, the deep red of the sunset on the far horizon would turn the river a coral colour.

We arrived at Thebes after twelve pleasant days of easy travelling. I was sad, although I was glad not to have to eat another dish of *ful* again; the soaked fava beans and onions spiced and served with flatbread had been served up to us on every day of the journey.

For much of the journey Robert had scribbled or sketched in his journal, but before we disembarked he again thrust *Modern Egypt* into my hands.

'I think we will head for Medinet Habu,' he said. 'Have a read and see what you think.'

I did not really want to wade through this dry tome, so I quizzed him. 'What is at this Medinet Habu, then?'

'The Mortuary Temple of Ramesses the Third.'

'One of the pharaohs?' I liked the idea of that; it suggested ancient Egyptian artefacts.

'Yes, and a very famous one too.'

'So this is where he is buried?'

'No, of course not,' he answered, as if it was obvious. 'He is buried in the Valley of the Kings, about four miles away — this is his mortuary temple. He had it built to honour his memory; he thought of himself as a god.'

'But Medinet Habu is an Arab name?'

He looked at me then, his eyebrow rising as if to acknowledge my insight. 'Yes, it is. You're right; it is a different rasher of bacon, isn't it?' he said playfully, and we shared a knowing smile.

We travelled by donkey from the west bank, the ten miles or so to Medinet Habu at the foot of the Theban Hills. We made camp and put up our tents on the outskirts of the modern town; this was intended to be the base for our explorations. The first thing next morning, however, Kamil the new dragoman came and said he had found us a cave to live in. I did not like the idea of sleeping on the hard stone, but he was right; the cave gave an even temperature, being cool in the day, and warm in the night. Its open front also ensured that light flooded in, and Robert was able to scribble to his heart's content.

Robert and I spent the rest of the first day exploring the site of the great mortuary temple. It was winter, but this was a desert climate; the temperature was still in the seventies, reasonably pleasant. It smelt like the rest of Egypt — of camels and sand, of burnt ash, not unpleasant, though without the spices of the souk to add that piquant odour. The place was so dry, even the air seemed desiccated; we were told that it had not rained for over a year, and I think it infected Robert's mood. The temple itself had not been excavated, and the sight of tomb raiders stealing and destroying its treasures upset him.

'Are you not doing the same thing, Robert?' I asked tentatively, biting my lower lip.

'No, of course not, John.' He looked at me intently. 'I am *saving* the Coptic manuscripts from poor and ignorant monks. I am not stealing them away for profit. Have we not seen that some of the ancient historical manuscripts have already been cast in the furnace just to keep the monasteries warm?'

I could see that he believed what he was saying, and I was in no position to be holier than thou. I shot him a sheepish glance, choosing my words carefully. 'But do you need to take them back to England to save them?'

'There is no university in Egypt where they can be studied,' he snapped. 'The expertise is in Oxford and Cambridge — don't you see that?'

I let it go as we wandered around, but then his spirits rose as he saw that there was also a Coptic presence on the site — this was what he was looking for. 'Edward Lane did not mention any of this in his book, John,' he said enthusiastically.

On the second day we set out from Medinet Habu with just the *kawass* and a few armed men dressed in Ottoman clothes, their curved swords at their waists, ready to protect us. The new dragoman insisted on coming too and his presence, likewise, was not really necessary; but I could see that he just wanted to take advantage of any opportunity that arose.

Within just a few miles, we came upon a rocky hill, upon which stood the ruins of an old Coptic monastery, its crumbling walls overlooking the unexcavated city of Thebes still visible below us and the Nile valley beyond that. There we found a handful of expansively bearded Coptic monks in their long black robes and black pillow-box head caps, with a small Coptic community living outside. I saw Robert's shoulders visibly droop.

'What is it, Robert?' I asked.

'More uneducated, half-starved monks, unaware of their abundant history. These monasteries used to be places of learning.'

Once again we showed our letter of introduction and met their leader — I did not think we could call him an abbot, there being so few of them, perhaps eight in all. He was a hunched-looking figure, worn and broken by his unenviable task of trying to keep the last of his flock together. He offered us tea and we sat with him on threadbare carpets in the ruin of an old building, as he lamented that his church had been destroyed.

But as he spoke, it became apparent that Robert was wrong about him: this was no ignorant monk. He could read and write Coptic, Arabic and Turkish; he had a knowledge of history, astronomy and medicine and knew the ways of the Franks. He was surprised that this Frank could speak and understand Coptic, and it seemed to encourage him to talk.

He told us that the monastery had been fully inhabited until about forty years ago; this area had been the home of many Coptic communities for centuries after Christianity came to Egypt — indeed, the home of the Coptic town of Djeme — and they had even built a church inside the prodigious Mortuary Temple of Ramesses the Third itself.

Robert's mood, I could see, was changed radically by the knowledge and wisdom of this old man. 'So was this monastery the site of great learning, before the arrival of the Arabs in the seventh century?' he asked in Coptic, leaning forward eagerly, but his enthusiasm was getting in the way of his translation.

The old monk's brow briefly furrowed in incomprehension. Then he seemed to understand. 'Indeed, it was,' he said with some pride, 'and even after the arrival of the Mahomedans, our learning was preserved.'

'So you still have the library?' The words flew from Robert's mouth, so eager was he.

However, the old monk seemed to recoil at the question. He was unnerved, I could see it. He put a brass cup to his lips to sip his sweet tea. He looked up at the *kawass*, who was standing at the back of us with the Ottoman bodyguards in their billowy trousers, waistcoats and turbans. Their right hands, as always, were on the handles of their sabres, ready to fight if necessary.

'The library is gone, I'm afraid,' he said. 'It was destroyed by Mahomedan bandits looking for treasure, who wrecked the monastery and took away all our precious relics.' Robert commiserated with him for his loss, and he seemed grateful for our concern. We left him when he indicated that he had to lead his small band of brethren in one of their daily devotions.

Back at the cave, we took an evening meal brought to us by our cook, prepared outside his tent. All the tents had now been relocated to some yards outside our cave. He had a more extensive repertoire than the cook on the river boat; he served us a dish called *tamiya*, which was deep fried balls, using mashed white broad beans and herbs, served with hummus in baladi bread, like a sandwich, with crunchy salad. We lit a lantern as the sun fell, then sat back, looking out at the majesty of Luxor and Carnac, with scorched mountain tops silhouetted in the background. I could see that Robert was eager to talk, though.

'Did you believe the old monk?' I could not see his features in the dim light, only the reflection of the flame flickering in his eyes.

'He is a man of God, is he not?' I said, lying down on my carpet for the night. 'I would have thought he would regard lying as a sin. I think I believe him.'

'Did you believe him about the library?'

I folded my arms behind my head as I thought. 'I've come to believe that all the monks we have met are hiding things from us, if that's what you mean.'

'So you see it too, John?'

'Aye, and I think I have brought the solution with us.'

'Rosoglio! You've brought some bottles with you?'

'Aye, I have Robert,' I said smugly. I could not see his face, but I knew he was smiling in the dark.

CHAPTER 18

The following day, Robert and I went alone to the ruins of the Coptic monastery, against the wishes of the *kawass* and our new dragoman, whom we had to order to stay behind. We took some of our provisions with us — a small sack of rice, some herbs and spices, and some dried fruit and preserves. The monks had an insignificant garden by the ruin of their once-proud church, but it was clear that they too were as undernourished as the monks at El-Sourian and were grateful for our gift. We ate their evening meal with them, and Robert engaged them in an extensive discussion about the history of the monastery.

I produced a bottle of rosoglio, and the bottle was quickly emptied by the monks as if we had brought them the most precious of gifts. I was more circumspect with the second bottle, making sure that the measures of the pink liquid I poured for their old leader were much more generous. He said it had been many years since he had tasted rosoglio and his appreciation was profuse; our plan to make him feel indebted to us was working.

Robert took the lead, translating for me at intervals; Coptic to English. 'Abbot,' he said, addressing their leader — I could see immediately that this worn and shrivelled old man took pleasure in being given this title — 'I am a scholar, like yourself. I have come many thousands of miles from the land of Britain to study your historical manuscripts, the oldest writings on the life of Jesus.'

'And I wish you well in your quest, my son. It is a noble journey you have embarked upon.'

Robert looked around at me, and I leant forward and filled the old man's brass cup again. Robert inhaled as he tried to pick his words carefully. 'Do you think that you can help me in my quest? Do you know where I can find these historical documents?'

The wrinkles on the old man's face intertwined as he thought for a minute; then he looked at Robert, who sat up straight in expectation. 'I believe that the monastery at El-Sourian has an extensive library.'

'I have already been there, Abbot,' said Robert, his shoulders falling.

I tried to suppress a laugh and Robert looked at me, first in rebuke but then in expectation. I knew what he wanted of me. I produced the last bottle of rosoglio I had brought, this one intended just for the old man.

After another half hour or so, the old man was clearly intoxicated, and Robert changed tack. 'We are fellow Christians, Abbot,' he said, looking deeply into those old but shrewd eyes. 'We have come this evening without our Mahomedan companions, to ask for your help.'

He seemed to drift away from us, as if stung by a potent memory. He studied the ground in front of him, then suddenly appeared to be alarmed at his own thoughts. He tried to use his staff to haul himself up, but he failed — a mixture of his age and the rosoglio, I thought.

One of his monks moved to help him, but he put up the palm of his hand. He settled back, as if resigned. 'I was a young monk working as a librarian when the Mahomedan raiders came here.' His words were wistful. 'I saved as much of the library as I could. I have carried the burden of its survival ever since.' His countenance changed, as though he was glad to unburden himself.

'We will respect your treasures, Abbot.' Robert's voice was soft and reassuring. 'I only want to study these great manuscripts of yours.'

The abbot's gaze fell upon Robert and then on me. I was used to men trying to see if I was genuine, and I attempted to assume that guise, the one that I had mastered, but for the first time it came with a pang of guilt. I knew we were being disingenuous.

'Come tomorrow evening, alone. No Mahomedans.' The old man's voice fell away at the end of his sentence. He then looked at the other monk, who helped him to his feet, and they made their way carefully to his cell.

The next evening, Robert and I made our way again to the ruined monastery, the sun low in the west. At first, we could not find the old monk, and we began to think that he may have forgotten his inebriated promise to us. Eventually, we persuaded one of the other monks to take us to his cell. When we entered, he was sitting in a corner on a frayed carpet, with two others. There was a small pool of light from a tallow candle, not really enough for us to make out who they were.

The old man held out his wrinkled hand and bade us sit, and we did so. There was still reluctance in his demeanour, I could see, but then he spoke quietly, and with immense dignity. 'I regard our library as a sacred treasure,' he said, fingering the wooden cross around his neck. 'I should not have admitted to you that it still exists.' His voice caught briefly as he spoke.

Robert turned and mumbled the translation to me. I leaned in and told him to re-establish his confidence in us; otherwise, we would lose our opportunity. But Robert evidently knew this already. 'Abbot —' the tone of his voice was sincere and heartfelt — 'you have carried an enormous burden for so many years. I consider my quest to be one with yours. *My* burden is to record all these ancient texts before they are destroyed forever; I think we travel the same road.'

The old man's eyes fell away as he contemplated Robert's words. Finally, he looked up. He was holding his breath as if trying to avoid the inevitable 'Very well,' he said, his voice hardly audible, 'I put you on your Christian honour to respect our treasures.'

Robert nodded, his noble countenance confirming his trustworthiness, and I tried to do the same after he translated.

'But I am afraid,' said the old man, 'that I am too infirm to take you to their hiding place.' He turned and looked at the two others with him. 'This is Hisham and his son Farid. They will take you there. You will go as soon as it is fully dark so that no one can follow you.'

Hisham, it transpired, was a carpenter from the Coptic village. He was a small man, perhaps six inches shorter than Robert and myself, whom I estimated to be in his mid-thirties. He was clearly very poor, his clothes little more than a short tunic, made of homespun goat's hair, and a felt skullcap, with some rags twisted round it for a turban. His son, Farid, a boy of ten, wore a similar tunic, but without the ragged turban. 'The old monk has made me the guardian of the old library and treasures,' Hisham said proudly as we set off into the night.

His son carried a lantern, but it was not lit; we navigated by the moon and the canopy of brilliant stars in the cloudless night sky. The journey was long and arduous, taking us first across the plain of Thebes and then to the hills and valleys above. I stumbled several times on the hard desert ground, my knees running with blood as the journey progressed. The terrain was difficult, full of holes, and Hisham explained to me that they were ancient tombs and mummy pits. They had been dug up by tomb raiders, he told me, emphasising that they were Frankish, but we had already seen Arab raiders doing the same thing. Then it got worse; we encountered skulls and bones. Hisham said that they were the ancient mummy bones — the bandages had been ripped away by raiders in order to steal the gold amulets and other ornaments that the ancients had been buried with.

The journey seemed endless in the blackness of the night, punctuated by the howls of a scavenging hyena in the distance. We had become used to long, tiring journeys, but somehow this trek took its toll more than the others, each step being treacherous lest we fall down some excavated hole. I was fatigued when at last we came to the top of one of these pits and Farid climbed down into it, the loose shale-like stones making him slide down, half on his sandalled feet and half on his backside, holding the unlit lantern high in the air to keep it from shattering. He descended into darkness, the bottom of the pit hidden from the moonlight by the lip high above it. We then saw a spark as he lit the candle in the lantern. Hisham bade me follow, and I tried to use the same technique as his son, sliding down the loose sides of the pit, adding to the grazes I had already accumulated. Robert was just as ungainly, whilst Hisham brought up the rear with more dexterity.

The boy lifted the lantern to reveal the entrance to an ancient tomb, half filled with rubble, and we crawled down through the tunnel after him, perhaps thirty yards or so until the rubble descended to a solid floor, still strewn with debris that I assumed had been blown in by the wind over millennia. I took two candles from my pocket and lit them from the lantern, and Robert and I followed the boy down the passage. A strange smell tingled in my nose. I breathed in deeply, trying to identify it; it had a resonance, something indefinable, and then I remembered. It was the same smell that came from the historical artefacts that Haroun had shown me; it was the smell of the ages.

And then the passage levelled out and opened up into a large chamber. The walls and columns were covered with hieroglyphics, the colours still vibrant despite their extreme age. But the chamber, I could see, was empty, its treasures having been raided long ago. Robert and I looked at each other, confused.

A thin smile crossed Hisham's features in the dim light. He went to the far corner of the cavern, where a small pile of rubble had accumulated. He then started to move it away with his hands, and his son helped him. We both joined in to reveal another doorway, no more than two feet high, and Hisham crawled through, the lantern lighting his way. I tried to follow, but then I needed to back out; I was bigger than him, and we had to remove more of the rubble. I tried a second time and my candle was extinguished in the crush, but I managed to squeeze my way through. Robert followed me.

We relit our candles and looked around this second chamber; despite its magnificence, it was also empty. We again went to the far corner, removed the accumulated sand and rubble, and squeezed through into a third chamber. Inside, the walls were white, but with pictures of the ancient gods in vivid colours standing tall above us, looking down on us from their ancient subterranean resting place.

Robert identified one as Osiris, the green-skinned god of the dead, but then pointed to the far end of the chamber. 'That's not right,' he said. 'That is a Christian altar; it should not be here.'

I followed his finger to a semi-circular stone altar — displayed upon it were the remnants of the Coptic library of the ruined monastery; it had been well hidden indeed. Robert rushed over and counted them — there were ten in all. He then set his candle on the ground and lifted down the first musty brown manuscript to study it. The carpenter and his son squatted down and I joined them; I was exhausted, and Robert's enthusiasm did not infect my tired limbs.

After a time, though, I went to him. 'Is this a historical manuscript, then?'

He was turning the worn cotton pages, spotted with yellow wax from ancient candles, deep in concentration, and did not look up at me, continuing instead to read and translate. 'Er — no,' he murmured distantly, poring over a page. 'Well, maybe; this is written on *charta bombycina*, a sort of cotton paper, so we know it is old — but not old enough. This is some sort of a martyrology.'

'A what?' I exclaimed.

He finally looked up at me and saw my confusion. 'Sorry, John; it's a history, but of the lives of the saints rather than a history of the life of Jesus.'

'The saints that were martyred, you mean?' I was beginning to understand.

'Exactly, John.' He turned back to the manuscript.

'So not what you are looking for?'

'Probably not, but there just *might* be something if one of the saints was a contemporary of Jesus — if they knew him and this document had some of Jesus's sayings. But that is probably too much to hope for.'

I left him to it for several hours, squatted down again beside Hisham and his son and dozed intermittently. But I also got the opportunity to talk to Hisham, and a notion took me. We left the tomb about an hour before sunrise, our return journey equally as hazardous as the outward one had been. I would not have found it again had I mounted an expedition in the daylight, but I suppose that was the intention of the old monk who had hidden his treasures there. I was weary when we got back to our cave; it was cool and enticing, and I slept for several hours on my carpet despite the hard rock floor beneath.

Over the next week, Robert went each evening to the tomb to study the manuscripts, but I did not go with him. I also persuaded him that he did not need the services of Hisham; his son was an adequate guide for him. I had other plans for Hisham.

He was poor, abjectly so, and the promise of some piastres was enticing to him. He said he had 'eaten stick' many times for not being able to pay his taxes to the *pasha* — 'eaten stick' being the phrase he used for a beating from a *kawass* or other Turkish officer. We made a pact: he would be my guide and we would go in search of ancient Egyptian artefacts.

CHAPTER 19

Pressing the sharp edges of my Arab stirrups into the skinny sides of my mangy donkey, and with the *kawass* on his own donkey and two of our Arab bodyguards walking beside me, I set off for the Coptic village just outside the ruined monastery to meet up with Hisham. We had already spent a week making contacts with various bands of grave robbers. The skilled ones, I had established, were working as agents for merchants back in Cairo or Alexandria, but the unskilled ones were our targets. They were destructive in their excavations and did not always know the significance of their finds, but I did not care; they were the men that I could do business with.

We had identified an Arab man by the name of Gamal. He had set claim to a hole in the ground, and he and his men were excavating it as an ancient burial site. He had other men armed with swords posted above, making a ring around the hole to defend his find from brigands who might steal away his treasures, but I suspected that he was just as much a brigand himself.

He came to meet us, a dusty, heavily muscled little man with a hard, wicked gargoyle of a face, but when he smiled he revealed, surprisingly, a perfect row of white teeth. He was dressed similarly to Hisham: he wore a short tunic, but without the ragged turban.

He led us precariously down into the hole to an excavated entrance. The half cleared tunnel descended into the darkness, but he was reluctant to take us into it — its secrets, I could see, he would keep from us. That was fine by me; I wanted to view what he had for sale in the bright light of the sun, not by candlelight deep in the bowels of the ancient tomb. The purpose of taking us down to the tomb entrance, it seemed, was to show us that he had sole access to this ancient tomb and to protect our dealings from unwanted eyes.

Hisham opened the negotiations, and I kept my knowledge of Arabic to myself. It gave me an edge; I did not want Gamal to know how good it was. We were led a few feet into the tunnel, where he had laid out the artefacts that he had for sale: a beautifully ornamented ancient bed, which was not very long, I noticed; and many stunningly decorated vases used to house the numerous things that the deceased needed on his journey into the afterlife. Although I could see the appeal of these artefacts, I thought that gold would be more attractive to ladies of society and the gentlemen who would buy it for them.

'Ask him whose tomb this is,' I whispered to Hisham.

Gamal skirted around the question, and I could tell that he did not know. I remembered what Robert had told me: the discovery of the Rosetta stone by Napoleon's troops in 1799 had led scholars to decipher the ancient Egyptian hieroglyphic scripts. This ability had been about for fifteen years or so, since the early 1820s. It was clear that Gamal was no scholar and could not decipher the ancient script.

'We are interested in the mummy,' declared Hisham on my behalf, but again Gamal skirted around the issue. He rubbed his hands across his whiskered chin, then clapped his hands and a number of his men came forward, each holding coarse pieces of roughly spun material folded over carefully. He took the first and unravelled it gently. A piece of the theatre, I thought, but the reveal was stunning: a blue amulet of a scarab beetle, beautifully carved as part of a golden necklace.

'It was to protect the deceased on their journey, *sidi*.' Gamal turned and bowed to me. Hisham pretended to translate for me; I nodded, deliberately keeping my face a mask, but I thought that perhaps he did have some knowledge after all.

Gamal clapped his hands again and one by one the precious items were brought forward and uncovered for my inspection. A golden belt with porcelain-like cowrie shells, elaborate gold earrings, bracelets, a sumptuously decorated box containing an intricate jet-black wig. They were not in the same league as the artefacts that Haroun had shown me back in Cairo, but they were desirable nevertheless.

I broke my silence and started to negotiate with Gamal directly. Briefly, his eyes widened in shock — I could see he was a little uneasy about my good Arabic — then a nervous white-toothed smile crossed that gargoyle face; I used that to my advantage. I attempted to purchase the golden necklace with the blue beetle amulet, the golden belt and the wig box; but the negotiations stalled, even though one of the painted vases was offered in addition to complete the deal.

I was not going to agree a deal, though, until I had seen what else he had to offer; I wanted my pick of his merchandise. 'I need to see inside the tomb,' I said condescendingly, as if my knowledge was superior to his. 'I want to see what you have uncovered, to make up my own mind as to what are the best finds.'

At first he just flourished his hand bellicosely in my face to gesture that what I was suggesting was out of the question, the way I had seen the merchants in the souk doing. His response was to bring down the price of his merchandise a fraction, but I resolved not to play his game. I gestured with my head to Hisham and we turned to climb out of the hole.

'*Sidi*,' he shouted after me, and I looked back over my shoulder at him. He rubbed his stubbly chin vigorously, then stepped outside of the tomb entrance, looking up at my armed Turkish guards and the formidable *kawass* in particular.

'Your men up there must go,' he said. 'I will only take you and your servant.' I was going to agree, but Hisham put a hand on my arm; it was a gesture telling me to be careful.

'But *your* men are also armed,' I said, fixing him with a hard stare.

He scowled, but then his face took on a sycophantic expression, and his body followed suit. With his head on one side, he seemed to shrink before me. He reminded me of the despicable Hakeem. 'Come back tonight, after the sun has gone down, unarmed, just you and your servant,' he said, giving me an uneasy look.

'And you will meet me, also *unarmed*, with just one man.'

He grunted his agreement in a low, throaty voice.

At the top of the hole, I advised the *kawass* what I had agreed and, for the first time since he had been with us, he became animated. He did not like the idea of my dealing with these men without him. He evidently saw them as the lowest of sorts. I made it clear to him that I had made my decision and my resolve was unshakable, and he saluted — hand to heart, to mouth and then to forehead — to show that he would obey. But somehow, this time, it had a reluctance about it.

I turned to go back to my lodgings in my cave, but he did not follow me. He stormed off down the side of the hole, remarkably keeping his footing, his dignity undiminished by the precarious nature of the descent. He marched up to the diminutive Gamal and raised his silver-topped stick, and at first I thought he would strike, but then I realised that he was reinforcing his status, making it quite clear to Gamal that, through him, I had the protection of the *bey*.

That evening, Hisham and I returned to the excavations, reaching the top of the hole just as the sun dropped below the horizon. We carried a lantern with us and lit it as the sky quickly blackened, the moon only just beginning to rise. We were met by Gamal and just one of his men and, as promised, they carried no swords; neither did they appear to have the Arab daggers at their waist, but I suspected that they may have been hidden.

I fixed Gamal with a hard stare. 'I have brought no money with me,' I told him at the outset. 'If your plan is to rob us, then there will be no reward in it for you. The only way that you will receive coin is for us to agree a price on your antiquities, and I will return tomorrow with my armed men and the money.'

'*Effendi*,' he said sycophantically, holding his own lantern up to my face, 'I am but your humble servant.' He gestured with his outstretched arm for me and Hisham to follow him.

He slid skilfully down the side of the hole with his man, and Hisham and I followed, me less adeptly. As we walked, our lantern exposed the walls of this ancient excavation like the spotlight on a carriage. I could see the antique chisel marks in the stone made by the long-dead Egyptian craftsmen, and even their geometric reference points marked out by the architect for them to follow. In silence we walked, deeper and deeper, the only sound made by our sandalled feet on the desiccated stony floor.

Finally, we reached an antechamber, and Gamal raised his lantern to reveal an undecorated room chiselled from the hard stone. It was about fifteen feet by eight, and under six feet high; I had to bend slightly, not quite able to rise to my full height. I could see where the antique bed had stood, but other than that there were merely numerous vases and pots. At first I was a little disappointed, until I realised this was not the burial chamber — that was at the far end, and had been enclosed behind a wall of stone bricks which had now been removed and loosely discarded about the antechamber.

We crawled to enter the tomb, the door being no more than three feet high. The tomb was about twelve feet long and perhaps eight feet wide, and a vaulted ceiling overhead was painted in a pattern of blues and greens to represent, I thought, the sky. The walls were just as brilliantly coloured in red, ochre and gold with images of the gods, as well as scenes to describe events in the deceased's lifetime. Somewhere amongst these images would be the deceased, I thought. It was remarkable how the vibrancy of the colours had not faded over the millennia. The tomb had apparently been packed with the deceased's property and things that he would need in the afterlife: chairs, pots, vases, the sarcophagus (within which was the coffin), boxes and jars, all elaborately decorated — although it had clearly just been ransacked. The sarcophagus lid had been removed, and so had the coffin lid within. Bones were strewn on the floor — the raiders had cut through the antique linen coverings to get at the jewellery, then just dumped the bones after removing the prized possessions. The amulets had been placed on the mummy for protection, but now they were the reason for its desecration.

My eyes fixed on an image on the wall; the mummy was apparently female. I had suspected this was the tomb of a wealthy woman. The theft of her jewellery from her body was the reason Gamal had no mummy to sell. He was little more than a looter, fuelling the black market, but then I was a part of that same black market and had no right to condemn him. He was just a poor man using his wits to earn a living. I knew Robert would disapprove, but he himself was walking a fine line when purchasing his Coptic manuscripts, even if he believed he was saving them for history.

I reasoned, however, that I could still use this as a bargaining tactic. I gestured at the chaos all about the tomb, my brow furrowed, and I was about to reprimand Gamal for his vandalism, when I heard a sound behind us — back in the antechamber, or perhaps even back in the tunnel.

My head shot round at the sound, and then I looked sternly back at him. 'Is that your men come to rob us, Gamal?' I spat.

Gamal had also looked behind us, and when he looked back I could see fear on his face, his eyes wide in disbelief. 'There is no God but God,' he mumbled, his voice quivering — but he was speaking to himself, not to me. Then his eyes flashed at me. 'These are your men come to steal from *me*!' he screeched.

I shook my head indignantly. 'Certainly not,' I hissed. We both listened for some moments, our eyes darting to the antechamber. I walked to the low door, crouched and crawled through inelegantly, lifting the lantern — but the antechamber was as we had left it. Gamal followed me in, hesitantly stood up and raised his lantern also. We stood like that for some moments; then I just shrugged and crawled back to the tomb, angry at my own foolishness. When we arrived, I realised that we had left Hisham and Gamal's man in total darkness, and there was now extreme fear on both of their faces.

'I see you have already removed the best pieces then, Gamal?' I said, but before he could answer there was another sound. This time, it was a high-pitched call, like the way Arab women ululate, vibrating their tongues in a wail of grief.

Terror took Gamal like a bolt of lightning. '*La ilaha illallah* — there is no lord worthy of worship except Allah,' he rumbled to himself over and over again, his eyes bulging, all the time making a sign of blessing. Then he prostrated himself and his man did the same.

I looked at Hisham; there was fear on his face too. I, too, was afraid — we were a hundred feet below ground; there should be no one and nothing to make such a noise. I was not a superstitious man by nature, but even I was in fear that this long-dead woman had come back to take revenge on us.

'We should go back,' I said, trying to stop my voice from trembling. 'There is nothing more for us to see here.' I moved to the doorway, but Gamal and his man inched their way to the far wall of the tomb, their back to it, their hands and fingers spread wide. In the dancing flame of the candle in the lantern, I could see beads of sweat rolling down the side of his distorted face. It was clear they were not going to follow us.

'Well, I am not staying here, even if you are, Gamal.'

'No, do not leave us, *effendi!*' he cried out.

'Then you must come now.' My voice was stern. I wanted to get out of there as quickly as I could. 'I will go through to the antechamber first,' I added encouragingly. I crouched down to the little door and moved through on bent legs, my torso almost doubled over. I lifted the lantern, afraid of what I might see, but nothing had changed. I spun in a slow circle, illuminating all four walls — yet everything was as we had left it. I shouted for them to come through, and Hisham followed and then stood behind me. At first Gamal faltered and sent his man ahead, and when he cried back he too inched his way tentatively into the antechamber.

The four of us stood there, trembling. I took the lead with Hisham following and went through the door of the antechamber into the long inclined tunnel that Gamal and his men had laboriously excavated. After I had gone about twenty feet, I looked behind me, but the only faint light I saw was still in the antechamber. I gave Hisham my lantern and went back to it; Gamal was still cowering there with his man, and they were holding onto each other.

'Come,' I grunted, waving them forward with my arm. They did not move. I walked back to them and grabbed their lantern; they were shaking so much that Gamal did not fight me for it. As I walked to the doorway, they followed so as not to be left in the darkness. I pushed them ahead of me so that I was at the rear with the second light and we started the climb up the inclined passageway.

After a slow beginning, we began to gather pace, eager to get away from the tomb. But then we heard another noise. It was a low growl that seemed to come from all around us. We all stopped and darted glances at each other, then up ahead of us and then behind, not sure from where it came.

I had never been a believer in ghosts and ghouls but at that moment, in the bowels of that cavern, I expected that we would be confronted by some ancient giant god, bent on revenge for our sacrilege. We had been challenging forces that we could not comprehend and we were in a city of the dead. The sound stopped after about seven or eight seconds, but the echo seemed to continue.

'*La hawla wa la quwwata illa Billah!*' screamed Gamal. 'There is no power and no strength save in Allah!' His man followed suit. They repeated it over and over again. Then their chanting changed to '*Inna Lillahi wa inna ilahi raji'un*' — 'We are from Allah and to Allah we are returning.' They thought they were about to die and were submitting themselves to God. I felt the perspiration running down my spine.

Then that throaty clarion-like sound started again, and up front Hisham let out a terrified cry and began to run up the tunnel. Gamal and his man followed, and I brought up the rear. Several times there were stumbles, but each time he immediately got to his feet and took off again, screaming. We all thought we were being pursued by some terrible apparition.

Then, at last, we saw the distant light at the end of the tunnel. Frantically, we scampered towards it, concertinaing up as I ran faster than Gamal and he, in turn, ran faster than Hisham. Finally, we emerged into the moonlight and we all scampered up the side of the hole as fast as we could. I bent over, hands on my knees, my heart in my throat, my lungs bursting.

After a few seconds, I looked up. Gamal was on his back, exhausted, trying to fill his lungs. His man was crouched down on his haunches, his head between his legs. Only Hisham, the oldest of us all, remained upright, though he was winded.

We were debilitated for several minutes, then Gamal rolled over, clambered to his feet and signalled to his man that they were going. 'Don't let them go without agreeing a price,' Hisham whispered in my ear. I looked at him incredulously; we had just escaped with our lives, had we not? 'This is a good time to make a deal,' he added, looking at me knowingly.

'How much for the necklace with the blue amulet?' I needed to take a large breath before going on. 'And the golden belt and the box containing the wig?' But Gamal did not want to discuss it — he just wanted to get away to safety, to thank Allah for his deliverance. I ran over and grabbed his muscular arm as he tried to turn away. 'I will offer you two thousand five hundred piastres for the lot,' I said forcibly. He tried to pull his arm free, but I tightened my grip. 'Our business is *not* concluded,' I added.

Then I saw his sweat-streaked face, his protruding eyes. The last thing he wanted to do was negotiate.

'Two thousand five hundred piastres for the lot — what do you say?' I squeezed his arm, the nails biting deeper into his skin.

'Yes, yes, two thousand five hundred piastres is acceptable.'

I let go of his arm and offered my hand for him to shake. He looked down, reluctant at first, then he spat on his hand and we shook on the deal. I had originally intended to offer my entire war chest of four and a half thousand piastres for the haul; I was now still left with two thousand piastres to make further purchases.

We watched Gamal and his man scamper away until the darkness swallowed them. I put my hand on Hisham's shoulder, gesturing my thanks that he had encouraged me to finalise the negotiations. I saw there was a grin on his face, and I was not sure of the reason behind it. We had done well in the acquisitions, but I was still mightily relieved that we had escaped with our lives. Was he just as relieved? He did not seem to be. I frowned in confusion and, at the sight of this, his grin widened into a broad smile. 'What?' I demanded.

His lips tightened, his tongue pressed up against his teeth and he forced a shrill whistle. From behind a mound, a small figure stood up and came towards us. I peered into the night as he emerged; it was Farid, his son, and he was holding something behind his back.

'What have you got there?' I asked him, nodding at his hidden hand.

From behind his back he produced some sort of a horn. He was grinning like his father. 'It is an ombeya,' he said. 'It is an elephant horn.' He lifted it to show me; it was made of curved ivory.

'It is a Sudanese war horn,' Hisham interrupted. 'Play it for *sidi*,' he said to his son. Farid put it to his lips, took a deep breath and blew. A deep, throaty note sounded, the note held steady by the young boy, the wailing clarion immediately recognisable to me.

'It was you in the passageway, with this — ombeya?' I asked, rubbing my whiskered chin. He stopped blowing and gave a small bow of confirmation. 'And the other sounds?' He let out a shrill ululating sound, his tongue vibrating rapidly in his mouth, his unbroken voice adding to the piercing sound.

I looked around at Hisham. 'And *you* knew all along?' He gave me a sheepish look, as if trying to stop himself from bursting into laughter. 'You just pretended to be scared?' I added.

'The more I pretended to be scared, the more they were, *sidi*,' he answered, as if he had pulled off a fine wheeze, which of course he had.

'Well, I never,' was all I could say. I gave a hollow laugh; I was the one who was supposed to be the rogue.

The next day, once I had paid Gamal for the artefacts, I went to see Hisham and Farid. I gave Hisham two hundred piastres as his cut, in addition to the few piastres I had agreed to pay him as my guide. His eyes widened in disbelief at the sight of so much money. I had not realised that it would be that much of a fortune to him — more money, he said, than he had ever seen in his life. He fell to his knees and bowed his head. I took his arm and raised him up.

He pulled his son to him, put an arm around him and hugged him tightly. His voice caught as he tried to talk; he needed to start over again before the words came out. 'I will never have to eat stick again,' he said finally, his eyes welling with tears.

I felt somehow uplifted, an emotion that was new to me. Generosity had never been a bedfellow of mine and, in truth, two hundred piastres was much more significant to Hisham than to me. Nevertheless, I felt good about myself.

CHAPTER 20

We were back in Cairo by the middle of February 1836. Our moods were different. I was carefree and relaxed, our visit to the Necropolis of Thebes had been a success, as far as I was concerned. I had the start of an excellent collection of artefacts to sell in London.

Robert, on the other hand, was subdued; the manuscripts he had found, except for the martyrology, had again all proved to be church books, liturgies for different seasons or homilies. They were of immense importance to the Coptic monks but had little historical value. He had studied, by candlelight, the martyrology for ten consecutive nights in that subterranean hiding place, but, striking as it was, it also held no historical significance. His only consolation was that he did not have to break his promise to the old monk that he would respect their treasures as fellow Christians.

While Robert made plans for our next expedition, I visited the tavern and gambled, increasing the two thousand or so piastres I had left to over three and a half thousand. I also visited the lovely Ebonee for my gentlemanly pleasures; perhaps I had not changed that much, after all.

Our next expedition, Robert explained, would be gruelling. St Catherine's Monastery was at the mouth of a gorge at the foot of Mount Sinai, the legendary mountain where Moses had received the Ten Commandments. He spoke of it in awe, saying that Emperor Justinian I had ordered it to be built in the sixth century on the site where Moses had seen the burning bush. On the third day of March, we journeyed eastwards to the city of Suez and from there we would make the long trip, crossing over to the peninsula and then down to Mount Sinai.

At Suez, I saw that the port was a poor sort of a place. Robert told me that this was the result of fighting between Napoleon and the British some thirty or so years ago, which had left it in ruins, and it was not yet fully recovered. Kamil, the new dragoman, was charged with finding us bearers and we required more than previously, the proposed journey being so much longer and the expedition much more comprehensive. He also suggested camels instead of donkeys in view of the vastness of the Sinai Peninsula desert and when we consulted with the *kawass*, he agreed. Kamil also went to the souks to purchase the extensive provisions that we needed.

We started our journey on the sixteenth of March, heading eastwards across to the peninsula. I, Robert and our two guides rode camels, as did the dragoman and the *kawass*. The rest of our party, the bodyguards and the bearers, followed on foot, walking beside the other camels that had been packed with our provisions. On this journey, wells would be further apart than in the Wadi El Natrun, and we had to carry much of the water with us, as well as fodder for the camels. But camels have an amazing ability to search out a place of water or grassland due to their extraordinary sense of smell, and without that we surely would not have been able to carry enough water for our expedition. Our trip south-eastwards down the vast triangular Sinai Peninsula would be over two hundred miles, and as each ponderous mile passed, I rolled with the lolloping metronomic gate of my mangy camel.

The Sinai was a wilderness of grandeur; mountains punctuated by valleys and wadis (dry river beds), vast dunes of soft sand and the occasional lagoon. The blazing sun was so bright that the world around us appeared in silhouette. It was hot, but it was not the blistering assault of the high summer. We still wrapped our faces with our headdresses to protect us from the sun and the blowing sand. As we peeked out of the narrow slits of material, we occasionally saw the motionless vipers and lizards or dawdling tortoises watching us as we passed by, perplexed at our unhurried progress. Once, a desert fox stopped abruptly to gaze at us, before scurrying away in its search for something to eat. Isolated strips of water with perhaps a solitary tree or even a flower broke the monotony at intervals.

It was in the early evening when the sun was on the horizon that the full beauty of this land became apparent. The sand now embraced the gentler light so that hues of white, yellow and ochre became evident, and in the distance the mountains now stood blood-red. The pale blue sky deepened to azure, turning cobalt at the horizon.

In the evenings, we did little but eat and then crawl exhausted into our beds, or lie on our carpets looking at the profusion of stars. The camels were watered from leather buckets, and fed from the fodder that they had themselves carried.

In geographical terms, we were now more than two hundred miles south of Cairo, over to our west across the Gulf of Suez, a northern finger of the Red Sea. It was on the seventh day of April, after twenty-two days in the desert, that I had my first sight of the Monastery of St Catherine; it was not what I expected. It was huge, a fortress of a place, with walls forty feet high. We rode around it, looking for the entry point, but could find none at ground level. The only entrance we could see was a sort of wooden portcullis suspended thirty feet high in one of the walls. Visitors, we were to discover, had to be hauled up in a basket.

We made our temporary camp below the suspended entrance, expecting the monks to send down the basket for us, but although we saw the occasional face at the parapet, they made no attempt to contact us.

'They must think we are Arabs,' I said to Robert, taking off my headdress as I looked up to a bodiless head that gazed down on me. I intended to show that I was a Frank, but I was heavily bearded after our long trek and I was unsure whether he recognised me as European or not. 'Wave your letter of introduction from the Patriarch of Alexandria at him,' I added.

'That won't help,' he said.

'Then shout up at them in Coptic.'

'That won't help either.'

I looked round at him and he gave me a red-eyed glance, biting his blistered lower lip. 'Why ever not?'

'This isn't a Coptic monastery.'

'Then what is it?'

'It's a Greek Orthodox monastery, under the jurisdiction of the Greek Orthodox Church of Jerusalem.'

'What?' I exclaimed. 'We have come all this way through the wilderness without a letter of introduction?'

'It would have taken months, John — to get a letter through to Jerusalem and back. That would have put the expedition back to the height of summer. It was not an option.'

'So what did you expect would happen when we got here?'

'I expected to be able to speak to the abbot and explain that we were scholars come to look at their library. I did not see a problem.'

'Look,' I said, 'let us make camp for the evening, and you can write a letter in Greek to the abbot. At least he will know that we are not Arab men.' It was all I could think of.

He nodded his agreement, and after another meagre meal of *ful* he sat scribbling in his notebook the intended letter. He made several attempts, I saw, but I was fast asleep by the time he was satisfied.

The next morning, we gesticulated at the head in the sky, waving the letter at him and shouting in Greek until we were hoarse. Nothing seemed to happen, and the face disappeared for some time; then it returned and the basket descended. Robert climbed inside, but they would not haul him up. I listened; my rusty Greek was good enough to hear the disembodied head tell us to just put the letter in the basket. I hauled Robert out, and the basket was raised with the letter inside it. Yet again, nothing happened for several hours, and we were just left in the midday sun to ponder what to do next.

In the mid-afternoon, the basket started to descend again, with a bearded monk as its contents. When he reached the ground, he climbed out and came to us. He was a very tall, lean man, at least two inches taller than Robert and me, and he towered over most of our guards, his long black habit and pillar-box hat adding to his perceived height. He introduced himself as Father Baptiste.

We offered him tea, he accepted and we went to our tent to keep out of the dazzling sun. I sat in on the discussion, straining with my long forgotten Greek. Robert was good, I had to admit. He explained that, as a scholar, he had studied the monastery and knew that it had been built between 548 and 565 AD at the site where Moses had seen the burning bush and that there had been a Christian settlement here since the third century. He also knew that Catherine of Alexandria was a Christian martyr, condemned to death on a wheel.

The monk nodded a sort of acknowledgement, then said, 'You should understand that although this is a Christian monastery, the site is also sacred to followers of Islam and Judaism.'

This was good, I thought. They must have received pilgrims from each of the religions; they will, for this reason, have a duty of hospitality to us. But Robert was ahead of me. 'I understand that you have an admirable library of ancient manuscripts, and I would be honoured if your abbot would give us permission to study them.'

The monk nodded demurely but then was silent for a time. 'The Archbishop of the Orthodox Church of Mount Sinai is based here at St Catherine's,' he said, 'and he also acts as the abbot here; he is a wise and powerful man.' He hesitated and looked at us for our reaction, and we both felt obliged to nod respectfully. He went on, 'He has asked me to find out about you.'

'As my letter said, we are scholars from England, merely wanting to study in your great library.' Robert's words were quiet and respectful.

'But England is a Protestant country, is it not?'

He looked intently at Robert and then turned to look at me. Robert and I exchanged glances — but what could we do? We knew the significance of the question. 'Yes, it is,' Robert answered truthfully.

'And are you also Protestant?' The monk's gaze was searching.

'We are, but we come as scholars, not pilgrims, father, you must understand that.'

The monk reflected, looking at the sandy ground before him. Then he sighed and we knew what was coming. 'Then I am afraid that the Archbishop commands me to tell you that he will not grant you admittance. The best I can do is to offer you some hospitality. I will have some fresh water delivered to you in the basket.'

That evening we were all subdued. Robert, because he could not continue his scholarly expedition, and the Arab bearers and Ottoman bodyguards because they had looked forward to a respite before heading back on the arduous trek through the wilderness of the Sinai Desert.

By the next morning, however, Robert seemed to have grown resolved. He gave instructions to make a permanent camp; we were settling in for a long visit. He adopted a stance as if he were an actor giving a performance. 'I'll be damned, John, if I'll go back defeated. I have not come all this way to be turned away.' He produced another letter and waved it at a face on the parapet. The basket was lowered and he put it in.

'What does it say?' I asked.

'It's addressed to the Archbishop himself. I have told him that we do not intend to leave until I have an audience with him. I have reminded him that we may be Protestant, and to his mind that may make us heretics, but we *are* Christian. I want to prick his conscience, John; I have asked him if he would deny entrance to Islamic or Judean pilgrims.'

We camped for nearly three weeks and, despite regular letters from Robert, we were still denied entry. Robert made a point of having a Christian service each Sunday, outside our tent; the congregation was restricted to just the two of us. We did not start until we saw faces at the parapet to witness us, and then we sang our hymns with gusto so that they must have heard us.

Father Baptiste came to see us at intervals to tell us that the Archbishop would still not see us, this constant denial making our days long and tedious. I liked Father Baptiste; he had such a genuine face, his features elongated by his lengthy greying beard. He shuffled uncomfortably as he sat on our carpet each time he delivered the rejection.

It was part of Robert's strategy to ask him searching questions. Were we not Christian? Were we not fellow scholars? Did we not deserve the same hospitality as Islamic or Judean pilgrims? It made Father Baptiste uncomfortable, I could see, but that was Robert's intention; he also made it clear that we were not going, and so the monk's awkward meetings with us would continue. He wanted him to speak to the Archbishop on our behalf.

But Robert's strategy had a flaw: our provisions were finite, and we needed to preserve some for the long trek back. As each day passed, we became more apprehensive and, despite Robert's attempts to seem upbeat, I knew he was concerned. Then, unexpectedly, Father Baptiste came to us and said that the Archbishop would see us.

We were hauled up in the basket and saw the inside of the monastery from the parapet. It was vast and all intact, with the fortified walls built around the main church, the Basilica of the Transfiguration, but there was also a chapel called the Chapel of the Burning Bush. I could see the monks' cells built along the defensive walls and the refectory, which I was later told was called the Crusader's Church. This was not, it was clear, a dirt-poor community like the Coptic monasteries.

I pointed to a strange, incongruous rectangular building at the south-west of the Basilica. 'Is that what I think it is, Robert?'

He followed my finger. 'Well, I never,' he said. 'It certainly looks like a mosque, if that's what you mean.' This was an unusual place indeed.

Father Baptiste introduced us to the Archbishop, who offered us tea and we accepted. He was younger than I'd expected, mature, but plainly not old — a small, rotund man, with a long sprawling salt-and-pepper beard. His simple habit was black, and if it were not for the series of rings on his fingers and the large golden crucifix that hung from his neck, I would not have identified him as an archbishop. Despite his status he had humbleness about him; it was surprising to me and my European expectations, as archbishops were usually powerful men.

Robert explained that he had studied from afar this splendid monastery and that he was privileged to see it for himself. The Archbishop seemed keen to add to his knowledge; he told us that the holiest part of the monastery was the large shrub that was said to be a direct descendant of the burning bush that was seen by Moses. He said that in the year 623, a document, the Actiname, was signed by the Prophet Mahomed himself, which exempted the Christian monks from taxes and military service and commanded Mahomedans to provide the monastery with whatever help they needed. This document was one of the most prized items in their library.

The audience was very cordial, a meeting of scholars, and Robert took the opportunity to bring the conversation round to the library. 'I understand that your library is the oldest in the Christian world.'

The Archbishop almost imperceptibly nodded his acknowledgement, then added, 'The monastery has been blessed: it has been here continuously since the sixth century and has never been sacked. The library is one of our treasures and our obligations.'

'Would you permit us to study your oldest manuscripts?' Robert searched out the Archbishop's astute eyes as he asked the question.

I saw the patriarch shoot a look at Father Baptiste; I hoped that he had already made the case for us. I was sure I saw a nuance in Father Baptiste's face as he looked back, as though he was urging acceptance. The Archbishop's forehead furrowed in thought. 'What do you hope to find in our ancient manuscripts?'

Robert looked down at the ground. 'Your Holiness, in England we read from a Bible that was translated in 1604. There is considerable debate amongst scholars and laymen alike as to whether the New Testament we read is an authentic record of the word of Jesus.'

'Why should people think otherwise?' the Archbishop challenged. I thought he was testing Robert, to see if he really was a scholar.

'Well, as you know, the Gospels of Matthew, Mark and Luke do not always say the same thing, yet they were all eyewitnesses to Jesus's life.'

'Surely the work of Bishop Athanasius of Alexandria means that their accounts are reliable?'

'But even then, that was in the late fourth century. That was more than three hundred years after the death of Jesus.'

'Yet his task at the time was to define a reliable fixed canon of texts; are you saying he did not do so?'

I looked at Robert; it was clear that the learned Archbishop was an astute man. I was right — he was testing him. Robert looked back at me as if to reassure me. 'I think we have to ask ourselves why Bishop Athanasius thought it was necessary.'

'And why do you think he did?'

'Well, until then there were many eyewitness accounts of the life of Jesus, and many early Christian Churches. The different Churches used different accounts of Jesus's life and sayings.'

'And how will studying our original manuscripts help you with that? I assure you, we do not have copies of these *other* Gospels that were rejected by Bishop Athanasius.'

Robert was silent. He had been outmanoeuvred; his justification had been dismissed. This devout man was just as much of a scholar as he was. 'You make an excellent point, Your Holiness, but the New Testament was written in Greek, and studying the oldest writings will enable us to test the validity of the Bible that we read in Britain.'

The old man nodded at that. 'Perhaps so.'

Robert jumped in to reinforce his argument. 'I want to prove that the word of God as we know it is reliable; it is a noble quest, is it not? I have recently been allowed to study a very ancient Coptic translation of St Matthew's Gospel at the Monastery of El-Sourian; I think it is the oldest translation that is known. I would like to reinforce this with manuscripts written in original Greek.'

The Archbishop sat up as if he had made his decision. 'Very well.' A rogue smile pulled at the corner of his mouth. 'You may study in our libraries, but your men are not Mahomedan *pilgrims* — they must remain outside the monastery.'

CHAPTER 21

Robert was elated; his strategy had succeeded. He set about his task with gusto, realising that our provisions were running low and that we had wasted so much time just to get admittance. We were fed at the monastery refectory, but this did not extend to our men. The only concession to them was that they were offered fresh water daily; the monastery had a continual supply from their 'Well of Moses', which tapped into an underground stream.

I left Robert to his studies, keen to explore the monastery. There was an extensive monastery garden where the ingenious monks had built tanks to irrigate the soil so that they could grow vegetables and fruit trees — olives, apricots and plums.

In addition to the renowned library, there was a gallery that displayed a collection of icons — the ones that were not needed to decorate the already lavish basilica — centuries of paintings of Christ, the Virgin Mary and the saints. These icons, although numerous, all seemed to have the same themes — the Madonna and Child, the body of Christ, the saints. Each generation had fashioned its own images. An abundance of haloed heads looked down on me imposingly, like a religious jury sitting in judgement. It was so unlike the Coptic monasteries we had seen; they were either in ruins or run by poverty-stricken monks. Despite its desolate location, there was an abundance here; the monastery was at the height of its powers.

I met with Robert on that first evening in the refectory and we ate with the black-robed monks. The food was delicious — a molokhia soup with pieces of seared rabbit in it. It was accompanied, as always, by a flatbread. Where they got their rabbits from, I was not sure. I was keen to tell Robert all about the things I had seen. He listened considerately, but I could see that his thoughts were elsewhere; all that resolve that had kept him going for the last three weeks whilst camping outside had drained from him in one day.

'Is something wrong, my Lord Robert?' I asked playfully, trying to lift his spirits.

His voice was uncertain as he scanned my face. 'They have hundreds of books, John; hundreds of them.'

'Well, that's good, is it not?'

I saw him bite his lower lip as he thought. 'Well, it would be if…'

'If *what*, Robert?'

'If I had the *time*, John.' And then the words just spilled out of him. 'The library is all over the monastery. It's never been catalogued. They have several librarians, each with their own bit of it. It's a mess: I would need a year just to sort it out.'

I took two ripe purple plums and gave him one, biting into mine. The flesh was soft and sweet and the juice ran down my chin. 'Cast your mind back, Robert,' I said. I saw his eyebrow arch in that way of his; then I saw his expression change — he understood what I meant.

'To El-Sourian, you mean?'

'*Exactly*, to El-Sourian. What was that like? That monastery hadn't had the services of a librarian for centuries, had it? The bulk of the manuscripts were just strewn across the floor. So what did you do?'

'I just started at one end and worked through it all, just sifting quickly, eliminating anything that was not old, original text.'

'And what did you eventually find?'

'An ancient translation of St Matthews's Gospel, John — I take your point.'

'So you do the same, don't you?' I advised, licking my fingers.

He bit into his plum, nodding. 'The library here is a hundred times bigger than El-Sourian's, but you're right. It is not a different rasher of bacon at all; once again, John, you come to my aid — yes, I will start tomorrow.'

For the next two weeks, I worked alongside Robert as his assistant. There were many beautiful illuminated books and manuscripts — though none that we saw was old enough. I was given the responsibility of identifying and eliminating church liturgies and passing anything else on to Robert.

It was getting hotter day by day, our labours becoming more uncomfortable. After two weeks, our task became urgent as our resources were running out. We had to think about returning across the desert to Suez and then on to Cairo, but we had sifted no more than a fifth of the library. We realised that the monastery contained thousands, not hundreds, of documents; it was an unreasonable task to even sift through everything.

We needed a new strategy. It was evident that the monks had respect for their library, but that did not extend to detailed cataloguing; any cataloguing was in their heads. So we questioned the librarians and asked them to bring us their oldest documents. But even so, what they brought us was not old enough. I began to suspect that, like their Coptic brethren, certain documents were being kept secret from us.

The oldest records that they brought us were some loose leaves, fragments of an ancient copy of the Old Testament. They excited Robert temporarily, but merely as a scholar. They did not advance his quest to find the earliest writings about Jesus.

A week later, we had to face the reality that our time had run out and that we had accomplished very little. Robert negotiated with Father Baptiste, on behalf of the monastery, to purchase the loose-leafed fragments of the Old Testament and, after consultation with the librarians, it seemed that they placed little significance to them and were happy to see them go.

We began our trek back on the last day of May in 1836, almost a year to the day after I had fled England. I wrapped my headdress around my face, looking out on the rock-strewn desert through a slit in the material. England — with its lush pastures, its verdant colours, its dewy smells — seemed a lifetime away. We had brought bearers with the expectation of returning with treasures, but they were now surplus to requirements; only one panier on one camel was loaded with the manuscript fragments. I suspected that Robert had only purchased them so that we would not return empty-handed.

The *kawass* and the dragoman seemed to share our sense of failure when we started our long trek back up the Sinai Peninsula. We were all subdued — even the hired bodyguards and bearers seemed to feel it. We all settled into the long, laborious journey and as the days passed, there was hardly a word spoken as we followed our guides across the endless rocky terrain and the dry wadis. Even at night I had little conversation with Robert; I left him to scribble in his journal by the light of the campfire and went to bed early each night. The only consolation was looking up at the cold night sky, as the temperature plummeted, to see a canvas of stars the like of which I had never imagined. I was usually asleep before our

Mahomedan servants had finished their prayers, prostrated towards Mecca on their prayer mats.

Despite the hardship of our passage, a sense of serenity fell on me, as if I were cocooned in a world without peril. But on the twelfth day of June, that feeling was viciously exposed as an illusion. A camel, I had been advised by the camel handlers, could differentiate between sounds and could recognise its owner's voice. Indeed, my camel had trekked sombrely for days, responsive to my voice, yet suddenly he became restless, giving bad-tempered grunts. I pulled on the reins forcibly to show him that I was in charge, as I would do with a skittish horse, but the animal was reluctant to settle. I peered out of the slit in my headdress and noticed that the two guides up front had stopped their camels and were looking eastwards. I followed their sightline with difficulty, my camel circling in its skittishness, to the blood-red mountains on the horizon; they seemed to be unusually visible today, as if they had crept nearer to us whilst we were not looking.

There appeared to be alarm in the behaviour of our guides, but I could not understand the source of their anxiety. I looked again, felt a rogue gust of wind, and instinctively closed my eyes tight to keep the sand out of them. When the gust had dissipated, I looked again at the mountains and realised that the wind was getting up — a storm, I thought. Then the full horror hit me. The mountains were getting closer; an icy cold shiver ran down my sweaty back as I tried to comprehend what I was seeing; it was *not* the mountains — it was a colossal wall of sand bearing down on us like some biblical tempest. I did not know what I thought a sandstorm would be like, but it was not this — an enormous barrage of sand climbing hundreds of feet into the sky. The whole panorama was altering before my eyes, and the scale of this transformation made us seem like ants to be trodden into the parched sandy ground.

A fork of lightning criss-crossed the darkening sky, followed immediately by a guttural rumble of thunder that made the ground vibrate; I felt it through my camel. The lead guide shouted at us to get to higher ground, and we drove the reluctant camels to the top of the nearest high rocks. I found out later that if we had stayed in a hollow, we might easily have been buried by the blowing sand. The *kawass* came to Robert and me, dismounted and told us to do the same. He put his camel at a right angle to the direction of the wind, and then crouched down behind it to shelter himself. All our bearers knew what to do and I saw them follow the *kawass*.

We could see what we had to do and also sat our camels down at a right angle to the coming tempest, as they had done. My camel instinctively knew what I intended; it brought its own head around the side towards me, sheltering in its own body. The *kawass* took his canteen and held it up to us, shaking it. I reached up, took mine down from the saddle of the camel and looked back at the *kawass*. He poured the water over his headdress and then wrapped it even tighter around his face; this time, he included his eyes. I realised instantly why we needed to do this: we had to avoid the sand pouring down our throats to suffocate us, or into our eyes to blind us. Robert and I did the same, and then we crouched down on the leeward side, tight against the fur of the mangy animals.

And then we waited, the fearful rumble of the storm gathering intensity. We did not have to wait long. I felt my camel roll slightly as the first gust hit it, and I feared that it would topple over and crush me, but it steeled itself against the storm. The noise was deafening in my swaddled ears, the shrieking howl rising and falling like some deranged banshee. We had no alternative but to wait it out.

I felt my camel jolt, and it let out a painful guttural grunt. I realised the chief danger was not suffocation by the stinging sand, but the concussive effect of heavy flying objects. My camel had been struck.

The minutes turned into hours. There was the occasional thud as something hit my camel, my heart racing each time it happened. Then I began to feel the weight of sand building up on me — I was being buried.

A tidal wave of memories besieged me; perhaps it was because I was facing death. I looked back at my life and saw a man of little consequence — a cheat, a fraudster, a swindler, a man without compassion for others. A man who had cheated the only real friend he had ever had.

And then an image of Samuel came into my mind, his large soulful eyes, his compassionate expression, his olive skin, his jet-black hair that he wore in a pigtail. He had one of those faces which, whilst not handsome, was warm and encouraging; the kind of look that attracted the fairer sex. But above all he was a man of innate honour, a characteristic that was absent in me.

God's retribution had found me, I thought, and I was worthy of it. Then, after two hours, the stormy winds started to ease, the high-pitched howling softened, and my fear began to subside with it — however, the feeling of self-loathing remained.

As the noise dissipated, I heard a paroxysm of coughing from our Arab bearers and Ottoman bodyguards as they struggled free from the grip of the amassed sand. I tried to do the same, but I was pinned by the weight of it. I brushed it away as much as I could and kicked with my feet, and they emerged from the dense mound. I struggled up, pulling on the reins of my camel, but it would not respond, its head semi-buried as I had been. At first I thought it had suffocated, and I walked around to the other side of it. The accumulated sand was even deeper, and perhaps this was the reason why it was making no attempt to get up. I swept away the layers of debris, then realised my folly; there was a tree stump stuck in its side, a trail of red running down its mangy fur. The creature was dead; it had given its life for me, a man not worthy of its sacrifice.

We made no further progress that day. We camped for the night, took stock of our remaining water, and made plans for the rest of our trek. My spirits had sunk far lower than Robert's. I was not good company for the remainder of the journey, and there was nothing in the long, monotonous days to distract my thoughts. We spoke but a few words each day. Robert at least had his journal to keep him company. I had nothing. I felt wretched, and knew I deserved my shame.

CHAPTER 22

Cairo in the height of the summer was blistering, and it did not help my melancholy. I needed something to take my mind off my depression, and so I reverted to my natural state; I gambled, I drank, I wenched with Ebonee. It helped only partially, occupying my mind in the evenings, but during the long hot days when I stayed indoors it just reinforced the feeling that I was a worthless man.

On my first night, I drank too much and lost two hundred of my two thousand-piastre war chest. It was my old folly: I was a skilled card player, but that skill evaporated as my mind became addled by the brandy and water. My cunning, though, was intact; I won it back, and more, the next night. The sea captains were anxious to play with me, seeing me as an easy mark, and I bested them in their greed. I had not planned it that way, but I played the trick masterfully, pretending to be drunk.

I felt good about this, but it was short-lived. I began to realise that the only time I actually felt good about myself was when I was helping Robert in his quest. What he was doing, I thought, was noble, and that nobility rubbed off on me. I decided that I too needed a noble quest.

I was already intent on acquiring antiquities to sell back in London, but there was no nobleness to it; it was merely a means to make myself rich. I realised that there was little chance of ever paying off my debts, though perhaps I could at least pay off the debts that I owed Samuel Medina — well, the monetary ones at least. I would regard that as my personal debt of honour. The incongruity of that thought hit me; in London society, it was gambling debt that was a matter of honour, yet a substantial debt to your grocer that resulted in him being unable to feed his family had no dishonour attached to it. It could remain outstanding for years.

I sought out Robert, eager for information about our next adventure, but found him in a reflective mood. He was sitting cross-legged on a carpet, there being no chairs in our lodgings, still scribbling in his journal, a leaf of manuscript before him on the floor. He was wearing a loose linen shirt without the stock. The armpits were soaked with sweat, and droplets dripped from his nose as he worked; I could see he was anxious that they should not fall on the precious manuscript.

'I have no plans for any further expeditions, John.' He looked up at me; there seemed to me to be regret in his eyes.

I was alarmed. 'Are you giving up on your quest then, Lord Robert?" Despite my own melancholy I had forced myself to call him "Lord" intending to be playful, but today, it did not come out that way.

He sighed. 'Our last three expeditions have uncovered very little, haven't they? But I have the prize of the Gospel of St Matthew from the Monastery of El-Sourian to take back with me.' He paused. 'Perhaps I should be satisfied with that?'

'Is it the sandstorm in the Sinai that has changed you, Lord Robert? I know we came close to death, but we are adventurers, are we not? Come, let us continue our adventures. You will regret not doing so when you get back to England.' I was being disingenuous, of course; I was not yet ready to go back to England.

He took a sharp breath and looked down at the floor. 'It is true that I will probably regret cutting the mission short, but I have no alternative, John.' He took out a letter from the back of another journal. 'I have this letter from the family solicitor;

it has been following me for months. It was posted to the British Consul in Venice last December. I left word with the consulate that I would be travelling in Egypt before we left.'

'Has something happened?' I asked.

'Yes,' he said softly. 'You tease me by calling me Lord Robert, but it turns out that you are right. Father died last December and I am the new baronet; I *am* Lord Robert, after all.'

'You need to take a few days to grieve before you make decisions, Robert,' I said hesitantly, but I was still being duplicitous: I still thought to talk him out of his decision. 'When did the letter reach you?'

'I have had it the best part of a week, John. I have already had time to think — you know I have responsibilities.'

I hesitated. 'Were you close to your father?'

'I have hardly seen him for the last eight years; first university, then the Grand Tour and now our expeditions in Egypt. It was my elder brother that he was closest to, he was more like him. Edward was a soldier, as father had been. I was the scholar, and I do not think he ever really understood me. But he was a good father; he let me pursue my own dreams and gave me a handsome allowance.'

'So he was a good father to you, even though you were not close.'

'True enough, John, but we had an understanding. He indulged my adventures, but my obligations to the dynasty were implicit in his support.'

'So you intend to go back to England?' I held my breath, awaiting his answer.

'Yes, John, I have to. I will hardly recognise the place, the estate workers, the servants — I will be a stranger to them.'

I sighed heavily. 'But it is six months since your father died; he will be long buried. Your solicitor will have appointed a manager to run the estate — is that not so?'

'Probably.' He looked up at me.

'Think about it, then, Robert; yes, you have to return home, but does it have to be right away? Perhaps one more expedition; let us go back to El-Sourian. I am sure the monks there are hiding things from us.'

He seemed unconvinced by my contention.

CHAPTER 23

Over the next three weeks, Robert was busy making arrangements to go back to England, crating up his precious manuscripts, his endless journals. I spent my nights gambling, and the stakes began to rise as the word got round the sea captains at the inn. What had been friendly games took on a more competitive edge. A different type of gambler was being attracted; this was good news for me. I was also becoming rather good at this variant of loo that was the preferred game amongst the sea captains.

My war chest rose from two thousand to four and a half thousand piastres, about forty-five pounds. I was trading with the antiquities dealers in the souk, although my purchases were not the prized relics that Amram Haroun had revealed to me. I had designs on the *Book of the Dead* that he had shown me, but at eight thousand piastres it was still way out of my price range.

I had a decision to make: should I stay here alone in Egypt when Robert went back to England, or should I go back with him? He was financing the expedition; if I stayed I would have to live off my wits, but then I had done that all my life; I was confident that I could continue to do so.

I spoke only briefly to Robert — most days we did little more that pass each other in our lodgings — and I slept whilst he worked and he slept whilst I gambled. Then one evening as I was preparing to go out, he came to me; I saw he had a letter in his hand.

'I am ready to go and look for a passage to Alexandria and then back to Venice,' he said matter-of-factly. 'Shall I book passage for you as well?'

'So you are decided.' My words were little more than a grunt.

He gave me an uneasy look. 'Yes, I have to go back to England — that is where my obligations lie.'

I cleared my throat. 'No, my Lord Robert, if you are to return to England, I will stay; I have unfinished business here. I intend to go back to the Monastery of El-Sourian. I mean to find what they were hiding from us.' I did not know where those words came from. I certainly had not been planning such a trip.

I saw him arch an eyebrow in that way of his, then his forehead creased in confusion. 'But you cannot read Coptic, John!'

'I know that, Robert, but the monks can, and I can speak Arabic to them. I'll find some way of identifying what I find.'

I scanned his face — was there something? My cunning kicked in; a door was slightly ajar, and I would push against it. 'Of course, it would be much better if you were with me; you are the academic, after all,' I added nonchalantly.

He started to pace up and down, staring at the floor. 'If we could get provisioned in three days, we could probably be there in two weeks…'

'I'm sure of it: take just the *kawass*, a dragoman and say, four bodyguards. We can act as our own bearers — a small expedition.'

He paced some more. 'We could be back in — two months, perhaps?'

'I am certain of it, Robert.'

The pacing continued. 'We have already sifted that mess of a library, so that does not need to be done again.'

'Absolutely.' I said no more, leaving him to struggle with his decision. I was a fisherman taking a rest, allowing a fish to play from side to side before landing it.

'I'm all packed and ready. I could be away from Cairo within a couple of days of getting back from El-Sourian...'

'I should think so, Robert.' I let the fish play some more.

He stopped his pacing abruptly and looked up from the floor. 'One last expedition, then; one last adventure together, John Campbell-John?' He seemed to want someone's approval to override the obligations he felt.

I gave it to him. 'Yes, my Lord Robert Babcock — let us have one last adventure together.'

Three days later we set out north-west from Cairo on the same route that we had travelled nearly a year before — our destination again the Desert of Nitria. At first, we followed the west bank of the Nile until we reached the village of Terrané, where we acquired two Arab guides complete with their camels to take us across the desert tracts of the plain. Once again, the *kawass* had got us three noble Arabian stallions from the governor's palace and Robert, the *kawass* and I rode at the head of eight donkeys, the first ridden by Kamil the dragoman, whom we had been able to acquire the services of at short notice. I suspected he may have welshed on another commission, regarding us as more profitable. Four armed bodyguards followed on foot beside the remaining eight donkeys that carried our provisions. A single bearer followed them, and he also acted as our cook.

Robert and I were armed with guns and pistols after our encounter with the rebels last time, but to be honest, if we were attacked again by such a large band, the weapons would be useless — though at least we could shoot wild fowl to provide fresh meat.

From Terrané we soon left the lush and fertile lands of the delta and entered the cruel desert and the Wadi El Natrun west

167

of the Nile. The backdrop was now nothing but a barren, rocky landscape as far as the eye could see, frying under a murderous sun. The temperature was rising to a hundred and ten degrees, its colour a monotonous vista of stony buff. In the evenings, when we made camp, the temperature dropped dramatically as the night hours extended, so we curled up in our tents to keep warm.

When we sighted the imposing stone wall and the soaring square tower of the monastery, it was inviting to our tired limbs; those long desert tracts were not getting any easier.

At the narrow iron entrance, Robert presented our letter of introduction from the Patriarch of Alexandria, which was now dog-eared, but afforded us entrance into the substantial inner square enclosure. Apart from the well-maintained church, the monastery was as neglected and derelict as I remembered. The old, blind abbot was sent for and he came with his constant attendant. He seemed glad to welcome us again; perhaps he remembered the food we had shared with them and particularly the sweet pink rosoglio that we had given them to drink. The abbot and his monks looked as thin and underfed as I remembered.

We wasted no time putting our plan into action. On the very first night we invited the old abbot and his senior monks to dine with us, as we had done on our last visit; they accepted eagerly. We had brought additional provisions for this purpose, together with more bottles of rosoglio. We could see the delight on their faces as they ate and drank; the meal our cook had prepared was nothing special, but there was spiced meat and I could see that, to them, it was a banquet.

Robert laughed and joked with them in Coptic. Sometimes we laughed and joked in Arabic so that I could join in. We exchanged compliments respectfully, but when the time was right Robert asked the question that seemed to change everything.

'Abbot, surely not everything in your famous library is contained in that one room. Do you have other books or manuscripts for me to study?'

His words were light, almost humorous, but any levity in that tiny room seemed to escape like a fleeing animal. Silence fell and the monks gave each other uneasy looks, their inebriation getting in the way of any circumspection. Robert and I knew at once that they were hiding things from us.

The old blind abbot knew it was down to him to speak for the monastery, and that required caution. He stroked his long white beard, then played with the ring on his finger. 'We are a very ancient community here, my scholarly friends, and God places many demands on us. Our library is imperfect in many ways...'

He left his comment hanging. I sought out Robert's eyes, but they were still fixed on the abbot. I looked back at him, but the milky opacity of those sightless eyes revealed nothing — his face remained expressionless.

Robert went to speak again, but the abbot just put up his hand. 'It is late and I am an old man — I am tired and I must go to my bed.' He leant on his cane and, with the help of his attendant, rose to his feet. He left without saying another word, and we all sat in silence. I saw Robert make a fist in frustration. The abbot, it seemed, was no fool; he had neither confirmed nor denied the existence of original historical documents. I just smiled inwardly; the game was afoot.

For the next few days, whenever we asked to see the old abbot, we were told that he was busy. We were allocated a young monk as our guide, Father Anoub, but he was chosen because he knew so little, and the answer to all of our questions was that we should talk to the abbot. However, he was never available — it was infuriating.

We dined with the senior monks each evening, trying to get one of them to be indiscreet, but without any luck — they were now on their guard. We took to wandering about the monastery without the young guide, talking to any of the monks who would converse with us. Our plan was to identify the monk whom Rokku had made contact with, the one who had told him there were other documents hidden.

We used the same technique as at the Convent of the Pulley, giving out little tidbits of food as an inducement with the implication that more would be forthcoming for information about the existence of the rest of the library. We expected that they would gossip with each other and the word would go round.

After about four days, we passed a group of three monks in a corridor and gave them each some figs. Before we emerged from the hallway, one of them came back to us. He was young, small and lean, and his beard was patchy, as though he had not yet grown into full manhood. His face was thin and sallow, pale for an Egyptian, but then he probably spent most of his days indoors. He hesitated and did not speak at first. He looked around himself, as if he did not want to be observed.

'Is the Maltese not with you?' A thin smile twitched expectantly.

Robert translated for me and we looked at each other, realising instantly that this was the monk we had been looking for. Robert returned his smile encouragingly. 'I am afraid that

Rokku the Maltese has died,' he said, his tone as soothing as he could make it. The young monk looked down, his face dejected, then turned to walk away.

'But he told us what you said to him,' I called after him in Arabic. He stopped and looked over his shoulder at me, his forehead furrowed; I could tell that he understood Arabic as well. 'You told him that there were other books, did you not?' I added hurriedly. He was unsure, I could see that, struggling with his faith and his responsibilities. 'I have a whole cured ham and a bag of rice — you look as if you need a good meal. Your elders have accepted food from us — why not you?' I did not want to let him off the hook.

He stood as if transfixed; hunger was obviously a great trial for him. Then we heard words, the sound of voices coming from the far end of the corridor. His head swung around, startled. He turned back, shooting us an alarmed look. 'Meet me by the tower just after sunset,' he said, then scurried away.

We were there by the tower, waiting for him after the sun went down. I carried a lantern but did not light the candle within, knowing that secrecy was required. Robert carried a roughly woven sack, with a shank of ham in it, and a bag of rice. After half an hour, our spirits were sinking; there was no sign of him.

'We did not even get his name,' I mumbled to Robert in the dark, looking up at the stars. It was dark; the moon not yet risen.

'We will find him again, I am sure we will.' I saw the shadow of Robert's shoulder shrug in the dark.

We both turned to go back to our cells, but then stopped and peered into the gloom. A spectral figure was emerging from the shadows, his black robes blending with the darkness of the night, obscuring his identity. He moved soundlessly across the courtyard, as if he was a morning mist descending a hillside. His head was bowed as he reached us, but he put out his hand and ushered me back. 'Quick, into the tower,' he said, his words apprehensive.

We did as we were bade; inside, there was not even the starlight to light the pitch blackness. I lit the candle in the lantern and held it up to the thin, sallow face of the young monk. 'We thought you were not coming,' Robert said.

'It was difficult to get away without being seen.' His eyes darted from Robert to me and back again as he spoke.

'My name is Robert, and this is John.' Robert looked at the monk, encouraging him to speak.

'My name is Father Justin,' he said, then bit his lower lip anxiously. He took out a candle from up his sleeve and lit it from my lantern. 'Follow me,' he stuttered.

We followed his candlelit form and, at first, he took us up a steep flight of narrow steps that led to a heavy wooden door, the sound of our footsteps echoing back to us from the stone walls. He pushed against it and it opened only reluctantly. Inside there was a circular stairway of worn stone steps, each one dipping in the middle from centuries of climbers. To my surprise, instead of going up, he turned to his left and descended the slender staircase, and we seemed to go round in circles for some time, down past several levels, so that we were deep into the bowels of the tower. When we finally emerged, again there was another heavy wooden door. I also put my shoulder to it, helping the frail Father Justin, and it creaked open sluggishly.

Inside, I raised my lantern so that the light would be thrown as far back as possible. It was a vaulted cellar of about thirty feet by twenty feet, dry, well-swept, and with colossal pottery vases stacked in rows on the left-hand side. 'What is this place?' Robert asked, perplexed.

'It is the old oil cellar,' answered Father Justin, as he rapped the knuckles of his free hand against one of the huge vases. It rang out hollow. 'But it was all used up many years ago, and the abbot has no funds to replace it.'

'But why have you brought us *here*?' Robert asked, peering at the shadows.

I looked at the young monk and saw only confusion on his face. He walked over to the wall on the right-hand side and hesitantly put out his arm. 'They were all here, stacked against this wall, on an elegant table.' He looked back at us, as if willing us to believe him.

'What were?' asked Robert.

'The sacred books — they were all here!'

'When did you last see them?' I joined the questioning.

'A liturgy was used in our Sunday service last week,' he spluttered. 'They were here then.'

'So just before we arrived,' I said, trying to piece together a timeline.

'Yes, yes,' said Robert, 'it is clear that the abbot has had them removed, to keep them from us.'

I leaned against one of the huge vases, my devious mind trying to find a way of using the situation to our advantage. 'Don't give him the food,' I said to Robert in English. 'In fact, give me the sack.' I took out the preserved shank of ham, unwrapped it, balanced it precariously on my bent knee, took my knife and cut off a large slice. I gave it to Robert, then sliced a piece and gave it to Father Justin. I cut a piece for myself and we all ate as we looked at the empty wall thoughtfully. I did this twice more but then made a play of wrapping the ham in its gauze and putting it back in the sack. I saw the look of longing on the young monk's half-starved face, the aroma of the cured ham still in his nostrils.

'The ham was intended for you, Father Justin, as a gift for showing us the historical manuscripts — but alas…' I left the words hanging and just gave the sack back to Robert symbolically.

'Let me see what I can find,' he answered quickly. 'I am sure I can find out where they have put the manuscripts.' He bit his bottom lip. 'Meet me here again tomorrow, at the same time.'

He was there before us the following evening and shepherded us into the tower as before. Again, we descended into the bowels of the tower, although not as far down. He produced a large iron key, unlocked a door and then entered a room; it appeared empty, apart from some bottles of communion wine. I thought it was supposed to be a wine cellar but again, very little was left. Robert and I exchanged glances, then looked at Father Justin.

'I have found where the sacred manuscripts have been hidden —' the monk dropped his head and looked at the floor — 'but I cannot take you there.'

I was confused, and I could see that Robert was too. 'So why have you brought us to this place?' Robert asked.

'I have taken an old manuscript from its hiding place.' Shame appeared to be lodged in his throat as he spoke.

Again, Robert and I looked at him, perplexed, but then he went to the far end of the room where there were two small, narrow doors that closed together in the middle. He pulled them open to reveal a dusty cupboard — and on the top shelf was an old manuscript. 'You can study it here tonight — but I cannot allow you to take it away with you. I will return it to its hiding place after you have gone.'

There were no tables, so Robert knelt and put the manuscript on the stone floor. It was encased in a wooden cover, which I could see had once been engraved, but the markings were mostly now obscured as the wood had darkened over the centuries to a deep, rich black.

'That looks very old, Robert,' I said enthusiastically, but he only grunted, gesturing for me to give him the lantern. I handed it down to him and then I sat on the floor, my back leaning against the nearest wall. Father Justin came and sat next to me with his candle and we waited, watching Robert in the small pool of light from his lantern.

He opened the wooden cover as if it was a precious piece of porcelain, touching the pages tenderly. Then he seemed to go rigid. He looked up at me, but I did not understand the expression on his face.

'Is it a Coptic text, Robert?' I asked.

'Aye, John, 'tis Coptic all right, but...' There was a catch in his voice. 'Come look at this,' he added imploringly.

I scrambled over on my hands and knees to see the manuscript. He raised the lantern off the floor so that more light fell on the first page. Then he pointed a shaky finger at the heading. 'What does it say, Robert?' I asked eagerly.

'I'll translate, John — it says —' he swallowed hard — 'these are the hidden words that the living Jesus spoke, and Thaddeus Jude wrote them down.'

'So it's an old historical manuscript, then — what you have been searching for?'

He looked round at me. ''Tis more than that, John — 'tis a new Gospel: the Gospel of Thaddeus Jude.'

CHAPTER 24

'Who was Thaddeus Jude, then?' I asked naïvely. We spoke in English; there was no conscious intention to keep Father Justin out of our conversation — we were just wrapped up in a powerful moment.

'Do you not remember your Bible studies as a child, John?' There was a mild rebuke in his words, but I could see he was being playful; his spirits were soaring. 'Thaddeus Jude was one of the apostles, the brother or possibly the son of James, and perhaps also the author of the Book of Jude, the penultimate book in the New Testament.'

'So this is important?'

'It is far past important, John — if this is genuine, then...' I could see that he was having trouble finding the words.

'How old do you think it is?'

'It will take better scholars than me to verify that, but...' He hesitated. 'John, do you remember what I told you about Bishop Athanasius of Alexandria?'

I paused. 'Was he the man who sorted out what should be in the Bible?'

'Aye, that is him John; that was in the late fourth century.'

'So he missed this book, then.'

'No John, he did not miss it. He *rejected* it.'

'I do not understand.'

'It is what the early Christian Church wanted.'

'Everybody singing from the same hymn sheet, you mean?'

He smiled at my choice of phrase, then said, 'Exactly, but now let us speculate; what if he wrote to all his abbots telling them what they should regard as strict scripture and what they should not? Now, suppose you were one of those abbots here all those centuries ago and you were told that the scriptures you had been using for the best part of two hundred years, and regarded as sacred, were now to be omitted — what would you think?'

'Well, I would not like it, I suppose.'

'Right, but if you continued to use them, you might be considered heretical. You would get into trouble; you might even be excommunicated.'

'Or worse — the Church over the years has not hesitated in putting people to death for heresy, has it?'

Robert nodded. 'So let us speculate further; what could the abbots of all these monasteries do? They could either destroy their old scriptures as ordered, or perhaps they could hide them.'

'And some chose to hide them, I see that, but would that not mean they have been hiding them for fourteen hundred years?'

'I think it means exactly that, John — and it means even more.'

I looked at him, puzzled.

'Don't you see, John? It means that we can date the original text to *before* the year 367, which is the recorded time of Bishop Athanasius's fixed canon. This will be a later Coptic translation, but even that is still likely to be before the year 367. So this could be the oldest known text ever found about the life of Jesus!'

I returned to the wall, sat beside Father Justin, and mused on what Robert had said. We sat together in silence, just observing Robert for hours as he read and scribbled furiously in his notebook. I started to nod as sleep tried to take me, but then I would snap awake at Robert's sharp intakes of breath as he read. Father Justin's candle burned down, the tallow solidifying on the back of his hand as it dripped down. After a time, he blew it out, saving what little was left of it; candles were valuable, even if his own was just smelly tallow and not wax.

I could see that Robert's thoughts had slipped away to another place; a place of fulfilment that his scholarship had defined for him. I felt happy for him, hoping he had found the object of his academic search. I also felt good about myself; for the first time in my life, I was part of something honourable.

And then, at about two o'clock in the morning, Robert's candle began to fail, becoming a congealed blob of wax in the bottom of his lantern.

'It's time to go,' I said to Robert. 'You can come back tomorrow.'

He did not want to go, but then he looked at the last flickerings of the dancing flame and shrugged his shoulders, realising he had no alternative. 'Are there more manuscripts of this age, hidden away?' he enthusiastically asked the shadowy figure of Father Justin.

Beside me I felt the young monk go rigid; his hunger was battling his shame. 'No, there are no more,' he snapped. 'The rest are just treasured liturgies.'

I knew he was lying, but I was in no mood to press him. He relit the last of his tallow candles and led us back up the stone stairway, the sack with the preserved ham and the rice I had given him tucked under his arm.

Robert returned to the old wine cellar for the next five nights, although I did not accompany him. By the end, he had filled four notebooks with his jottings and translations. I thought he would be pleased, but I saw him becoming more and more uneasy as each day went by.

'What is the matter, Robert?' I asked him one night, as he was preparing to go again to the wine cellar.

At first he was reluctant, but then it was as if a dam had broken. 'Do you remember what I said was my reason for looking for historical documents?'

I cast my mind back. 'You want to show that the Gospels that we read today are historically accurate.'

'Exactly, John, I want to find proof that they are the words *from* God, if not written *by* God; it's a major tenet of our Christian belief.'

'So what is the problem?' I asked.

'Remember, the apostles were basically preachers taking the word of God to the world. It was oral; they only set down their teachings when they were getting older and facing death.'

'So how does that devalue what they have written?'

'Some would argue that this delay in writing it down was enough time for the story of Jesus to be corrupted, but to the extent that Matthew, Mark and Luke were all eyewitnesses, *my* view is that little is wrong — as long as all the eyewitnesses say the same thing.'

'And do they?'

'There are some differences, but essentially, yes they do.'

'Differences?'

'Yes, only Matthew refers to the Magi, astronomers following a star to Bethlehem to bring gifts to Jesus, born the King of the Jews. Only in Luke is the account of Joseph and Mary travelling from Nazareth to Bethlehem for the census, and Jesus is born there and laid in a manger. Angels proclaim him a saviour for all people, and shepherds come to adore him.'

'But despite that, the accounts of his life are essentially the same?'

'Essentially.'

'So where is your difficulty?'

Robert frowned. 'This Gospel of Thaddeus Jude is the problem. Why was it rejected? He was also an apostle, so why is it not as significant as the canonical Gospels?'

'And what conclusion have you come to, Robert?'

'John,' he paused, his concern evident. 'John, it simply does *not* say the same things as the canonical Gospels.'

'What does it say, then?'

'It is not about the story of Jesus's life at all; it is just about the things he said. The problem, John, is that although many of the sayings and parables that Thaddeus Jude refers to are the same as in the Bible Gospels — the parable of the fishermen and the parable of the lost sheep are there — *many* are not. They will be new to Christians, and his account is much darker than the Bible in tone; it is not as optimistic.'

'But surely that is good — it will give us a better understanding of Jesus and his teachings.'

'Or a total rethink of his teachings. The basis of this Gospel is that you find God by looking for the light inside yourself; only then can you light up the world.'

'So a bunch of scholars such as you will argue interminably about what Jesus meant. It won't change the faith of the rest of us.' I saw his forehead furrow. I realised I was belittling his scholarship, his quest for knowledge — a mission that I had also begun to embrace, and now I had derided it in a few words. 'My apologies, Robert,' I said with all the contriteness I could muster. 'If what you are saying is true, it will disturb many devout people. They will have to reconsider their faith; I can see that now.'

Robert turned, pacing up and down the small cell he had been given, his anguish apparent. I thought I had wounded him deeply, but then his next words astonished me. 'There is something in what you say, John. Not everybody is as committed as I am.'

'So why *are* you so uneasy, Robert?'

He stopped, sought out my eyes, and came and gripped my arm. 'The more I read of this Gospel according to Thaddeus Jude, the more something becomes increasingly apparent. John — he portrays Jesus as *just* a teacher, as *only* a guide.'

'Well, he was, wasn't he?'

'Aye, 'tis true, but ... John, he does not portray him as a *divine* teacher. He does not refer to Jesus's divinity at all.'

I blew out my cheeks. 'You mean he does not see Jesus as holy?'

'No, John, he does not; blessed maybe, but not divine.' He ran his hand through his long, greasy hair. 'He does not call him Lord nor Christ, as the other Gospels do.'

'What about the virgin birth?'

'No, nothing at all about it.'

'Death and resurrection?'

'No, that is not mentioned either.'

I was beginning to understand his dilemma. He had set out to prove the truth and reliability of the Bible story of Jesus, but he had discovered a document that did the precise opposite. 'Robert, this will test the very faith of all Christians, will it not?'

'John, it will set an explosion that will eclipse anything that Mr Guy Fawkes and his friends could ever have envisaged.'

Robert spent three more uneasy nights studying the Gospel of Thaddeus Jude to the point that he had filled another notebook with his jottings, translations and sketches. He slept most of the day and asked me to use my cunning on Father Justin to try and get him to bring other historical manuscripts — but despite offering him more and more provisions, he would not budge.

'Do you think it is because he understands the significance of this Gospel? Is that what makes him reluctant?' I asked Robert.

'No, I do not. I think it's just the pang of his conscience. If he really knew, he would know the danger of showing this to us. It would not just be conscience; it would be fear.'

'And the abbot?' My eyes widened.

'He is a different rasher of bacon; he knows all right. That is why the manuscripts are hidden — the extreme care, the anxiety of a burden handed down to him from centuries past.'

'So how do we negotiate with him?'

'With extreme care, John, but I want this Gospel. It must be taken back to England.'

With some anxiety, we invited the abbot and his senior monks to another meal. At first, the old abbot declined — still, it seemed, determined to keep his distance from us. We persisted, but he only agreed to come when we indicated that it would be a farewell meal — I assumed because he would finally get us out of his silver hair.

We had the last of the rosoglio at hand and the evening became convivial as the sweet pink liquor flowed; the abbot had the largest measures, we again made sure of that. It was hard to see the extent of his inebriation, as his face was always a mask, but his voice rose and he chuckled, and we took it as a good sign.

'Have your studies been successful then?' he said, without any concern in his voice. He turned to Robert, but of course he did not see the expression on his face.

Robert had rehearsed his words carefully all day; he had been waiting for the right opportunity, and the abbot had now given it to him. 'Exceedingly so, if a little disturbing,' he said quietly, as if it was a military manoeuvre.

'In what way?' the abbot asked, his voice suddenly lower.

'You are a scholar yourself, abbot,' Robert said. 'Do not the differences in the texts of the Gospels disturb *you*?'

'A little,' he answered vaguely, 'but then there are many more comparisons than differences — the discrepancies are only minor.'

'But would you call the different text in the Gospel of Thaddeus Jude *minor*?'

It was as though a clap of vindictive thunder had sounded. The heat of the day had not yet dissipated and had still bathed us all malevolently throughout the meal — but now it seemed to vanish and was replaced by a sharp chill.

'I know nothing about a Gospel of Thaddeus Jude,' the old abbot said, his inebriation suddenly expelled.

'Then you must let me show it to you. It is hidden in your church tower.'

There was a paroxysm of coughing from one of the other monks, and no matter how much he tried to control it, he failed. The old abbot stroked his white beard but remained silent. A secret that had been kept for over a thousand years was now exposed; he must have realised that. The bitter taste of betrayal must have been heavy on his tongue. His forefinger and thumb traced back and forth across his forehead. He attempted to find words, but none came; he only made a disdainful sound.

Robert spoke gently to him. 'Perhaps it is time to lift this burden from you,' he said.

All eyes fixed on the old abbot. He sat upright and he suddenly looked even older than his years — yet that mask remained. 'You do not comprehend what you ask of me.' His unseeing eyes looked straight ahead.

'I think I do,' Robert answered. 'You mean the leaders of the Coptic Church, the Patriarch of Alexandria himself, would not understand this ongoing secret. They would regard you and your monastery as heretical.'

The abbot turned his head towards us; I could see he was taken by an elemental terror.

Robert spoke again, soothingly. 'It does not have to be that way. Let me take the book back to England, and I promise you that I will keep the place of its discovery secret. As far as the world will be concerned, I found it in an old desert ruin. The Gospel will be saved, and a great weight will be lifted from your shoulders.'

'I need counsel,' the old abbot mumbled. 'Would you gentlemen step outside whilst I consult?'

Robert and I rolled sideways and got to our feet. We left and stood outside the door, and I asked Robert to fill me in on the detail of the conversation he had had with the abbot in Coptic. He had been whispering out of the corner of his mouth to me, and now he filled in the gaps. But the silences had been as informative to me as the words, and my understanding had been correct.

'Did you mean it when you said that you would keep secret the place of discovery?' I asked.

Robert shot me an unforgiving look. 'Of course I meant it. Do you not know me by now, John? I am a man of honour, am I not?'

I looked down at the gloomy floor in the half-light. 'My apologies, Robert, 'tis true enough; you are a man of honour.'

He put his hand on my shoulder, to show that my apology was accepted. 'Do you think he'll let the manuscript go, John?' Robert held his breath, fixing me with a stare.

'It will take more than the rosoglio this time, Robert, but you have made a compelling argument; fear is a potent force. But there is still time to sweeten the offer, if they are wavering.' At that, the heavy door opened and a black-clad monk gestured for us to enter. Robert nodded respectfully and I followed his lead. We sat on the carpet again, and for some time we all sat in silence. Then the old abbot's assistant spoke for him.

'The abbot has for many years been forced to lie about the sacred documents that are hidden in our library. He is a man of God; lying is not something that comes easily to him. It pricks his very conscience.'

That was good, I thought, he would be glad to get rid of the manuscript — but I had misunderstood what was being said.

'How much are truth and honour worth to *you*, gentlemen?' the monk added pointedly, staring at both of us in turn.

Robert took a sharp breath. 'There is a phrase in my country: "an Englishman's word is his bond",' he said, straightening his back. 'I will give you my solemn word and take an oath on the Bible.'

The assisting monk stared fixedly at Robert, then leant into the old abbot and whispered in his ear. The other monks mumbled to each other, and their counsel passed down their seated row to the abbot.

I needed to do something. I spoke in Arabic. 'Your oil cellar is empty, Abbot, and there is little in your wine cellar.'

'We are a poor community,' the abbot said, 'but then self-denial is good for the soul.'

'You speak wise words, Abbot, but it must trouble you that your brethren are so undernourished. Words alone will not sustain them.' It was an underhand thing to say, but I was intent on playing on his conscience. At first he did not reply and I looked at him, gesturing for him to respond, though of course he could not see me. I looked at his assistant next to him and saw that he understood, but it was not his place to speak. I needed to press home my advantage. 'Abbot, Robert here will pay you handsomely for the Gospel text, but what if he was also to refill your oil and wine cellars; we will send a caravan back as soon as we return to Cairo.' I looked round at Robert; there was surprise on his face. I had no idea of what funds he had left, so I leant in and whispered in English. 'Rothschild's bank has an agent in Cairo. He can arrange for the funds to be transferred if you run short of gold or piastres.'

He considered my comments briefly and, after a moment, he nodded. The abbot's assistant whispered in the old man's ear, yet his face remained implacable. He began to play with the large wooden crucifix hanging around his neck, rocking forwards and backwards as he contemplated. Then he moved his hand and toyed with the ring on his finger, turning it round and round. But he started to nod as he contemplated; I looked at Robert and saw that he had seen it too.

'Very well,' the abbot said eventually. He leant into his assistant and whispered, and a heavy Bible was called for and passed down to him. 'You must both make the solemn oath to protect our identity, as you have promised. If you do so, then I will allow you to take the Gospel away with you.'

We did so; the old man then rolled on his carpet and was helped to his feet. His mask had slipped, and we saw that he was weary.

CHAPTER 25

The journey back to Cairo, across the panorama of endless desert, was tedious as well as searing. The heat made us all irritable, but for Robert there was something more. I could see that the words in this new Gospel were still causing him concern; he was not sleeping at night, despite his exhaustion. We arrived back in Cairo on the last day of September 1836, where we bathed for the first time in weeks, shaved, cast off the Ottoman dress and wore our breeches and linen shirts, though it was still far too hot for a frock coat.

That first evening we took to our beds early, clean but still exhausted. However, on the second evening, we dined together in the Christian quarter. It was an excellent meal, seared pigeon stuffed with rice, wheat, red onions and coriander, and served with a crunchy diced salad. I devoured it, but Robert played with his food, and I could see he was still troubled, hardly saying a word.

'Would you like me to organise the caravan back to the Monastery of El-Sourian with the oil and the wine we promised them?' I said.

'Huh?' he answered, at first just toying with his fork. Then he looked up at me. 'Oh, yes, thank you, John; that would be a great help.'

'I'll go to the souk with the dragoman tomorrow, then.'

'Yes, John, please do that.'

I sucked at my lip, unsure what to say next. 'You are still troubled by this new Gospel, Robert, I can see.'

'No, I'm fine, John,' he answered, sitting upright.

'You say that, but your face tells a different story — what is it?'

He looked at me. 'I wanted this manuscript more than anything I have ever wanted in my life, John. It vindicates this whole expedition; I believe it to be a second- or third-century Coptic translation of a first-century text. An eyewitness account by somebody who was there with Jesus, one of his apostles.'

'Well, surely that is good; you have an original historical document to test against the Bible that we read today in England.'

'Aye, it is what I dreamt of finding, but now that I have it, it terrifies the life out of me.'

'But you told me when we started that there was no guarantee the historical documents would support the Bible stories we read today. You were prepared for that.'

'Aye, true enough, John, I *was* prepared for that — but not this, John; not this.'

'Cheer up, Robert; this will make you famous when you get back to England.'

'No, John, it will make me *infamous*.'

'You are over-egging the pudding; people's faith is strong enough to withstand this.'

'Mine is not, John; my own faith is already shaken. This Gospel does not just throw light on errors in the Bible; it suggests that the whole *premise* of the Bible is wrong. According to Thaddeus Jude, Jesus is a spiritual guide who will lead you to God and heaven. He is a religious leader, not a divine leader. He is a prophet, not a god — John, I am afraid to take this back to England.'

'But it is just *one* document, Robert. Set against the many others that describe Jesus as divine, it is insignificant.'

'It is only one document that has been *found*. How many more were destroyed on the orders of Bishop Athanasius and his like? How many more are hidden away for fear of them being branded as heretical doctrine?' He turned, his gaze burning into me. 'John, this is an entirely different Christianity from the one I was taught, that which I have believed in.'

'For goodness' sake, Robert, you are making far too much of this.' I did not try to hide my exasperation.

He reached out and took my arm, squeezing it tightly. 'John, if I had taken this document back to England in the Middle Ages, I would have been put to death.'

I shrugged — I could not find the words. It was clear to me that I was not the man to ease his mind; it would take a scholar to debate this dilemma with him. He turned his head and stared off into the distance, his thoughts taking him away again. We finished our meal in silence.

I went to the souk the next day with Kamil. He was wearing a clean, crisp tunic and I saw that he too had felt the urgent need to wash himself after the long desert trek. He was quite noble-looking, but when it came to bargaining he was still as cunning as any rough bazaar merchant, negotiating considerable discounts on the substantial quantities of oil and wine that we were purchasing. If he was also getting paybacks from the traders, I could not detect it — although I strained to listen with my now good Arabic to catch him out. I was under no illusions, though; I knew him to be a conman, but I accepted that his roguery did not stop him getting Robert a good deal for his money.

I went to see Robert with the final tabulations. He looked pleasingly on the figures and said he thought he had enough silver and gold coins left, but he *would* need to visit

Rothschild's agent to get more funds transferred so that he could buy passage for himself back to Venice.

The next day the two of us, along with the *kawass*, went down to the souk to seek out the money exchangers. Robert had brought with him from Europe silver thalers and golden guilders, because they were international coins of a fixed weight of silver and gold. Nevertheless, the money exchangers went through their routine of weighing the coins, scraping to assay the quality of the silver and gold before they changed them for piastres. It was a large bag, many times bigger than the purse that he had brought the thalers and guilders in.

When we left I felt, at first, a little exposed, despite the presence of the *kawass*. Robert and I were both dressed in European clothes: white breeches and linen shirts without our stocks at the collar. I stroked my admirable Joseph Egg percussion pistol at my hip, which I had brought for added security. It was, I suppose, a conspicuous act, the pistol a warning to any thief that we were a formidable trio. Deep down, I was not fearful of being robbed; the souk was chaos, but a pickpocket was more likely than a robber. The *kawass* and I walked in front of Robert as a sort of guard.

We made our way through the labyrinth of narrow streets inside the souk, made narrower as the patrons displayed their goods reaching out three or four feet from their shop fronts. We were forced to step around them endlessly, and had to stop many times because of the sheer number of people also trying to make their way. There was the piquant aroma of herbs and spices, the scent of flowers and fruits, casting away the foul smells of the hot streets. The souk was a wonderful, vibrant place; I loved to visit it.

At one corner, we were halted as an old man was leading a donkey piled high with his wares, and we stepped back to let him through. I was not sure that I would ever fully recall exactly what happened next, there was so much confusion. It started with an angry bray from the filthy animal as it followed its master through the throng. At first, I smiled at it — it was cantankerous in the heat and we could relate to that. It seemed to be annoyed by the wall of people that it was trying to negotiate. It then stopped abruptly, stubbornly refusing to move. The old man came around to the front and pulled on its reins, but the animal backed away just as hard as he pulled, hee-hawing its throaty defiance.

I shuffled from foot to foot as I waited impatiently. Suddenly, I heard a sharp cry of pain; at first I was not sure if it was the donkey or somebody else — it did not sound like part of the donkey's repertoire. I looked behind me to see if Robert was safe and saw his bag of money tightly gripped in his right hand. But there was incredulity writ large across his face. His left hand was behind him, and then he brought it around to the front and held it up to his face. It was covered in blood.

'John,' he said hesitantly, disbelief on his features, 'I think I have just been stabbed.'

I stepped back, behind him, looking for a wound. I saw that there was a red stain emerging on the seat of his white breeches. 'Jesus Christ, Robert!' I said irreverently. 'You *have* been stabbed — in the buttock.'

We exchanged dumbfounded looks; why would anybody do that? It did not seem to make any sense. I looked up and down the alleyways for some sign of the culprit, but all I saw was a wall of faces staring in our direction, probably unaware of the stabbing, just impatient at the delay. I looked behind us in the direction we had come, to the next corner, only about twenty yards away. There was something there: an unpleasant face wearing an expression of challenge. And then the face cracked into a sour smile — it looked disdainfully at me, and a bony finger rose and made a throat-cutting gesture across its neck.

Recognition hit me like a storm wave crashing against a defiant cliff face. The grim features, the hunched shoulders, the narrow, black-bearded jutting jaw; it was the face of Hakeem, our erstwhile dragoman.

The cutting gesture was a taunt, of course, but I did not rationalise that — I just set off after him. There were so many people, and I shouted after them to get out of my way, but in my haste I yelled out in English. Hakeem ran from me, down the side alley and out of my sight. By the time I got to the corner, he was at the next corner, waiting so that I could see him. I thought of him as a man of maybe fifty, but his agility belied that assumption. He took off again on his stick legs, and I ran after him.

He turned left again and disappeared from view until I reached that corner and looked down the next side alley. There he was, waiting again; he was toying with me, I realised that, yet I assumed I could outrun him, and I continued the pursuit. At the next corner, though, there was no sign of him; I walked down, looking all about me, but he seemed to have vanished. I realised that he knew this souk like the back of his hand. I would never find him.

I had some trouble retracing my steps, but eventually I found Robert and the *kawass*. There was now a crowd around them, gossiping at the sight of his blood-stained breeches.

'You did not catch the rogue, then, John,' winced Robert through clenched teeth.

'No, he was too nimble for me; he knew the souk too well, but I know who it was. It was that scoundrel Hakeem.'

We both tried to see some sanity in this bizarre situation but failed to do so. We looked at the *kawass* for guidance; Robert translated that the attacker was Hakeem, the dragoman. The *kawass* just shrugged, nodding his head at the same time, as if it made perfect sense to him. I gestured for him to explain. 'It is revenge for dismissing him, for his loss of face,' he explained matter-of-factly.

'But why stab me in the arse?' Robert's forehead furrowed in confusion.

'You have to understand Ottoman law,' the *kawass* explained. 'You are a man under the protection of me and Muhammad Ali Pasha. You are not some insignificant Maltese bearer; the consequences are more severe.'

I still did not understand him, and there was silence for a few moments.

The *kawass* went on. 'Under Ottoman law, if you stab somebody above the waist, it is regarded as an attack with intent to kill, and that is serious. But if you stab below the waist, it is accepted that there is no intent to kill. It happens every day in the souk; that is how disputes are settled.'

'So it's regarded as no more than the restoring of face by teaching me a lesson — it's about humiliating me?' There was disbelief in Robert's words.

The *kawass* nodded.

With the help of the *kawass* and me, Robert limped around the souk to settle his accounts with the merchants for the oil, wine and donkeys for the caravan back to the monastery at El-Sourian. We then helped him back to our lodgings in the Christian quarter, and I tended his wound as best as I could. It soon became apparent that a stab wound to the buttock had added insult in addition to the pain. Every time he tried to visit the toilet, the wound would reopen. There was also the discomfort of lying on his front on his carpet for hour after hour.

I sent for a doctor the next day, an educated Turkish man. There was solace in his expertise. I had come to realise that they were more competent than British doctors. He looked at the wound with concern and said that it was small, but had gone deep. Some sort of stiletto blade had been used. He cleaned the wound, applied a poultice and left a physic for me to give to Robert.

However, the day after, Robert started to display signs of a fever, and I called the Turkish doctor again. He diagnosed the sepsis but said he was a fit young man and should be robust enough to fight it off.

The fever got worse, though; Robert's heart was racing, and at times he became delirious. And then he started to have trouble breathing, and he had spasms where the wheezing turned into terrible gasps for air. He would ask me to sit him up so that he could free his airways, but each time I did, the wound on his buttock burst and wept, and a new dressing would need to be applied. When I did so, there was a terrible stench from it. I also noticed his feet and legs had started to swell.

The doctor called again and said that his lungs had filled with fluid, probably a consequence of the infection travelling to his kidneys. His organs were starting to fail; he was losing his fight for life, it seemed. He speculated that the blade used to stab him had been tipped with some substance that had poisoned his blood. I had little doubt that it was so; Hakeem had already shown himself to be a callous man.

An unpleasant thought took me — at first it was just a feeling, but slowly it gathered pace until I was consumed with a powerful guilt. I had been walking in front of Robert in the souk, side by side with the *kawass*, to protect him from thieves, to protect his money. However, Hakeem had come from behind us — had I been the intended victim? I was the one who had accused him of the murder of Rokku; I was the one who had dismissed him, causing him to lose face. The conclusion seemed undeniable to me — Robert had taken the poisoned blade intended for me. My friend, my honourable friend, was dying in place of his unworthy comrade.

That evening, as I was trying to feed Robert some broth, he reached up and grabbed my arm tightly. He was more lucid than he had been all day; he knew that he was seriously ill, I could see.

'I fear that this will be the end of me, John,' he rasped forcefully, his red-rimmed eyes blazing.

'If you can survive a prolonged sandstorm in the Sinai Desert, you can survive this, Robert,' I answered, trying to be as positive as I could.

'You must get the Gospels of St Matthew and Thaddeus Jude back to England for me. Take them to Professor Jaynes at Cambridge University. He will know what to do with them. Make sure that I have the credit for the discoveries.'

'It will not come to that, Robert,' I mumbled, giving a hesitant smile.

His grip tightened on my arm. 'No, John, promise me you will do that for me, for our friendship.' Those red-rimmed eyes implored me to affirm.

'I will, Robert, I will,' I conceded.

His body relaxed. It brought on a paroxysm of coughing and each retch caused him pain, I could see, but my affirmation had eased his mind. 'Go to Rothschild's agent; tell him to contact my lawyers in Nottingham. They will arrange funds to be sent here for my burial and to pay for your passage home. I know you are a wanted man back in England —' he paused as he retched again — 'but you are a cunning bugger, John Campbell-John; I know you can do this for me.'

The fever raged for the next few days and the doctor called daily, applying various poultices to the wound and physics to help him fight the impurities in his system. I did not go to see Rothschild's agent, clinging to the belief that Robert's struggle for life would be successful. Despite being a scholar, he was a tall, robust man, with a powerful life force, a man of action who had travelled the world with confidence.

One evening as I tried to feed him, I heaved to sit him upright, but there was no help from his failing body, and I realised that his strength was fading fast. I eased my own body behind him and he leant back against my left-hand side so that my right was free to try and spoon some hot broth into him.

He swallowed the steaming liquid eagerly, and at first I was encouraged; perhaps this was a good sign. But he soon gestured that he had had his fill, and barely a third of the broth had been taken. Then he just seemed to relax into me. His hand came over to my arm limply and he patted me, as if to acknowledge our good fellowship, the bond between us.

'Time has a way of taking us off guard, John; I thought I had lots of it left. You will remember your promise, remember where you must take the Gospels?' he croaked.

I nodded at him, smiling to reassure his anxieties. 'Yes, to Professor Jaynes at Cambridge University.'

'Good, good man; I know you will not let me down.' I gripped his arm to reinforce my promise. 'People will hate me for this, John,' he mumbled uncertainly.

'No, no, you will be hailed as a great scholar, a great adventurer. Bringing back an original first-century text is no mean achievement. You will be hailed as a hero.'

'Thank you, my friend,' he wheezed, 'but I fear I will not be remembered as a hero. This new Gospel of Thaddeus Jude goes to the very heart of faith in Jesus as the Son of God. It disturbs me greatly, John; I fear that I will be remembered as a figure of loathing. I will be remembered as the infamous scoundrel who dared challenge the faith that Christians hold dear.'

His words faded, and he was quiet. I looked down and scrutinised his face; there was a faraway look in his eyes. He had drifted away to some other place, but I could see that he was wrestling with this dilemma. The academic in him wanted to present this original historical document to an unsuspecting world, but the Christian in him was fearful of the dreadful consequences. I reached around and wiped his mouth with my handkerchief; I saw there were beads of sweat on his forehead, and I wiped those away too. Then I stroked his luxurious dark hair, my heart heavy.

CHAPTER 26

Robert died the following day, on the tenth day of October 1836, far away from home. I was with him to the end, and when it did come it was — thank God — relatively peaceful. The doctor said that the poison in his system had caused his organs to fail one by one. The *kawass* left and returned an hour or so later, with a Christian Coptic monk and a helper, another Copt. I had not asked him to do that, but I was grateful for his intervention, for the body had to be prepared.

His cadaver stank of stale sweat, bodily secretions, and loosened bowels. The armpits of his linen shirt were black with the accumulation of days of dampness. The Copt sat up Robert's lifeless form, and removed his shirt and then his breeches. He washed him gently, first in rose water, his light hands thorough in their cleansing. Then he produced a sweet-smelling oil and began to rub it deeply into the skin, using circular motions to ensure that it was fully absorbed. Bit by bit, that reek of death receded until Robert smelt fragrant.

The Copt then produced a long Egyptian-style white linen shirt and dressed the body in it, and then laid it down. The monk said some words over him, though I did not, of course, understand Coptic. I looked down at Robert, but he did not look at peace. It was as though he was speaking to me, telling me he was a British gentleman. I sought out my cut-throat and gently shaved the dark accumulated stubble from his face, leaving only his moustache, which I trimmed as stylishly as I could.

It was still not right, though — the long Egyptian shirt was not suitable for him. I went to Robert's chest and then to mine, but there was not a clean shirt nor a fresh pair of breeches between us. I sent the Copt to the souk to find a laundry and he returned in under two hours, the offer of a few extra paras enough inducement for them to launder a shirt and breeches immediately. The Copt helped me dress the body, and a sense of relief coursed through me as the sight of a fine English gentleman emerged.

Yet there was one last thing that niggled at me. I looked at his left hand, at his ring with the green agate and the image of the eagle. It was one of the things that defined him, I mused. My mind slipped away, to the other things that made Robert what he was: they were now embossed on my grieving memory. The way he arched his eyebrow. Its many nuances so that it could either ask a question or make an ironic remark. His favourite phrase, *another rasher of bacon* — I smiled inwardly at that. I wanted something to remember him by, but wondered if he would want to take the ring into the afterlife, like some long-dead pharaoh. I exhaled deeply before making my decision. Robert, I thought, would not object; he would be happy to bequeath it to his friend. I removed it delicately; his little finger was bloated, but he gave it up easily. 'Thank you, my friend,' I said out loud.

I arranged for a Christian funeral, though the body was not buried: it was wrapped and put in a tomb, which was the custom amongst the Egyptian Christians. I was, at first, the only person present, but then the *kawass* came to pay his respects, despite being a Mahomedan. The *kawass* was a man of incredibly few words, who never engaged us in any unnecessary conversations, but there was respect in his eyes, and his luxurious moustache appeared to quiver with emotion; he had had some sort of bond with Robert.

So had I — a very powerful one. He had called me his friend before he had died. I had always believed that funerals were all about the closing of a door so that those left behind could move on with their lives. However, I realised now that this was not a universal truth. It was as though I had inherited that troubled mind that had tormented Robert in his final days. This was spiced with my feelings of guilt that I was not worthy of the sacrifice that Robert had made on my behalf.

I had always shunned close friendships; they came with obligations, and such duties got in the way of my roguery. I saw all people as possible victims, the source of funds. I had had only one real friend in my previous life, and I had wronged that man grievously. Now, I realised, however undeserving I was, I had had another: Robert had shown me friendship, but he had also left me with obligations. This was new to me and I wanted desperately to fulfil those commitments, yet I found the thought of Robert being remembered as a figure of loathing a difficult one to cope with.

Over the next few days, I felt as lonely as a single boat bobbing on a vast ocean. I uncrated Robert's notebooks, put them in order, read many of them, and came to understand something of the depth of his scholarship. But the latter ones reflected that dilemma that had afflicted his mind in his last days; the dilemma that I had now inherited.

I wrote a letter back to England advising, as sympathetically as I could, of his death, but there was no father or other relative to send it to. I tore it up and wrote a more formal one to his lawyers in Nottingham; he had given me their name and address in one of his less delirious moments. Again, I did not send it — something stopped me, something at the very edge of my comprehension, but it was enough to stay my hand.

Then a new dilemma took me, a more practical one. Before he died, Robert had asked me to go to Rothschild's agent to arrange for more funds from England, but I had not done so in the hope that he would recover. If I went now, I reasoned, why would the agent act on my request? I had no written authority to act for poor Robert. I was not repatriating his body — that was impractical in this fiery climate. Why would he arrange funds for *me* to return to England? Would the claim that I was transporting Robert's treasured religious antiquities mean anything to the agent? Would he act on my word as an English gentleman?

That term *English gentleman* tweaked a nerve somewhere deep inside me. I stabbed my thumb into my chest. 'Huh, you, gentleman,' I grunted. No, I was no gentleman. 'This situation is another rasher of bacon altogether,' I mumbled to Robert warmly as if he was still alive. At last, a happy, reflective thought. I turned and sought out Robert's purse; there were about a dozen silver thalers left. Just enough, perhaps, to get a boat back to Alexandria, but not a passage back to Venice and from there back to England. I sought out my own purse. I had just over four and a half thousand piastres, possibly enough to get me back to Venice and then England, but I would then be penniless — and it was my war chest for the purchase of antiquities.

A thought came to me. What if I were to go to Rothschild's agent and pretend to be Robert? Yes, that *would* be another rasher of bacon entirely.

CHAPTER 27

I went to see Rothschild's Cairo agent, dressed in Robert's best frock coat, and did indeed introduce myself as Lord Robert Babcock. His clothing fit me like a glove and helped me in my impersonation, but I need not have bothered; I was already a skilled impersonator. I knew that people rarely questioned what was in front of them; if I looked and played the part of a wealthy gentleman, then I was always accepted as such. The previous evening, I had studied Robert's handwriting in his journals to the point where I could make an acceptable stab at his signature.

I was offered a chair, and I took it, relaxing into the leather seat. I missed the comfort of chairs. The agent was a small, dapper man dressed in European clothes — a black frock coat with a pristine white stock at the collar. I expected him to be European but he was Egyptian, though he spoke excellent French. His face was leathery, his eyes large and deep-set. Despite my rusty French, I negotiated his questions with ease and gave him the addresses of Robert's lawyers in Nottingham and of his bankers. The only thing that threw me was when he asked how much the letter of credit was to be for; I had had in my mind just enough for passage all the way back to England and my accommodation on the way. But then a roguish notion suddenly sprang into my mind; what about those ancient Egyptian artefacts being sold by Haroun? It was, of course, unscrupulous of me, but it seemed that my old self was hard to shake off. Impersonation was what I had always done — and when I did it, my conniving mind was always calculating the angles, maximising the potential swindle. I had become this paradoxical mix of a scoundrel trying to do a noble deed. I thought back to the artefacts for sale. The trader wanted twenty thousand piastres for the golden necklace — about two hundred pounds.

What I said next took even me by surprise. 'Shall we say six hundred and fifty pounds?' I did not really know where that figure came from. I saw the agent's eyebrows rise in disbelief.

'Why so much?' he stuttered.

'Ancient artefacts can be expensive,' I answered matter-of-factly, as if such sums were a mere frippery to me.

He coughed to clear his throat; the amount I had asked for had evidently changed the whole nature of our meeting. 'Would you like a pipe?'

I accepted, but I thought it was more for him to contemplate the transaction. We both smoked in silence for a while, and then coffee was ordered.

'I will have to write to London, of course, with your written authority, and then await their instructions. It will take at least a month, maybe six weeks.'

I nodded as I exhaled.

Whilst I waited in Cairo, I drank and gambled at the shabby bar. I was being drawn back into my former life, I could see that, but I told myself that I was just marking time whilst waiting for Robert's letter of credit to arrive. My overriding aim, however, *was* to get Robert's findings back to Britain so that his work would be acknowledged and honoured. I was quite genuine in that, but there was something I was denying — deep down, I knew I enjoyed my roguery.

I went to see Haroun. The tomb statue and the exquisite death mask had been sold, but the wonderful *Book of the Dead* and the magnificent golden necklace were still for sale at eight thousand and twenty thousand piastres respectively. I negotiated twenty-five thousand piastres for the pair — about two hundred and fifty pounds. He said that he was expecting another consignment of the finest quality artefacts, and I told him that I would be interested in viewing them when they arrived.

Egypt always woke at first light, and then went about its day, its commerce, its agriculture. It slept when night fell, but not I. In the Christian quarter, I spent late nights drinking, gambling, and wenching — so that when dawn broke, I ignored it and slept until noon. But that sleep, despite being alcohol-fuelled, was far from peaceful.

One night I dreamt of Britain: preachers in their pulpits, distorted angry faces spouting fire and brimstone words at their cowering congregation — and the subject of their spleen was the malevolent Lord Robert Babcock, that villain who had unleashed on the world that heretical manuscript, the Gospel of Thaddeus Jude, the Gospel that dared to suggest that our Lord Jesus Christ was not a deity but just a teacher, just an ordinary man. Before my dreaming eyes came a succession of spiteful faces, spitting vindictive words at me. I woke in a panic, in my darkened windowless room, my heart beating and great beads of sweat on my troubled brow. I composed myself and turned over again; but when sleep returned, there were more irate faces shouting their bile at me. *Why me?* I cried out to them in my dream. *You, you,* said a series of vehement, hysterical faces. *You, you, Lord Robert Babcock.*

I spent the next day troubled. I knew the persona of Captain John Campbell-John was an invention, yet somehow I had become him. Was I now becoming Lord Robert Babcock? Was I concerned about the reputation of my academic friend or of myself, as his imitator?

The following night I was haunted by the face of the apostle Thaddeus Jude; it started as a diffused image but then coalesced into a large, grey-bearded face in a long white robe. The skin was heavily lined, the body bent, the eyes wide, with a sympathetic look. He was beseeching me to believe him. The voice was soft but pleading. *Jesus was our teacher, our guide to the eternal life.*

I tried to debate with him; in my dream, I was again Robert. *John was an apostle and in his Gospel he says that Jesus is our divine and beloved Lord,* I challenged him. *Why do you say differently?*

The old face creased into a kind smile. *The apostle John, my friend, died before his Gospel was completed; he was so very old when he wrote it.*

Yet he was just as much an eyewitness as you, I said imploringly. *Even an old man would not confuse our divine Lord with a spiritual guide.*

But he did not do so, he said gently. *These words were not his; they were written by the men who finished his account after he had died. They are not his words.*

I continued my debate with the image before me, growing more and more distressed as my points were all countered.

The following night, I drank and gambled much later than I normally did, trying to avoid the terror that sleep brought. I eventually fell onto my divan just before dawn and slept for about an hour — then the cruel dreams returned. It started with that aged bearded face of Thaddeus Jude, but it was not spiteful. It was kind, smiling warmly at me. Words emerged from trembling lips as his expression changed and desperation appeared in his eyes.

Why do you not believe me, Robert Babcock? Am I not also an apostle? Am I also not a witness, just like Matthew and Mark? Are my words not as important as Luke and John?

But ... but you do not say the same things as the Bible Gospels, I said desperately.

Many of the parables that I recount are also narrated by my fellow disciples, Matthew, Mark and Luke. I was there with them; I was also a witness. Does not my Gospel also tell of the parable of the light under a bushel? Thaddeus Jude went on.

Aha, I said, *but that parable is about the light being seen and not hidden.* I thought I had him.

That is so, Robert Babcock, the spectral face, nodded kindly.

So surely the light refers to Jesus himself? I was sure that I was right in that; I had discussed this very point with Robert after he had first read Thaddeus Jude.

No, my son, the light is not him; it is his word, his message.

I could not seem to win the debate with this apparition. Every time I tried to say what I had been taught as a child, or what Robert had told me, my arguments were rendered impotent. But then, I had never lived my life according to this Christian creed — so why should these dreams have caused me so much distress? Thou shall not steal, though shall not covet, commandments I have disregarded all my life. Thou shall not commit adultery — well I have done so at every opportunity. Worst of all, I have not honoured my father and mother.

So who was I distressed for: me or Robert? Was I trying to put the case for the believers in Jesus or were they Robert's words. These dreams were to go on for many more fitful nights.

CHAPTER 28

It was December the twentieth, 1836, when Rothschild's agent advised me that the letter of credit had arrived from Rothschild's Bank in London. He advanced me the money, partly in Egyptian piastres but mostly in pure gold and silver coin. At first, I thought that I would prepare to return to England in the new year of 1837, after celebrating Christmas; then I changed my mind, realising there was no one with whom to celebrate it.

I went immediately to see Amram Haroun and settled the account for the *Book of the Dead* and the golden collar. I also purchased some exceptional golden amulets that he had recently received.

I hired a boat to take me north on El Bahar to Atfeh and then on to Alexandria. I hired porters to crate all my belongings — the Egyptian artefacts, Robert's Christian manuscripts and his notebooks — and take them to the boat, and I was ready to sail on Christmas Eve. My only companion was to be the *kawass*, who would return to the palace of Boghos Bey at Alexandria.

I slept on the boat the night before, as the reis had advised, ready to make an early start on Christmas Eve morning. But in the night, terrors stung me like the most vicious of hornets. In my dreams, I tried to plead with Thaddeus Jude, but he disregarded my words as his own words had been rejected all those centuries ago. It was as though I was the carriage of his revenge. *I — Robert Babcock —* though in the dream, I did not shout out that I was not that man.

When I finally awoke with a heart-pounding start, I sat up on my carpet, temporarily disoriented in the open canopy at the back of the boat. It took some moments for me to restore the identity of John Campbell-John — itself a fiction, of course. I looked around as reason slowly returned to me; over the rail I could see a flock of birds, swirling about the vessel. I stood and watched them skimming the water, realising that the reis had already cast us off and was manoeuvring us out into the centre of the Nile to catch the flow northwards to the sea. The *kawass* was already up and had brought me some hot, sweet coffee, and we sat cross-legged on our carpets and drank in silence.

I had thought that the nightmares would go away when my journey home started, but now I knew they would not. My resolve had been breached — my resolve to make good on my promise to Robert to take home not only the early copy of the Gospel of Matthew, but also the disturbing Gospel of Thaddeus Jude.

I heard the rumble of thunder in the distance and my hands, involuntarily, curled into fists at the sound of it. I jumped to my feet, went out onto the centre of the boat deck, and looked around for the reis. He was sitting above the canopy behind me, acting as a steersman until the vessel was safely on its course.

'Turn the boat about, reis!' I shouted at him, pointing back upstream. 'I have some unfinished business to take care of.'

Two days later, on St Stephen's day, I rode out north-west from Cairo. At first, I followed the lush and fertile lands of the delta, intending to then veer off and enter the desert and the Natron Valley west of the Nile. I had only three companions, the *kawass* and two hired bodyguards. We all rode handsome

Arab stallions that the *kawass* had again acquired from the Habeeb Effendi, the Governor of Cairo. Our destination was the monastery at El-Sourian.

The resolve that had taken me on that Christmas Eve morning had spurred me into action. I had made Robert a deathbed promise that I would get the two manuscripts back to Britain, and I had been striving to keep that pledge. But I knew then that I would not best serve his memory by doing so. The Lord Robert Babcock I knew was a fine and honourable man, a man of scholarship and intellect; he would not want his honour tarnished by the Gospel of Thaddeus Jude. In his dying days, his much-troubled mind had been consumed by a dilemma; the scholar in him wanted to present to the world the words of Thaddeus Jude, but the humanity in him had realised that those very words would test the faith of many believers. It was a dagger aimed at the heart of Christianity.

I left the valuable artefacts with Haroun, who agreed to look after them for me, and arranged for the reis to wait for me, having paid him for his trouble. The *kawass* was entitled to be angry with me; we had kept him away from his home in Alexandria for over a year, and at the last minute I had turned the boat around. However, his sense of duty to me, and ultimately to the *bey* and Muhammed Ali Pasha, was unshakable. It was he who had advised me to risk taking such a small party, travelling by horse alone and not being slowed down by camels and donkeys. We were four mounted men with just a packhorse in tow, carrying the very basics of provisions to sustain us all the way to the monastery. We had only one further item of cargo: the manuscript of the Gospel according to Thaddeus Jude, which was carried in the saddlebag on my horse.

When we reached the village of Terrané, we did not hire Arab guides but headed west into the desert, trusting our own navigation. As we had been to El-Sourian twice before, we would hopefully remember where the watering holes were located. We travelled faster on horseback without the camels as our guide, and the aim was to get to the monastery in just ten days. We got there in nine.

When we arrived, our horses were all but spent, even though we had rationed our own water between waterholes to give them more. We too were also spent, dishevelled, sand-worn; we must have looked to the monks like the raiders we had encountered on our first trip, our dirtied headdresses wrapped around our faces so that we could only see through a thin gap. The monastery appeared like a beacon from a distant lighthouse and guided us to it, in the same way. I presented my dishevelled body at the narrow iron door by the large square tower. I could see that the monks were fearful of my appearance, so I unwrapped my headdress, shaking off the sand. I realised that I had not brought the letter of introduction with me, but my anxiety eased immediately as the monks at the gate recognised the eccentric Frank.

The *kawass* took the horses for a well-earned drink and the four of us followed. I drew a pail of water from the monastery well and poured it over my head to wash away the sand, then ran my fingers through my greasy, curly hair, sweeping it back from my forehead. I left the horses in the charge of the *kawass*, who fed and groomed them before giving them a well-deserved rest.

I asked to see the blind abbot immediately, but was told that he was at his devotions and could not see me. By the evening he was still avoiding me, suspicious, I think, that I was back again to raid his secret library. I took to my bed irritably, but soon fell into a deep fatigued sleep where no night terrors interrupted my slumber. They had been absent each night of our journey, and I knew I was doing the right thing by Robert.

I awoke late the next morning, my limbs still weary and stiff from the prolonged ride; however, my mind was calm and clear. I was given honeyed flatbread from the monastery refectory, which was frugal, yet I found it an unexpected delight after days in the desert. I asked to see the abbot again, but the answer was still the same — only the excuses were changed. By the evening, I knew I had to confront all this evasion. I thought about sending the abbot a note, but I could neither read nor write Coptic, nor even write Arabic, despite now speaking it passably well.

I went to the church and watched the daily devotions, listening to the calming chants of the monks until I saw one that I recognised. He was the one who acted as the blind abbot's eyes and was his guide. As he walked to the door to leave with his companions, in step with the peal of the tower bell, I stepped out in front of him. He was looking at the floor, as if in some spiritual place, but I sought out his eyes. He gave me a tentative, hesitant smile, and I returned it. I walked alongside him to the exit, as the church was not the place for a confrontation.

Out in the courtyard, I shielded my eyes from the powerful sun and saw the monk's eyes narrow for the same reason.

'Why will the abbot not see me?' I asked forcefully.

'He is a busy man at this time of year,' he answered, his words hesitant. 'It is the Feast of Epiphany. It is one of the seven major feasts of our Lord.'

I had not realised that it was Epiphany — I should have, I supposed. It took the wind out of my sails, but I was not to be put off. I had a strategy in mind, and that was to heap guilt on the old abbot. What I was not sure of was how important Epiphany was to these Coptic monks. 'And your feast will be more sumptuous this year, now that your oil and wine cellars have been replenished,' I said pointedly.

'Yes,' he murmured. 'That is so; you and your companion have been most generous.'

'Do you not think that our generosity should be matched with your hospitality? Do you not believe that we deserve that? I only want a short meeting with your abbot.'

'Hospitality is your right,' he said, looking directly into my eyes for the first time, 'but today there must be many chants, many readings, many prayers sung in joyous tune. It must all be done according to the Book of Lakkan; if it is not all done today, then we must start again tomorrow. They must all be said.' His words made me hesitate; perhaps the blind abbot was not avoiding me, after all. But I still held his gaze defiantly, and he looked down once again. 'Perhaps I can get him to see you briefly.'

In the late afternoon, I was led into the abbot's meagre cell. He was dressed in his finest vestments as part of his participation in the feast, but that mask of a face still greeted me. He held out his hand, gesturing for me to sit. I did so with a parcel on my lap. I saw him twitch at the sound of my setting it down safely. He started to speak to me in Coptic, but I interrupted him in Arabic. 'Robert Babcock is not with me,' I said.

'You come alone?'

'Yes, Robert died a few weeks ago.'

The abbot made the sign of the cross. 'I will pray for his soul,' he said. 'He was a generous man. The oil and wine arrived a few weeks ago, as he promised it would. What did he die of?' The abbot fingered his wooden crucifix.

'He was stabbed by a mean-spirited man, then died of poisoning to the blood.'

'There is much wickedness in the world.' The abbot's words drifted away introspectively.

I coughed to change the subject. 'Do you know what is written in the Gospel of Thaddeus Jude?' I blurted out.

'Sayings of our Lord,' he replied. 'I too am a scholar, if not as illustrious as your friend.'

'Does the book not disturb you?' I was not sure if he would understand what I meant.

The old man twitched his head sideways. 'You mean he does not call Jesus "Lord"? It has been the subject of much discussion over the centuries. But it is a topic kept for scholars, not the brethren.'

'I can understand that; it goes to the very root of faith. But if it is so precarious, why has it been kept all these centuries?'

'Because the words are still Jesus's words, a first-hand account of them. They are not devalued because he does not call him "our Lord".'

'I had not thought of it that way,' I mumbled.

'And Thaddeus Jude does not actually say that he was *not* our Lord, he just does not call him *Lord.*'

I was silent as I thought about those words. It was a debate that Robert could have entered into, but not I. My dilemma was unresolved, and I steeled myself to face it. 'Robert was much disturbed by the writings,' I said. 'I have made this journey to return the book to you. I think that it will be best preserved in your keeping. Your scholars are the people to study it.' I heaved the manuscript over to his lap, and he held it close to him as if it were the most precious thing in the world.

'It is a burden to me,' he said, 'but one that I am happy to endure.'

CHAPTER 29

We arrived back in Cairo, exactly a year to the day after we had first set sail for Luxor. I went with the *kawass* immediately to the dhow and was relieved to see that the reis had kept his word and was waiting for us. I enquired when we could set sail northwards up the Nile to Alexandria, and he indicated that we could depart the following day — he was anxious to get away after waiting for so long.

I thought for a few moments then suggested that I needed another day, to give me the chance to recover my Egyptian artefacts from Haroun. I was going to agree on the twenty-second, but the *kawass* — he of little words — put his hand on my shoulder and said that he had some business to take care of on behalf of his master, Boghos Bey.

'How long will you need?' I asked. We had spoken in Arabic since Robert's death. I realised that I had arched my eyebrow in the way Robert always had.

'Three, maybe four days,' he said, looking at me over the silver head of his cane.

I looked back at the reis and suggested that he be ready to sail on the twenty-fourth, and the *kawass* nodded his agreement.

Over the next three days, I concluded my business with Amram Haroun and had everything packed on board. I also took a hot bath and had my wardrobe laundered at the souk — some of my clothes were blackened with accumulated sweat from the desert journey. On the night of the twenty-third, I slept soundly in the open cabin at the back of the dhow; there were no disturbing dreams like those I had encountered the last time I had slept aboard.

I was woken early, to the sounds of the sailors making ready to sail, and I breakfasted on *ful* and hot, sweet coffee. We were ready to set sail within an hour of the sun rising, setting a coral tint on the lazy waters of the Nile. However, there was no sign of the *kawass*.

The reis indicated that we should set sail anyway, but I held up my arm to stay him. He mumbled some words, no doubt rude ones, then went to his position as steersman and sat by the rudder in his place on top of the open cabin. I expected that the *kawass* would not be long delayed, but the hours dragged on. In the middle of the afternoon, the reis relinquished his position as steersman, came down onto the deck and gave instructions to his men, without consulting me. We would spend another night in Cairo.

The next morning the pattern was repeated. We were ready to sail within an hour of the first rays of the striking dawn, but still there was no *kawass*. The reis made no attempt to hide his irritation, for I had kept him waiting for weeks already. The day dragged on and despite the weather being more comfortable in the winter sun, I could not enjoy it. By mid-afternoon, it became apparent that we would spend a further night tied to the quayside.

By mid-morning on day three the reis was ranting at me, waving his hand in my face to emphasise his frustration. I pointed out that I was paying for his time whether we sailed or not, but this did not seem to placate him.

Just before noon, a large, powerful man appeared down on the quayside. He was dressed in a striped kaftan over the Arab *galabeya*, the long shirt-like garment down to the ankles, and he had a turban wound around his head. He was a strange sight, but then I noticed the magnificent jet-black handlebar moustache lavishly extending either side of his face.

It was the *kawass*. Gone was his embroidered long-sleeved jacket, his shirt of deep jade, his billowing trousers, his draped turban, his *kilij* and his *kurbash*. The only thing he carried that I recognised was his long silver-headed cane.

He walked up the gangplank and came straight to me, throwing down a dirty off-white garment as if it were a trophy. I looked down and saw that it was blood-stained; I looked back at his cane and saw dried blood on that too. He thrust back his broad shoulders and expanded his muscled chest.

'Where have you been, *kawass*?' I asked hesitantly — I was unsure of exactly what was happening.

'I have been at the souk, *sidi*,' he answered, as if it were obvious.

'But why, and why like this?' I pointed to the kaftan and *galabeya*.

'My master, Boghos Bey, gave you his protection.' His words were matter-of-fact. 'Sheik Robert — I did not protect him for my master. I could not go back until my duty was done.'

'And what duty have you performed in the souk?'

'I have been looking in shops, at market stalls, at the money changers, the laundries. I have been in cafés — waiting, smoking, drinking coffee, spying.'

'But what have you been looking for?'

He seemed confused by my lack of understanding. 'I have been looking for Hakeem, the dragoman.'

I looked down at the shabby blood-stained garment at my feet. It was the toga-like one-piece garment that Hakeem had worn, the one that swept around his body. I looked back up at the *kawass*. 'You have killed him?'

'I have restored my master's honour,' he said succinctly.

I was not revolted by the killing; I thought I may have done the same if I had encountered Hakeem. He was responsible for both Robert's and Rokku's deaths, after all, but I was shocked by the arbitrary nature of the *kawass*'s actions. However, retributive justice was a feature of Ottoman Egypt; it followed what the Quran and the Bible said — the old law of an eye for an eye, a tooth for a tooth. The *kawass* had set himself as judge, jury and then executioner to dispense the *pasha*'s justice. He had done his duty.

The *kawass* changed back into his regalia and stood resplendent in his elaborately embroidered rust-coloured jacket worn over his jade shirt, and his billowing trousers, separated from his shirt by the ornate belt. On his head, he wore that deep-jade turban of the sort that looked like a draped headscarf. On his left hip, he wore his curved *kilij*, and on his right hip he carried his curled hippopotamus hide *kurbash*.

The reis manoeuvred the dhow into the centre of the river to catch the flow northwards. The *kawass* stood on deck, his shoulders back, the sun on his face. I thought he too felt that his own honour had been restored.

PART 2

CHAPTER 30

Nottinghamshire, 1867

This journal, I start today, the day after my sixtieth birthday. It is a dangerous document; it will put the inheritance of my children in doubt. It is not for publication, and I must entrust it to my eldest son Edward, who can decide what to do with it after my death. And yet, I am compelled to write it, to put the record straight. Sixty years is a good age, but it brings my own mortality into sharp focus. Nevertheless, I would state at the outset that I am of sound mind and what I tell is the truth.

My name is Lord Robert Babcock, the eleventh Baron Carberton. I live at Carberton Hall on the Carberton Estate in the county of Nottinghamshire. Except that is not my real identity; my actual name is Captain John Campbell-John, the military second son of an English country squire. Except that is also an impersonation; my real name is Edward John, the illegitimate son of a country squire and the governess he hired to teach his children.

I met the real Robert Babcock in Venice in 1835 when I was running away from my creditors back in England. Robert was a true scholar, a man educated in the classics, a man who wanted to adventure in Egypt, a man who had an honourable quest: to seek out historical books to prove that the words we read today in our Bibles are the real words of our Lord.

I can see him now: tall, perhaps an inch taller than me, with dark brown hair, long sideburns and a small manicured moustache. The shadow of his beard was dark on his face; he had large, expressive hazel eyes that proclaimed his honesty.

He was ruggedly handsome, and athletically built. My, we were a pair; we turned the heads of all the ladies.

But we were so different; I was a rogue and a chancer, an imposter, a man without empathy for his fellow man — a man who lived on his wits rather than doing an honest day's toil. Robert, on the other hand — ah, Robert was such an admirable man, with a powerful thirst for knowledge. He was the exact opposite of his appearance; he looked like a dashing young cavalry officer who would fight a duel for the hand of a beautiful young lady — and yet he was an academic who liked nothing more than to study.

Robert was killed in Egypt; he died on the tenth of October 1836 in Cairo. On the brink of bringing his momentous discoveries back to Britain, he was murdered in a trivial act of revenge, to *save face*.

My impersonation of him began as no more than an act of expediency. I had promised him on his deathbed that I would get his discoveries back to Britain, but I did not have the money to do so. It was simply pragmatism: I forged his signature to get funds sent back from England. However, if I am writing this account to put the record straight, I now have to make a full confession; I also took the opportunity to line my own pockets by requesting much more than I needed.

With Robert's discovered Gospel of St Matthew and my own collection of ancient Egyptian artefacts, I set sail north up the Nile delta from Cairo in January 1837; then, in early February, I took passage back to Venice from the port of Alexandria across the blue waters of the Mediterranean. I arrived back in London on the seventh of March, the wind swirling and icy on my tanned face, spring still not hinting at its arrival. I felt the chill after spending nearly two years in North Africa. My unpaid debts meant that I was a wanted man in London, of course, but the long voyage had given me time to plan a strategy. I allowed my beard to grow but kept up my impersonation of Robert Babcock. My infantry captain's uniform was jettisoned overboard in the murky waters of the English Channel — the persona of Captain John Campbell-John would put me in danger: he had to die.

When the ship docked, I walked down the gangplank as Lord Robert Babcock, wearing a charcoal-grey frock coat and a linen shirt with a white stock at the collar, all freshly laundered before I left Venice. I did not have a greatcoat, however, and I shivered in the wintery wind. I took a hansom cab and directed the driver to take me to a letting agent. I was looking for a quiet lodging and suggested Rathbone Place in the new West End, as I had previously had a lady acquaintance on that street and knew it to be quiet but fashionable, so that a fine gentleman such as I would not look out of place. Luckily, there was a house available on the street. I asked the driver to load my two chests and the crate containing the Gospel of St Matthew, and I went straight away to view it.

The house was furnished, so I took a one-year lease immediately and sent for the remaining crates from the dockyard the following morning. Rathbone Place was to be the base of my operations from then on. I knew I had to stay away from the drinking and gambling establishments, where a skilled card player such as I would be remembered and recognised. I knew I would find this difficult, but I kept reminding myself of the life that Robert would lead.

CHAPTER 31

The first part of my strategy was to fulfil my promise to Robert or at least partially meet that pledge, having already returned the Gospel of Thaddeus Jude to the monks at the Monastery of El-Sourian. I wrote to Professor Jaynes at Cambridge University under Robert's name explaining that I (Robert) had travelled extensively in Egypt and that I had returned with what I believed to be a second-century Coptic translation of the Gospel of St Matthew. I asked for his help in validating it, saying that I believed it to be the oldest copy of a Gospel ever found. I also said that my companion John Campbell-John would deliver the manuscript for me, as I had family matters to attend to.

After I had dispatched the letter, a sentiment took me, casually to begin with, but it would not let me go; it pricked my conscience. Why had I continued with the pretence that Robert was still alive? Cambridge was many miles from London; surely there was no real danger there. I told myself that I still needed protection; I was safer being Robert Babcock than John Campbell-John — in London that was true, but in Cambridge? Deep down, I knew it to be a weak justification.

I took the mail coach to Cambridge, the crate containing the Gospel of St Matthew held firmly on my lap, having refused the driver's offer to strap it to the back of the coach. At first, this was no problem, as the ride was comfortable, if noisy, with the iron-clad wheels rolling over the cobbled London streets. However, when we left the city and got to the uneven dirt roads, I felt like I was being tossed about like a rag doll. I had trouble keeping my hand on the crate with the other holding the hanging leather loop. The journey was long and arduous, but I knew the preciousness of my cargo, so I concentrated on the countryside passing by outside the window.

Professor Jaynes met me at his door with overwhelming enthusiasm. His rooms at the university were as I had imagined — wood-panelled and covered in bookcases, although there seemed to be more books stacked on his desk and in piles on the floor than were actually on the shelves.

He bade me sit down and I sat before him. He was a small man with a thin, sallow face, as though he never went out into the sun — unlike myself, with my face still bronzed. The room had a strange paradoxical mix of smells, beeswax and, I thought, urine. He was old, perhaps seventy, but his eyes were lively, his mind obviously alert.

'And how is Robert? I have not seen him in ten years.'

'Well,' I lied. I had been given another opportunity to end the pretence, but I had rejected it. It was not a rational decision; it was instinctive.

'The best student I have ever had, you know.'

'I am not surprised,' I said. 'He is the most knowledgeable man I have ever met.'

'And you, sir,' the old professor went on, 'are you a scholar as well? Have you studied these ancient writings?'

'Only as a layman,' I answered honestly. 'My knowledge has all been learned from Robert. No, sir, I am a military man. My part in the expedition was practical and strategic.'

He nodded politely but then went quiet, his eyes twinkling in anticipation. 'Well then,' he said eventually, 'let me see the manuscript.' He stood and took most of the books off his desk, making room by stacking them on the floor. I placed the crate on the cleared desk, took my penknife from my pocket and levered the lid open. The professor let out a long whistle at the sight of it. He lifted it out like the precious document that it was. 'Do you read Coptic, Captain Campbell-John?'

'No, sir, but Robert has explained to me what is written. Do you think he is right — that it is from the second century?'

'It will take me many weeks of study to determine that, Captain.'

He turned the pages delicately, throwing rapid questions at me as he did so. Surprisingly, I was able to answer most of them, but for those I could not, I suggested that he write to Robert for the answers, intending to study his journals before I replied.

Back in Rathbone Place, I visited the apothecary and purchased a preparation of katam dye. Now that my hair was clean, my natural colour of dark blond had become more apparent. My beard was naturally darker and was now speckled with grey, so it was less of a problem. I mixed the preparation with warm water and lemon juice as the apothecary had recommended and applied it to my hair, and it did indeed deepen to an acceptable dark brown. I must have still been very anxious about being recognised.

I needed to go about; I had the antiquities to sell — a glorious *Book of the Dead*, and a superb golden necklace that I had purchased from a Jewish trader for about two hundred and fifty pounds. From an Arab tomb-raider, I had bought a golden necklace with the blue amulet of a scarab beetle, a golden belt with porcelain-like cowrie shells, and a sumptuously decorated box containing an intricate jet-black wig. I had paid two and a half thousand piastres for them — about twenty-five pounds collectively. At first I did not know how to find potential buyers; antiquities were not something with which I was familiar. I consulted the London trade directories and made a note of a possible dealer, but I vaguely remembered that the British Museum had a collection of ancient artefacts, and I made an appointment with the antiquities curator there.

'My name is Charles Pettigrew,' the curator introduced himself in the foyer of the British Museum. He was a tall man with stooping shoulders and small beady eyes, the right one holding a monocle. His manner was dismissive initially: he made no effort to hide the fact that he was a busy man, that he had other duties to attend to. I was not even invited to his office. I said very few words to begin with; I was not going to pander to this officious man. I carried several small crates and boxes, but also a leather portfolio over my shoulder. This was the easiest to open; I put the other containers down gently, undid the buckle on the portfolio and reached inside.

Gently and deliberately I took out the magnificent golden collar necklace. It was wrapped in tissue paper and I delicately peeled each layer back to reveal the true splendour of it. I saw his eyes widen, at first in disbelief and then in wonder. His manner changed; I was invited to his office and offered sherry. When everything was displayed, his sycophancy knew no limits.

He studied them in great detail as I sipped the sherry; he seemed in no doubt as to their authenticity. 'The museum is definitely interested in your finds, Lord Carberton,' he said matter-of-factly, although I knew he was trying to suppress his enthusiasm. 'How much are you asking for them?'

I took out my silver snuffbox, the one with the miniature of the real Robert's father painted on the lid, put a pinch on the back of my hand, and snorted some up my right nostril and the remainder up my left. I then took out my kerchief with a flourish and wiped the excess off my nose, all the time making him wait. 'Two thousand five hundred guineas,' I said disdainfully, while returning the kerchief to my pocket casually.

The monocle dropped from Pettigrew's eye and he sat up straight in his chair. 'You cannot be in earnest, sir,' he said.

'I am completely in earnest, sir,' I replied, holding his stare intently. 'These are the finest artefacts ever to come out of Egypt. I wager they are finer than anything you have here at the British Museum. And, what is more, the *Book of the Dead* identifies the name of the deceased. The two major items are not just the result of indiscriminate tomb-robbing; they are from scholarly excavations.'

He sat back. 'I will have to consult the trustees of the museum,' he said, his voice little more than a whisper.

'You do that, sir,' I said as I began to put the artefacts away. 'You do that.'

CHAPTER 32

The next part of my plan was to write to Robert's land agent. I asked him for a list of all the people employed at the Hall and on the estate and their ages. I suspected that he must have scratched his head at the latter, wondering why I wanted that information. Nevertheless, he dutifully supplied it, but I remembered something Robert had said: *the estate workers, the servants — I will be a stranger to them.*

The reply was encouraging — the house had been virtually closed down. The kitchen staff, as well as the maids and the footman, had been laid off. There were now only three employees left at the Hall, the housekeeper, the butler and one solitary maid. The agent advised that the housekeeper had been offered another position and she was working out her notice. The butler's age was given as sixty-three.

The estate workers were more problematic; many of them were of a similar age to Robert and may have been there as he grew up. I took the view, however, that they would not have come into as close proximity to him as the house servants would have. I had been in this position many times before. I was happy that my impersonation skills would be sufficient to deal with them; if I presented myself as Lord Carberton, then I would be seen as Lord Carberton. I knew people accepted what was presented to them — that principle had been the bedrock of my schemes in the past.

The land agent said he was looking forward to *meeting* me as, it seemed, he had been appointed by Robert's father after Robert had left on the Grand Tour. He had not met Robert before, an unexpected gift indeed. He invited me to come and see the estate accounts, which were ready for my inspection. I decided it was still too dangerous to visit the Hall, though, and I replied that I had business in London and instructed him to come down to see me.

George Davies arrived at Rathbone Place the following week. He was younger than I had expected, perhaps twenty-eight, and had taken over from his father as the land agent after he had retired. He had a round, expressive face with penetrating pale blue eyes, hair inclined to brown and a healthy complexion. He was neat in his person, with a polite way of speaking. He gave off an air of reliability.

I went through the estate ledgers with him. The manor farm was showing a healthy profit, and all the tenant farm rents were up to date. The estate, it seemed, was running efficiently. I pondered, as I went through the figures, over how this man had been left to execute the estate without supervision — there must have been endless scope for deception, to line his own pockets — but he was, it seemed, an honest man. I wondered if I would have been the same in his position; deep down, I knew the answer.

I now moved my plan forward. I instructed him to close down the Hall completely. The butler was to be given a pension and a cottage purchased for him in Nottingham, far enough away so that he would not be a problem. George thought this was generous in the extreme, and said that he was delighted that I was such an enlightened master.

The next day, I instructed a London firm of lawyers to take over from the lawyers in Nottingham. I was eliminating, one by one, all possible chances of being recognised as an imposter.

I had thought that finding buyers for the Egyptian artefacts would be difficult; it was a world that I knew little about. I learned, however, that the world of antiquities was a very small community indeed. My visit to the British Museum had caused a stir; the whole community was abuzz with it. I did not need to go looking for these dealers: they came to me.

I had four messages sent to my door asking for the opportunity to view my finds, and I invited them all round at the same time. I displayed all of the antiquities in my drawing room and watched their faces intently. I answered their questions intelligently, surprised at how much I had learned from Robert, and allowed an auction to unfold naturally. But I did not finalise the sales there and then; I knew how to play these dealers off against the British Museum.

A month later, the sales had been completed: the magnificent golden collar necklace and the superb *Book of the Dead* went to the British Museum, for two thousand guineas, raised by subscription from their patrons. The rest went in individual lots to the dealers and raised another nine hundred guineas. I was, once again, a wealthy man — but this time not from gambling. I also had the estate rents that would now be a regular income.

For once in my life, however, my own pleasures were not foremost in my mind. I was a self-centred man, but for those past two years I had been overcome with bouts of melancholy. I had stolen from the first real friend I had ever had, Samuel Medina. I knew the amount to the penny — a colossal sum, an amount that I never imagined being in a position to repay. I set out to find him, thinking it would be easy as he had been the most famous man in England when I had fled the country, the great boxing champion — but when I went to his house, there was someone else living there. I had to find him; however, as I was known by all in the pugilistic world — I had been Samuel Medina's promoter, his second in the ring — I had to be circumspect.

I consulted my solicitors, and they sent out runners to discreetly make enquiries. They did their job well and established that he lived at an address in St Giles, a very impoverished part of London. My mood darkened at this information; I assumed that he had had to sell his house to pay the debts I had left him with.

I went under cover of darkness to visit the address, still anxious that I would be recognised. It was in a rundown street; there was an acrid stench from the rubbish — ashes, offal, dead animals, the contents of chamber pots that had missed the night soil collectors, overflowing cesspits. Why had Samuel been reduced to living in such a place? He was the Champion of All England; he could command vast purses whenever he fought.

I knew I had found the right house — there were candles glowing in the window. *Ah*, I thought to myself, *of course, it is Friday night, the Jewish Sabbath*. Samuel always observed the Sabbath, and he would have celebrated it with his wife. I knocked, heard movement within and then the door opened slowly, the candlelight painting me with its dim glow. There was my friend Samuel, in shadow; I saw his forehead furrow as he took in the man before him, then I saw the realisation spread over his features. He gave a hollow laugh. 'You!' he said fiercely. 'John Campbell-John!'

'Aye, 'tis me.' I held my breath. He gave me a hostile stare and set his jaw hard as if about to speak — then he slammed the door in my face.

It would have been easy to go, yet my shame was still hanging heavily on me — I had to put right my wrongdoings. I knocked again, but he continued to ignore me. I kept on tapping, the force increasing until I was hammering, whilst at the same time shouting his name through the closed door. I jumped back as he angrily pulled it open.

'Be gone with you before you wake the neighbourhood!' he exclaimed, slamming the door shut again.

I started tapping again; I kept the volume down but persisted. After a time, the door opened again.

'Be gone, I tell you!' he yelled, the words tapering away when he realised he would awaken his family.

'Sammy boy, let me in. I need to talk to you.'

'But why should I want to speak to you?'

'Because...' I said, then paused; I could not find a creditable reason. I had rehearsed the words in my mind all day, but now they deserted me. 'Because ... you were the best friend I ever had, and I treated you grievously. I need to ... to ... make amends.'

Slowly the door opened. 'You had better come in and sit down.' I doubted he could have explained why he invited me in — I could see from his face he was in turmoil.

'Thank you, Sammy boy.' I entered cautiously.

I saw him taking in my appearance, my elegant frock coat. 'You always were a flash bugger, John Campbell-John.' His voice was low and throaty.

He indicated a chair, fetched two tankards of ale and gave me one. We drank slowly, sitting in silence by the crackling fire, staring into the dancing flames. I looked up at him. 'You have lost weight, Sammy boy,' I said tentatively.

'Aye, well, I have been ailing,' he answered curtly, then added, 'and do not call me Sammy — only *friends* can all me that.'

There was so much anger in him; it was plain to see. He did not want to look at me; he just stared into the fire or into his tankard of ale. 'You have not forgotten me, then,' I said, twitching a nervous smile, trying to lighten the mood.

He leaned forward and prodded a stiff finger into my chest. 'You do not forget embezzlement — you do not forget betrayal.' He worked his mouth and spat a gob of spittle into the fire.

'Betrayal is such an ugly word, Samuel. Was I that bad, then?'

His hands curled into fists. 'What would you call it?'

'It was just self-preservation, that's all. I had to ... well, go to ground for the sake of my health, so to speak.' I looked down at my feet nervously.

'*Your* health!' exclaimed Samuel, his anger barely contained, the words sticking in his throat. 'What about *my* health? I was imprisoned because of you.'

'What? Debtors' prison?' Shame lodged in my throat as I uttered the words.

'Aye,' said Samuel, 'the King's Bench Debtors' Prison. Thanks to you, John Campbell-John, you bastard! You left *me* to pick up *your* debts, didn't you?'

I looked down and picked at my fingernails. 'I'm sorry, I didn't know. Or perhaps I didn't want to know. Besides, all you had to do was fight to pay them off. Why did you not just do that?'

A log shifted on the fire. There was a crackle of sparks and the smell of singed matting. Samuel peered into the embers. 'They wouldn't let me.'

'Why not?'

'Sir Oliver Ruddle — that's why not!'

'That bastard — what had it got to do with him?'

'He was the leading creditor; he bought up all my debts and swore out a charge against me. It was revenge, you see — he couldn't get you, so he was intent on getting me. He had lost wagers to us so many times in the past that he wanted me in prison more than he wanted his money back.'

'How much?' I asked nervously.

'I sold everything I had and reduced the debt to two hundred and thirty-six pounds, seven pence, and offered to repay that out of the receipts from my next fight. But Ruddle would have none of it. I was portrayed in court as a man of low birth, of little character. I saw the judge sneer at me, and then he rejected my offer. So I was in debt but wasn't allowed to fight to get the money to pay off those debts.'

'How long were you in prison?' I asked timidly.

'A year and a half.'

'*A year and a half!*' I was staggered. 'You must really have hated me.'

'Oh, yes, I hated you, all right.' He grimaced. 'My family were starving whilst I was in prison. My hatred helped me to endure the ordeal. We'd spent so much money when we had it, and then suddenly I could not raise a farthing. I even fought from the prison, but the marshal took nearly all the profit; he was making so much money from the fights that the last thing he wanted was for me to pay off my debts and be discharged. But then it got worse.'

I was unable to meet his eyes. 'How?'

'Gaol fever, typhus. It is a miracle I survived; most men do not. You can see from my physique I am still only half the man I used to be.'

'Oh, Samuel, my dear old friend; you are right to hate me.'

'Aye, I hate you all right. The only reason I am not still in prison is that my wife cajoled, coaxed and pleaded with everyone we know, to give or lend us money; it was demeaning.'

'I can understand that, Samuel. You are the most honourable man I have ever met.' I tried to divert this uneasy conversation, giving a dry chuckle. 'But we did spend money, didn't we, Sammy? We lived liked princes, though, didn't we?'

'Oh, yes, we did that right enough, but perhaps if *you'd* paid your dues along the way…' Samuel turned his mouth down. 'If you had, then things may have turned out differently.'

'Yes, so many regrets, Sammy boy, so many regrets. But so many great memories as well.'

'Well — yes, I suppose so.' His words were reluctant but heartfelt. We both fell silent for a while. Suddenly, Samuel smiled. 'Do you remember when we first met?'

'Oh, I do, Sammy boy — how could I forget? I remember it well, Sammy boy — I remember it well. A spring morning and a brash young boy wanting to fight the world.' I could see much of his anger was, despite himself, draining away at the fleeting memory, at these thoughts of happier times.

'Have you come to pay me back, then?' Samuel asked at length.

'Aye, I have,' I answered quietly but earnestly.

His eyes widened, then his expression darkened again. 'Do not mock me, sir.' His words were thick with menace.

I took an envelope from the inside pocket of my frock coat and handed it to him. He opened it suspiciously. I watched his face crease in disbelief.

'Is this what I think it is?'

'Aye, 'tis a letter of credit from my bankers.'

'But it is for two thousand, one hundred and seventy-eight pounds, seven shillings and eight pence!'

'It is the sum that I owe you, to the penny.'

'But where did you get such a sum? It is dishonestly come by, I take it?'

I was not offended. 'You know me well, Samuel, but in this instance it is not. It is *honestly* come by.'

He stood, momentarily bewildered, then marched to the foot of his stairs and shouted up, 'Rebecca, come down quick! I have something to show you.'

His wife came down the stairs almost immediately, pulling a robe around her nightgown. 'What on earth is the matter Samuel?' she asked, but then she saw me. '*You!*' she exclaimed.

'No, Rebecca,' Samuel said eagerly. He thrust the letter into her hands and she read it. I could see she did not, at first glance, see the significance of it. She read it again, her face finally showing her understanding.

'I have come to repay my debt to you, Rebecca,' I said.

CHAPTER 33

In the desert, I had learned that progress was slow and relentless, one foot after the other, stride after stride, mile after mile. Unrelenting advancement, a goal achieved by enduring struggle, the reward for sustained effort. But three months after I arrived back in London, quite the opposite happened; fame ambushed me. There had been no sustained effort on my part — I did nothing to encourage it and did not see it coming.

Professor Jaynes at Cambridge University authenticated the Coptic Gospel of St Matthew as a second-century translation of an original first-century text, verifying it as the earliest known copy of a Gospel. He wrote to me to confirm this and he also published his findings in university journals. Other eager scholars came excitedly to study the manuscript; it was a sensation and that notoriety was picked up by the daily newspapers. Robert had told me that there were already suspicions amongst scholars that the Gospels might be unreliable because the Gospels of Matthew, Mark, Luke and John did not always say the same thing. Now it emerged that there were even differences between what was said in St Matthew in the King James Bible and what was stated in this second-century translation.

A debate erupted amongst the scholars as to the significance of these differences, disputes as to the confidence that could now be placed in the words in the King James Bible. This debate was taken up by the newspapers; there was nothing more provocative to the British than the subject of religion, and letters were sent to the editors on all sides of the argument. The new Gospel was published, and sold over a million copies, provoking more debate this time in the non-scholarly public. The interest kept on mounting; it was the subject on everyone's lips, from the drawing rooms of London society to the public houses, from the coffee houses to the factory floors. I now knew that I had done the right thing in returning the Gospel of Thaddeus Jude to the abbot of the Monastery of El-Sourian; if these minor differences were causing such a stir, then the indication that Jesus was not divine would have unleashed a maelstrom of wrath and resentment.

Professor Jaynes gave my name (Robert Babcock, Lord Carberton) as the adventurer who had found the Gospel in the remote deserts of Egypt. The newspapers came to my door; I was the centre of attention in all this controversy. I was spooked by it all — I needed anonymity, not fame.

At first I ran from my sanctuary at Rathbone Place and took lodgings in Cambridge, but the university town of Cambridge, I found, was itself consumed with this new Gospel and its consequences. The very fact that it contained ancient edits challenged the universal belief that the word of God, as contained in the Bible, was unchangeable. The word of God could not, by definition, need revision. Even the most devout of believers could now see that this was simply not true.

When I went about from my lodgings, this debate was inescapably all about me. I sat inconspicuously in a Cambridge coffee house, overhearing a heated discussion on the very subject of the consequences of the ancient amendments. I listened intently. Cambridge, however, did give me time to think and take in everything that was happening. I came to a decision: I was an imposter, I had been all my adult life and I knew the rules of impersonation. One faces the world head on, presenting an image for people to latch onto. I decided that I would use this newfound fame to *cement* my impersonation; the more people who saw me as an adventurer nobleman, the more secure it would make me — and the more I was perceived as Robert Babcock, the more Robert Babcock I would become.

I went back to London and gave the first of a number of interviews. They could not get enough of me. I told the stories of my travels, embellished as only I could. But then, I had seen so much first-hand; I told them of, amongst other things, pyramids and tombs, deserts and palm trees, and languid boat trips on the Nile. Yet I dared not mention the name of my companion Captain John Campbell-John, for fear of inviting interest from my villainous creditors. Nor did I forget the promises I had made to the monks at the Monastery of El-Sourian; I kept that source from my stories.

I liked all this attention and embraced it; it sat easily with my personality, but there was danger in it, a hazardous course to negotiate. I was sent invitations to dinner parties at the finest of houses, some of which I had been to before, as the gaming tables had been a feature of many a dinner party. It was usual at ten o'clock for the dancing to be interrupted and two small tables erected in the coffee room. I had been a regular attendee, using my wit and cunning, as well as my card playing skills to gamble at these tables. I was still tempted to accept, but I had the sense to politely reject these offers on the grounds that I was presently engaged in academic pursuits; I would surely have been recognised.

And then that falsehood became truth; I was approached by a publisher to write the story of my adventures. At first I hesitated; the real Robert Babcock was the scholar, not this imposter. However, the thought took me; after all, it was not an invitation to write an academic account — it was to be an account of my exploration. A resolve took me; yes, I would do it. I also had Robert's journals to fall back on, but yes, why not?

I set about the task with enthusiasm and found that the words just fell out of me. I was not restrained by the real Robert's academia, the need to accredit my sources; I just told my story and did not baulk at embellishment. A year later it was published — *Travels and Discoveries in Egypt* — and it was an immediate success, going to several reprints. My name became synonymous with Egypt, with adventure, and other expeditions were planned to follow in my footsteps.

Soon after its publication, Professor Jaynes died. He caught a winter chill, but it turned into pneumonia and it took the frail old academic. I was genuinely sad; I liked his enthusiasm. He had immediately recognised the embellishments in the book and blamed me (John Campbell-John) for influencing my friend Robert Babcock. I smiled at the memory and, despite my sadness, I recognised that another obstacle had been removed; he was one of the few men who would know me as an imposter and not the real Robert Babcock.

I chose my public appearances wisely — ignoring society and the season — restricting them to scholarly audiences. They were not the type I would normally have chosen. I would have loved to have drunk with John Barleycorn and gambled with good old John Bull. But there were still ladies about to pursue at these gatherings, if not those from high and low society that had previously been my target.

It was at a musical evening in Cambridgeshire that I met the Anglican Bishop, George Newstead, dressed in cassock, apron, breeches and gaiter, a rotund, blotch-faced man, with copiously bushy eyebrows and a boundless enthusiasm for knowledge and the finer things in life. He monopolised me all evening, wanting to know everything about my adventures in Egypt. He ate prodigiously all through our conversation, slurping claret as he did so and encouraging me to keep up; I was happy to oblige. We were regularly shushed as we spoke whilst the musicians tried to play.

I was a little drunk when he introduced me to his daughter, Charlotte Alexandria Newstead. I took a look back at him, not believing that such a beauty could be his daughter. He laughed robustly. 'Takes after her late mother, Lord Carberton,' he snorted.

'Now, Father,' she admonished him, 'you promised me that you would not drink too much tonight.' She dabbed at a claret stain on his cassock. 'It's a good job you are wearing black, Father.'

From that moment on, my libidinous eyes did not leave her. Her face had an ancient Egyptian look, her hair almost raven, and she had large dark eyes that seemed to hold me under a spell. She was nineteen but looked older, already a woman.

My thoughts went back to Ebonee, a prostitute in Cairo, to that first image of her lying on a divan at the far end of a room, beckoning me to enter. I remembered her loose trousers, her long-sleeved silk shirt embroidered with gold and pearls, the semi-precious stone-covered headdress, from under which hung the long tresses of her jet-black hair, plaited with sequin-adorned silk.

I imagined Charlotte Alexandria with the edges of her eyes blackened with surma in the way Ebonee's had been. I looked at her evening gown, fashionable, proclaiming her as a respectable English lady, with a very wide neckline off her shoulders, short puffed sleeves, mid-length white gloves, and pleated panels of fabric arranged horizontally over her bosom and around her shoulders. Her raven hair was parted in the centre and dressed in elaborate curls, loops and knots extending out to both sides. But I could not get a different image of her out of my mind; an Egyptian picture. It was as though I was a capricious artist who was painting her on the wrong canvas.

Despite my drunkenness, I behaved honourably and was charm personified. I later paid court to her according to the rules of polite society, visiting her with chaperoned correctness. She became my wife the following year. I insisted on calling her Alexandria and not Charlotte — a habit, she said, she found charming.

CHAPTER 34

The constant fear of being recognised by the thugs of Molly Jasper seemed to intensify after meeting Alexandria and making plans to marry. I was no longer a lone wolf able to live by my wits; my whole world had expanded.

My previous life now seemed incomprehensible to me. Had I *really* lost two hundred and eighty-nine pounds on *one* hand of cards? Molly Jasper's house took responsibility for any gaming losses at their establishment. My name and debts were now inscribed in their ledger, the all-knowing ledger. Molly stood as surety for the loss and would have paid it in my absence, but they would collect from me — and there was no time limit on their pursuit. That fear of recognition was like a stone in my shoe; every step brought it back to mind. I cowered from strangers in the street, suspecting recognition in their eyes. I took hansom cabs wherever I went and when this was not possible, I walked in alleyways rather than the main thoroughfares.

This was no way to live, I thought; after the sale of the Egyptian artefacts, I now had the funds even without using the rents from the tenant farmers. I would like to say that my actions were motivated by altruistic beliefs, but that would be a lie; I was motivated by fear, the threat of retribution, and the need to wipe the slate clean for the benefit of Alexandria and my proposed new family. I instructed my solicitors to contact Molly Jasper and discharge the debt. It was the most unusual of commissions for them, and they were told not to reveal the source of the payer — my name, Lord Carberton, was never to be mentioned. It turned out to be the easiest of commissions for them; Molly Jasper asked no questions — he was just happy that his ledgers were balanced and that the money was in his coffers.

Another constraint had been removed, although I still owed vast sums; of course, John Campbell-John had lived like a king and had a wardrobe of the finest clothes and a string of horses to show for his profligacy. I was still in debt for both. But that was not the end of it: I owed my jeweller, my lacemaker, my bookmaker, my gunmaker, my shoemaker, my bookseller, my saddler, my coachmaker, my embroiderer, my hatter, my watchmaker and a huge amount to my wine merchant. I had left them all to stand the losses when I had fled. I had committed the cardinal sin of all gamblers; I had chased my losses. I had attempted to clear the enormous arrears with ever increasing bets until the stakes required were so immense I was unable to raise them.

I could have welshed on these other debts; my new identity protected me from them. Charges, I assumed, had been sworn out against John Campbell-John, but in the absence of that man, there was no one to answer them, and the courts were unable to prosecute me. Nevertheless, I set about paying these overdue unpaid arrears, one by one, until they were all cleared. I had been back in England for a year and a half when they were all finally discharged, just before my marriage to Alexandria. I took pleasure in that action. If the repayment of the arrears owed to Molly was motivated by fear, then the discharge of the other debts was not; I was intent on making my new life a nobler one.

We took our honeymoon touring the continent: Paris, Vienna, Florence and then Rome. Alexandria took to exploring and studying art and culture like a duck to water. She had an enquiring mind and wanted to know all about everything we saw. But she also, I found out, had a robust constitution; the long hours of travelling, the endless corridors of museums did not fatigue her. At Rome, Alexandria indicated a wish to see Venice as I had so often spoken of it, so we travelled there. It brought back so many memories for me; it had been the start of my adventures in the Levant. It did not end there, though; she expressed a desire to also see Egypt. I tried to explain the hardships that would be involved, but she was not to be put off.

It was so enticing to me that I agreed, and we set about planning our expedition. We set sail from Venice, as I had done with the real Robert Babcock, and spent a year and a half in Egypt. I did not go looking for early Coptic manuscripts, but we spent our time looking for ancient Egyptian artefacts. Alexandria was a great help; her French was better than mine. I renewed my acquaintance with Amram Haroun, the Jewish scholar and trader, an acquaintance that is still in place today. He asked no questions about my change in identity; if he suspected a switch, he did not say. He is my agent in Cairo, and I have spent my life since pursuing my passion for all things Egyptian, either ancient or modern.

On the way home we travelled to Jerusalem, at Alexandria's request. She wanted desperately to see everything of that historic city. However, the visit had to be cut short, as she fell pregnant. Robust as she was, I wanted her to be cared for in England and our child to be born there as well. Our son Edward was born in Rathbone Place, London, much to Alexandria's displeasure; she wanted me to take up my position as Baron Carberton at the family home in Nottinghamshire. I was still nervous that it was too soon and made excuses that I needed to be near my publisher and the antiquities traders.

I finally relented, though, and we moved to Carberton Hall in 1845. Since then, I have lived here as Robert Babcock, the Eleventh Baron Carberton, a country gentleman living off the estate farmland and the rents from his tenant farmers. I have brought up my children here, Edward, John and my daughter Cleopatra. I also have some fame as an explorer, an expert and trader in Egyptian artefacts. I toyed with the idea of studying the Coptic language, but that would have required a tutor, and the first question he would surely have asked was how was I able to find Coptic manuscripts if I could not read them? So I allowed my reputation as a scholar of ancient Coptic manuscripts to wane, as I knew it would not stand up to investigation.

Now, as I put down my pen, my secret has been told: who I really am. I hope I will not be diminished in Edward's eyes when he reads this account. I confess I have been a profligate, self-centred, unempathetic man. I am still an imposter. But I hope that I have changed along the way; that there has been a redemption of John Campbell-John.

If that redemption is real, then I must acknowledge the reason for it. I stole the identity of Robert Babcock, that is true, but when I started to live as him I also took on his admirable character. Little by little, I began to behave as he would have. I have always asked myself that question — what would Robert have done?

Robert, dear Robert, as I look down on your ring on my little finger, I hope that I have lived your life with honour, as you would have done. A different rasher of bacon, to be sure, but I hope still a worthy one.

HISTORICAL NOTES

The travels and discoveries of Robert Babcock are based on the Bible hunting of Robert Curzon (16 March 1810 — 2 August 1873), Constantin von Tischendorf (18 January 1815 — 7 December 1874) and Émile Amélineau (1850 — 12 January 1915). Although Curzon and von Tischendorf were contemporaries in life, they travelled in Egypt at different times.

Curzon, in particular, left behind a published account of his travels in his book *Visits to Monasteries in the Levant.* This was a goldmine for me, as not only did it recount his travels, but it has detailed descriptions of the people he met, how they dressed, what they ate, their manners, etc. It gives an outline of the different officials within Ottoman Egypt down to the *kawasses.* It also describes in great detail his adventures and the terrain that he had to endure, and many of his travels have formed the basis of the adventures of John and Robert. But what's more, it gave me an insight into the Egypt that he encountered in the 1830s: an eyewitness account of the period in which I have set the story. Many of the ideas of John and Robert are based upon Robert Curzon's interpretations.

The story of Ouardi, who was shut up in an enchanted palace to keep her from her lover, Prince Anas el Ajoud, was also taken from this journal, although I have not been able to track down this story anywhere else.

My internet research suggests that cotton paper was a nineteenth-century invention, yet Robert Curzon says in his book back in the 1830s that he discovered ancient manuscripts on cotton paper. Whichever is correct, I have used cotton paper in this story. This cotton fibre paper is known to last for many hundreds of years without appreciable fading.

In the late fourth century, Bishop Athanasius of Alexandria set about defining a fixed canon of texts about Jesus, which led to the fixed canon that we know today. Up until then, the different branches of the early Christian Church used many different accounts of Jesus's life and sayings. These other gospels and writings used in the early Church were then discarded.

The *Sayings of Jesus* were actually discovered much later than Robert and John's adventures (the Oxyrhynchus papyri in the late nineteenth century by Grenfell and Hunt and much later, in 1945, with the discovery of the Nag Hammadi texts) and are attributed to Thomas, another of Jesus's disciples. This is one of the texts used by Christians before the adoption of the fixed canon by the early Orthodox Church. They were hidden because they represented unauthorised versions of the Bible, which would have been considered heretical and would have got the monks into trouble, excommunicated or worse; it put their lives at risk.

The finding of the Gospel of Thaddeus Jude by Robert and John is purely fiction and although it did not exist, it is very loosely based on the non-canonical Gospel of Thomas found at Oxyrhynchus in the late nineteenth century by Grenfell and Hunt. Robert is greatly troubled by the contents of the Gospel, feeling that it would send shockwaves through the Christian world. This is precisely what happened after the Gospel of Thomas was published some sixty years later.

The actual identity of Thaddeus Jude is disputed by some scholars. He is clearly not Judas Iscariot, who betrayed Jesus. Both Jude and Judas were common names among Jews of the time. These names, of course, come to us as translations from Aramaic, into Greek and then into other languages such as English or French, which blurs the issue further. Luke, in his Gospel, identifies in his list of apostles Jude of James; whereas Matthew in his Gospel lists Thaddeus in his place. Again, any errors in this story are mine, but I like to think they may also have been errors of Robert's own scholarship.

If you are interested in further reading on the subjects touched on in this book, I can recommend the following:

A New History of Early Christianity by Charles Freeman

Ancient Egypt: Art, Myth and Life by Joann Fletcher

Sinai: Landscape and Nature in Egypt's Wilderness by Omar Attum

The Comprehensive New Testament by J. Clontz and T. E. Clontz

The Gospel of Thomas and Christian Wisdom by Stevan L. Davies

Lost Scriptures: Books that Did Not Make it into the New Testament by Bart D. Ehrman

The Five Gospels: What Did Jesus Really Say? The Search for the Authentic Words of Jesus by Robert W. Funk and Roy W. Hoover

Nag Hammadi Codex II by Bentley Layton

The Fifth Gospel: The Gospel of Thomas Comes of Age by Stephen J. Patterson, James M. Robinson, Hans-Gebhard Bethge

A NOTE TO THE READER

Dear Reader,

Thank you for getting this far. I hope you enjoyed *The Lost Gospels.*

Nowadays, reviews by knowledgeable readers are essential for a writer's success. If you found this book entertaining, I will be in your debt if you would consider leaving a review on **Amazon** and **Goodreads**. I love hearing from readers, and you can contact me through my website: **www.stephentaylorauthor.com**.

Thank you!

Stephen Taylor

Sapere Books is an exciting new publisher of brilliant fiction and popular history.

To find out more about our latest releases and our monthly bargain books visit our website:
saperebooks.com

www.ingramcontent.com/pod-product-compliance
Lightning Source LLC
Chambersburg PA
CBHW060913250626
47159CB00008B/2984